(a girl called) Karma

SM Thomas

Written by:
SM Thomas

Published by:
A.R Hurne Publishing

Edited by:
Allison Reinert, A Favorite Pen

Cover Art by:
Beth Godfrey

ISBN
978-1-7385686-4-2

Dedication:

Dedicated to Nanny Joe - who supports all of us unconditionally in whatever crazy pipe dreams we choose for ourselves. xx

Dear Reader,

I don't necessarily agree with trigger warnings - and this isn't quite that - but I just wanted to take the time to write to you before you dove into Karma and Zoe's story.

Within these pages you will find stories you may find upsetting or uncomfortable. And perhaps the reason behind those feelings are that you can relate, or that you know of someone who can relate. Because unfortunately real life, much like fiction, contains many different types of people and not all of them are kind.

If you have ever suffered at the hands of another please know that you are not a victim, no matter how they may have made you feel, you are a **survivor.** They may have broken you but you can and you will rebuild.

They will forever be a monster but you can be so much more. You <u>are</u> so much more.

Please remember that it's just a bad day, just a bad moment, not a bad life. There are people and organisations you can reach out to if you need to. There are still kind people in the world. People who will love you, heal you and bring you back to **yourself.**

Don't let the monster's win.

Thank you,
SM Thomas

Contents

Prologue: 1

Chapter One: Zoe 4

Chapter Two: Karma 9

Chapter Three: The Farm 14

Chapter Four: Zoe 18

Chapter Five: Target #15 24

Chapter Six: Zoe 32

Chapter Seven: Zoe 41

Chapter Eight: The Farm 48

Chapter Nine: Zoe 54

Chapter Ten: Zoe 59

Chapter Eleven: Target #23 68

Chapter Twelve: Zoe 75

Chapter Thirteen: Karma 81

Chapter Fourteen: The Farm 86

Chapter Fifteen: Zoe 89

Chapter Sixteen: Zoe 95

Chapter Seventeen: Zoe	100
Chapter Eighteen: Zoe	109
Chapter Nineteen: Target #25	116
Chapter Twenty: The Farm	119
Chapter Twenty-One: Zoe	123
Chapter Twenty-Two: Zoe	131
Chapter Twenty-Three: Zoe	139
Chapter Twenty-Four: Zoe	141
Chapter Twenty-Five: Karma	148
Chapter Twenty-Six: The Farm	153
Chapter Twenty-Seven: Target #30	156
Chapter Twenty-Eight: Zoe	161
Chapter Twenty-Nine: Zoe	166
Chapter Thirty: Target #31	174
Chapter Thirty-One: Karma	179
Chapter Thirty-Two: The Farm	186
Chapter Thirty-Three: Zoe	188
Chapter Thirty-Four: Target #32	194

Chapter Thirty-Five: Zoe 200

Chapter Thirty-Six: Zoe 206

Chapter Thirty-Seven: Karma 213

Chapter Thirty-Eight: The Farm 217

Chapter Thirty-Nine: Target #38 220

Chapter Forty: Target #38 225

Chapter Forty-One: The Farm 233

Chapter Forty-Two: Zoe 236

Chapter Forty-Three: Zoe 242

Chapter Forty-Four: Karma 247

Chapter Forty-Five: Zoe 251

Chapter Forty-Six: Zoe 256

Chapter Forty-Seven: The Farm 260

Chapter Forty-Eight: Karma 264

Chapter Forty-Nine: The Farm 270

Chapter Fifty: Zoe 272

Chapter Fifty-One: The Farm 278

Chapter Fifty-Two: Zoe 280

Chapter Fifty-Three: The Farm 283

Chapter Fifty-Four: Karma 286

Chapter Fifty-Five: Karma 292

Chapter Fifty-Six: Zoe 294

Chapter Fifty-Seven: Karma 296

Chapter Fifty-Eight: Zoe 302

Epoilogue: 307

Acknowledgements 311

(a girl called) Karma

Prologue:

It was simple enough.

A small dose of the compound was dropped into the target's drink, not enough to cause a blackout but enough to infiltrate the bloodstream. A barista, restaurant worker or barmaid were always a good call for Stage One and they were the lucky ones. By the time the body was discovered, any traces of the drug had long left their system. There was never a trail back to those working in Stage One. They often had too much to lose, families to provide for or to protect. So they were granted a kindness.

A friendly offer of help when the effects began to kick in. A sudden feeling of light exhaustion, confusion, and anxiety and they'd willingly accept help from a stranger. Especially one so nondescript. They always made sure to only use plain members of the web for Stage Two, somebody easy to forget. Occasionally, they got interviewed by the police, but they were always pictured on CCTV for the rest of their day, providing an airtight alibi. Always.

Put the victim in a taxi, make a show of talking to any witnesses about your Good Samaritan deed for the day and be on your way. Disappearing back into your life, knowing your debt has been cleared. That you've paid it forward. Stage Two had it easy as well. More often than not their debt had been a smaller one, still heinous, but a lesser evil when you took in the web.

The car was hired using a credit card in a name no one owns. Delivered and picked up at an address that no one lives at. Driven by somebody with an axe to grind. Those in Stage Three were close enough to the inner circle that they could see the bigger picture - they believed in the cause and wanted to do all they could to help. Well, just about all they could. Stage Three participants didn't have the stomach for the final part and nobody was forcing them to. They took enough risks driving the target to their final stop, disguised by some of the best makeup artists the web had taken on over the years. You look hard enough and you'll find broken people everywhere.

Stage Four was when the fun began - when wrongs were righted, and the target was made to confess their sins. It could be a quick stage or a long one depending on the anger of the person running the show, depending on what their victim asked for. Nobody minded either way, so long as justice was served.

A large dose of the synthesised 'venom', as the police would grow to refer to it, would be injected using a two-pronged syringe and once everyone was satisfied the target would become an empty shell. The monster would feel their body grow rigid in a matter of seconds as paralysis tore through their bloodstream, a token of the Indian Krait. And then they would feel their stomach gurgle and vomit would warm their oesophagus, a nod to the Pit Viper, and then they would lie and choke on their own regurgitated meal with nothing but their own terror for company. Until eventually, it was over.

A calling card would be left and everyone who once thought the world of the deceased would know the truth. They would know that their 'loved one' was the thing of nightmares. That it was their face that had haunted somebody every night since they first encountered them.

They would know that Medusa only comes for the guilty.

Chapter One: Zoe

"I just don't understand why you have to travel with her, Zoe," Jake protests, his face twisted into an expression he presumes is pleading, in reality, it just infantilizes him.

"This is the opportunity of a lifetime. Do you know how many podcasters would kill for this opportunity?" I shoot back at him as I pull my backpack over my shoulders. We've had this same conversation so many times since I received the email from Karma's team confirming I'd been chosen to podcast her story. Honestly, I could run this argument on fast-forward and it would still reach the same conclusion.

It may have been two weeks since the email landed in my inbox but I still haven't quite let myself believe that it's real.

I started my podcast two years ago on a whim. In lock-down, the company I'd been working for made redundancies and although it had stung at the time to see my name on that list, it turned out to be the push I needed. I pooled together my savings, made use of the 0% purchase rate on my credit card, and sourced the best recording equipment I could find - and then I just started talking. And surprisingly, people listened.

True crime was a no-brainer as the topic of the podcast.

I'd always had an interest in the darker side of society. As a child my nose could always be found in a book and that book was more often than not inappropriate for a girl my age. Try as my mum did to steer me towards lighter stories, I always preferred the company of vampires, monsters and eventually murderers.

Ted Bundy was the first serial killer I read about, so cliche I know. Despite the queasy feeling that grew in my stomach I couldn't fight my interest in picking apart his psyche. Trying to work out what made a person sink to such levels of depravity, I poured over every book, article, and documentary and eventually fell down the rabbit warren of true crime.

Even as I was completing my college course in creative writing, I'd do so with the sound of podcast episodes about cults as background noise. I was, and still am, desperate to understand the mindset of the people who unleash cruelty on the world. If I understand it then I can avoid it. The more victims I read about the less likely I am to become one myself, or at least that's how I justify my macabre interests.

"Couldn't you just commute?" Jake whines and I shake my head. I'm so tired of having the same conversation, of giving the same justifications.

We've been together for eighteen months and he still doesn't see the importance of my work. Just because he walks into an office building and sits at the same desk day in and day out doesn't mean his work is more important than mine. I have regular listeners, nearly three thousand of them, and the monetisation of my podcast is only growing each month. By telling the exclusive story of Karma Jones' life on my podcast I'm ensuring the longevity of my career. These will be episodes that people seek out, that they re-listen to and tell friends about. I've been full of hope since the email from her team landed inviting me to be the one to tell her story.

At the moment the money I make from the podcast stretches far enough to cover my monthly outgoings; just. With an exclusive update on Karma and The Farm I might actually be able to start cushioning my savings account again, I might even be able to afford to hire a proper studio to record in rather than the dinky spare bedroom I contort myself into at the moment.

"I can't turn down this chance Jake, and I can't keep having this conversation. It's only for a couple of months." I cross my fingers behind my back, hoping that this time he will understand, that this time he will support me.

"I don't know if I can wait that long," he replies, pride swimming across his face. He really thinks this is his ace to play, that an ultimatum over the state of our relationship would sway me into obeying his wants and needs.

I've come to realise over the last few months that Jake always likes to get his own way. There is no give and take with him. We always eat the food he prefers, watch the shows he's heard about and hang out with the people he's friends with. My wants and needs are secondary and this conversation is the nail in the coffin for our relationship. He can't even put me first in this one crucial moment. He can't see how important this is for me.

"Well, that's your decision," I reply, making a show of pushing my set of keys to our flat into my pocket. The lease is in my name, he moved in six months ago and we've never updated it. Perhaps deep inside my mind I knew this wasn't a relationship that would outlast my tenancy agreement.

"I can't believe you would throw away what we have, for a podcast," he sounds angry now, injecting the right level of hurt into his voice. Jake has always been very clever when it comes to manipulating people, but this time he will fail.

"And I can't believe that you can't support me. This chance could change everything for me - for us. If I get this right the podcast will skyrocket." This is my last attempt at pulling us from the ditch he's pushed me into over and over again.

What Jake doesn't realise is that the more he argues with me, the less I love him. The more I see the imbalance in our relationship and so the less powerful his ultimatums become to me.

He never tells anyone about my podcast or my achievements with it, it's as though he's ashamed. Whenever I dare to bring it up in public he loudly tells people it's an expensive hobby and likes to make out that he supports me financially whilst I'm off on a creative whim. That's not true though. I've never lived on his money, I would never live on anyone's money but my own and I don't like how his pretences make me feel. Jake makes me feel smaller, lesser than those around me and I think I deserve better. I know I deserve better. Everyone does.

"It's just a podcast, Zoe. It's you, sitting alone in that room talking shit. It doesn't matter."

And with those words, he's shown me how he truly feels about the work I care so much about. When I first started making episodes I used to ask for him to listen to them as I wanted his opinion and I actually cared about it. That was a long time ago though. I've given up on asking for him to take an interest and I know he never will. It's just a silly podcast about dead people.

"If that's how you feel then I suggest you use this time apart to find somewhere new to live." Even though I've wanted to speak those words for so long, they still scare me. I imagine ending a relationship will just about always feel sad, no matter the circumstances.

To his credit, Jake nods his head in agreement. He knows our time together has reached its natural conclusion. He's only been so pigheaded about my trip because he was trying to veer us from the course of this breakup. To keep us together a little longer than we ought to be. Life, in a lot of ways, was comfortable together.

Returning his nod, and finding no tears brimming in my eyes, I walk out of the flat, close the door on my relationship and take a deep breath.

These interviews better be worth it.

Chapter Two: Karma

Karma Jones was the young girl who broke the internet.

At just eleven years old, she escaped a long-standing cult, The Farm, and found help for the other children who were being held captive. Summoning up courage that was beyond her years, she walked five miles, barefoot, in the midnight rain. Never faltering in her journey, knowing that every second counted.

In the days following her escape from The Farm, news sites carrying her story suffered from long loading times because of the number of people desperate to find out about the strange little girl and the heroic journey she undertook.

The first thing Karma Jones requested after the legal investigation into The Farm began was to apply for a birth certificate. She wanted to be legitimised in the eyes of the law, for there to be evidence that she existed. On The Farm, births weren't recorded in any sense; there were too many deaths of mothers and babies, and Father thought it best not to keep reminders of that lying around.

When the police raided The Farm, they found nearly fifty children, ranging in age from infants to eleven years old. All were malnourished and loopy from a cocktail of drugs, all showing physical symptoms of abuse and all with the names that had been flung at them by adults who didn't care what they were called. Some, like Karma, kept their 'birth name'; others spent hours pouring over online naming dictionaries until they found one they felt comfortable with, and some just chose the name of the officers who had cared for them. Dates of birth, and therefore ages, were guessed as best they could, given nobody had educated the children on dates let alone thrown any of them a birthday party. And birth certificates began to arrive in the post at safe houses up and down the country.

The children had all been split into groups of five, as authorities realised it would be too mentally damaging to split them entirely. Those children had only had the love and reassurance of each other for so many years, and to sever those ties entirely might cause irreversible damage. But to house all of them together was logistically impossible, not to mention dangerous. The members of The Farm were still out there in hiding, and it would be so easy for them to find the large group of children and destroy the evidence they possessed in one fell swoop. At least if they were split up into smaller pockets around the country it would make them harder to trace. Less noticeable to dangerous eyes.

The children weren't allowed contact with the outside world, other than the queue of doctors, psychologists and social workers that paraded themselves through the houses' doors every morning. All of them were desperate to help where they could, and to insert themselves into one of the biggest criminal stories of their time.

Each of the safe houses was separated by miles of geography for the children's protection and recovery. So, after the evidence was gathered and concrete plans for their futures were put in place, most of the children grew up never knowing what had happened to their counterparts who were kept away from them. Never knowing if they changed the name they knew them by or where they'd been adopted out to. It was a necessary cruelty though, the law decided. A way to protect all forty-nine young lives from The Farm.

Father and his followers had all absconded into the night. There wasn't a single person working on the case who doubted that those children's lives were at risk. They had been rescued from a burning barn, thankfully one that was too damp from a well-timed downpour to fully alight. The children were found huddled in the centre, arms and feet bound to each other to create one giant human knot. They had been abandoned to die once Father learnt of Karma's escape. Once he'd realised the police would soon follow.

Those children would have perished that night had it not been for her actions. Somehow, she managed to escape from the knots that bound them, fought the cocktail of sedatives in her bloodstream, climbed from a high window and walked five miles barefoot to find somebody who could help. Someone she could trust. The first door she tried knocking held no answer but the third was flung open by an elderly woman. A fierce seventy-two-year-old matriarch with silver hair down to her waist, who instantly saw the pain in the young girl's eyes and called the police.

She sat by Karma's side, holding her hand silently, as she listened to the eleven-year-old bravely divulge the location where her friends were being held. And she rode alongside Karma in the back of the police car when she agreed to travel with the armed response unit to The Farm, all the while this woman was in awe of the child beside her. The woman had never known somebody to be so brave under such pressure. She had to bite back tears as she listened to Karma idly explaining to the officer driving them about the abuse she'd been subjected to. The child shared the information as though it was just an interesting tidbit about her day, as opposed to the heinous crimes that had taken place.

Joanna Klein knew two things the day she opened her door to find Karma standing on her porch. That everything she had known about life had changed. And that Karma Jones was going to change the world.

The two of them had fought to stay together. Joanna put in multiple applications to become Karma's legal guardian but the powers that be decided against it. It wasn't reasonable to expect a woman in her seventies to raise and nurture an eleven-year-old child who'd been through so much trauma. Plus, in unspoken sentences, they were all aware that Joanna's best years were behind her and she didn't have many left.

Karma had shaken with tears on the day Joanna was escorted from her foster home. Joanna had been invited for a welcome meal, a way to ease Karma into her new family, and she hadn't been shy about expressing her disdain for their set-up. She noted the way the woman babied Karma, treating her as though she was a glass statue about to break, the way the man kept his distance from the child, not quite sure how best to approach his latest ward. It was clear to Joanna as they all made a show of passing the potatoes around that this child was too damaged for them to love.

She knew, as well as Karma did, that she was the only one who could help heal this little girl. Who could hear her truths without shrinking away from them, ugly and violent though they were? She proved that on the night Karma had turned up on her doorstep, in the way she bit back tears and apologies as the girl shared her story. The child didn't need her empty apologies.

Even at age eleven, she knew that the hand she'd

been dealt was unfair. And that apologies would never make it right.

What the child needed was love, support and justice. All of which were lacking in her foster home.

Father had never been caught. Nor any of the twenty inner circle followers Karma had named to the police. They all vanished into the void and the handful of lesser devout sheep had killed themselves before a sentence could ever be placed upon them. There would be no legal justice for the children of The Farm.

Joanna had been so taken aback by the unfairness of the situation that she'd tried to leave and take Karma with her, instructing her to pack her bag. As Joanna waited at the bottom of the stairs the girl did as she was told, happy to finally be going to live with someone she trusted. But by the time Karma finished packing her Paw Patrol backpack, there was a police officer at the door. She watched with large cold tears pouring from her young eyes as her only friend left in the world was marched away from her foster home, never to see her again.

Needless to say, Karma was removed from that home within a week. She spent her days terrorising the couple who'd taken her in, the ones who had robbed her of Joanna. Her tiny body was full of anger at the injustice of her life.

She bounced from home to home until finally, she turned eighteen and was in charge of her own life.

With hope in her steps, she picked her way towards Joanna's house, hitching rides across the country where needed until finally she was back on the doorstep she found sanctuary at so many years ago.

But it wasn't Joanna who answered the door.

Joanna had died two years before Karma had finally returned home to her.

And Karma was broken all over again.

Chapter Three: The Farm

Peter Walker always knew he was an unusual man.

And it wasn't just because his mother told him often and passionately about how special and unique he was. Because she did do that, but most mothers do. It's part of their job description.

No.

Peter's sense of grandiosity was one that grew alongside him as he went out into the world and noticed that other people weren't quite like him. They were different from him. Less bright. Less imaginative. Less passionate. Just…less

At the age of fifteen Peter found God. Or rather, as he liked to think of it, God found him. And in the pages of the Bible he found the rhyme and reason behind this feeling of 'other' that he'd lived with his whole life. He found that he was the second coming. It was the only logical explanation as to why his fellow men seemed so below him. Because he wasn't like them. He was special, chosen and anointed for a higher purpose.

When he shared his discovery with his mother, the true meaning behind his life that he had found, her face had drawn tight, which wasn't flattering on a woman her age. It caused her eyes to show in high definition the years of stress she had lived through. The arguments with his father. The affairs she smiled through. The loneliness she'd felt at raising him whilst his Dad worked tirelessly to achieve freedom for the guilty in order to keep them in the life they'd grown accustomed to.

Peter didn't like to see his mother age so rapidly, but there was a thrill to be had at being the one who caused such an emotional shift in a person. It showed Peter the true power of words, and more importantly how he could wield them to affect another.

But he loved his mother, in the same way one might love a hamster, and he didn't want to cause her pain so he never spoke about it again. But the truth of his existence hung in the air between them every day.

Sometimes Peter wished he had kept his relationship to God to himself rather than sharing it with the one person he thought might have understood, might have been proud of his higher purpose. Instead, she grew skittish around him whenever she caught him with a Bible in his hand, but what had Peter truly expected? His Mother was just human. She couldn't begin to understand the power that ran through her only child's veins.

Every year he grew more and more sure of his theory. Spotting miracles peppered throughout his youth that could only be explained by having his true father, God, looking out for his latest son.

The way the car had mounted the curb and killed his friend instead of him. The last minute change of plans that meant he avoided the bombing of the train he had been booked to catch. The attention of women so far out of his league that were somehow drawn to him despite Peter never chasing them.

Yes. God was always looking out for Peter and that meant he was special.

On his twenty-first birthday he walked past a homeless teenage girl, begging for scraps at the side of the road and that was his sign. A sign that he'd finally been given the purpose God had laid out for him. He needed to bring peace to those who needed it most. He needed to bring the wayward in-line and create a Utopia.

As though the universe was confirming his thoughts, his mother died quite suddenly. A faulty gas cooker had caused her to asphyxiate in her sleep. These things happen, humans are only temporary and Peter didn't shed a tear for the woman who had loved and raised him. She was in a better place now. She was being cared for by God.

Her death, as if a final gift, created an opportunity. Peter found himself the heir of one hundred acres of family land, and his dad didn't care enough to fight him for it. By this point in time the relationship between the two of them was non-existent, his mother the only thread that held them together. With her death the two men parted ways, never to speak again. The land his mother had left him was destined to be used to create a better world for lost souls.

It was unkempt, full of forestry but that suited Peter just fine. He knew that the outside world wouldn't understand the process he had to go through in order to better their lives. They would have to wait for the final results. Only then would society understand Peter and his importance.

He knew he was young.

Much younger than those who had tried to create a better society than him before.

Charles Manson had been thirty-four when he tried to make a change.

Jim Jones had been close to Peter's age when he

attempted to bring a better message to the world, in his mid-twenties, but he hadn't had the power of God on his side.

David Brandt Berg, an old man in his forties, had left it far too late to try and right the wrongs of the world.

They had all failed in their plans to create a better society. But Peter Walker would not.

Peter Walker knew what he had to do and he had the time and the balls to get it done.

The first thing Peter did, shortly after the ink from the executor's signature had dried, was build a series of small shacks on the land he'd inherited. He buried them deep inside the trees and bushes, away from prying eyes that might try to interfere in his important work.

The second thing Peter did was return to the street corner where he walked past the homeless teenage girl. She was his sign, his driving force and as such, she deserved to have a founding role in the better world he was destined to create.

Chapter Four: Zoe

I throw my backpack down onto the hotel bed and take a look at the room around me. So, this was going to be home - at least for tonight. And then after that it would be another hotel room, just as bland as this one, in another town and so on and so forth.

I was surprised when I'd been given the name of the hotel we were staying in tonight. It was just a bog standard chain hotel. I sort of assumed that Karma Jones, the sought-after speaker that she was, would be able to choose somewhere a little more upmarket to lay her head.

Today, before attending the first of Karma's lectures on what was to be a two-month tour of the country, I'd finally get to meet the woman behind the name. I was perhaps just a touch obsessed with Karma and her origin story. My third podcast had been about The Farm and the manhunt for the adults who had run it. I spent hours reading every article, blog and forum post I could find about them, especially about the person the children had been made to call Father.

There was nothing concrete about him though, just

endless theories about what might have happened to him. He was clearly a man with very useful friends that had helped him disappear from existence. All I needed was a thread though, if I could find something useful to grab a hold of then I knew I'd be able to unravel all the secrets that were keeping him hidden. It never came though. Wherever he was now was stitched up tightly.

It was as though he'd vanished into thin air the night Karma had escaped. There wasn't a single reported sighting of him. Then again, all the public and the police had to go on were descriptions of him from the mouths of babes. And after what he'd put them through I wouldn't be surprised to hear that they couldn't describe his face in accurate detail. Young minds block out nightmares as best they can.

The sexual, physical and verbal abuse that those children had received at the hands of the adults around them still brought a catch to my throat. Karma had been the oldest of them all at eleven when she'd escaped, and so far she was the only one who'd spoken out about parts of what they'd lived through. The other forty-eight children who escaped that night had been happy to live in anonymity ever since. Karma had divulged, during one lecture, that she was in touch with her 'siblings' as she called them and that she respected their right to live quiet, comfortable lives after all they'd been through.

Karma began speaking about her experiences openly the day after her eighteenth birthday, the day she was legally an adult and able to make her own decisions. The various foster families she'd lived with over the years had discouraged her from telling her story publicly, perhaps afraid of the horrors she could verbalise. A lot of people were uncomfortable when she first started out, the young girl was so full of rage despite the poetically detached way she was able to speak about her life before she was rescued. It resonated in her at every public function and only those with a strong stomach managed to stay the whole way through her early talks.

Twenty years later and Karma has been on a journey to adjust her public persona, she keeps the vitriol to a minimum at her events and has long since given up blaming those who failed her and the other children.

Because they had been failed.

The Farm had existed just outside of a small town, and the town had been full of whispers for years about Father and his followers. And yet nobody brought those rumours to the police, stating in later years that they were afraid of what The Farm would do to them if they did. It was true that crime rates rose in the town whenever an 'outsider' drifted too near the land owned by Father, but the fact of the matter was that grown adults had put their own safety above the lives of the children they must have known existed.

To this day residents of the town are still the biggest donors to the foundation Karma set up on her twenty-first birthday to provide support for others who had lived through physical abuse. For other people life has failed. Guilt is always a reliable driving force.

Now Karma was one of the most in-demand non-celebrities in the country. Her schedule was booked at least eighteen months in advance, and she donated 60% of her earnings from her public engagements to the Foundation. She shares her time equally between the corporate and philanthropic sides, regularly attending and running survivor's workshops and taking the time to engage personally with everyone who attends. Karma was the poster child for survivors of abuse and she took her responsibility seriously.

It would be her fortieth birthday next year and she'd decided to mark the occasion by promising to tell her full story, in all its gory detail, on a podcast. She announced that it would be the first, and last time she would speak in complete detail about all that she'd lived through.

We received slithers of the truth over the years via her public talks, but she'd never given a legitimate interview to any publication. Nor had she released a tell-all biography. The true crime forums I participate in went wild when the news hit. Finally we'd know the true depths of The Farm. Finally we'd know the woman behind the legend.

I had applied on a whim to be the host for her story and surprisingly, despite the amount of applicants who all had far bigger audiences than me, I'd been the one Karma had chosen. And still, to this day, I can't believe it.

I'd beaten out national broadcasters, celebrity broadcasters and social media influencers to be the one trusted to tell Karma's story. Perhaps that's what one of my first questions would be to the woman I admired so much: Why me? Why my podcast?

Then again, if I asked that question, then I risked highlighting my nerves at being trusted with the story the world was desperate to hear. My subscriber count had doubled the day I was announced as the winner, and it has been growing over the last two weeks. People were gagging to be amongst the first listeners, and I'd had countless emails begging for early access.

All of which I turned down; the contents of my contract had made it crystal clear that all episodes were to be released simultaneously to the general public. Karma didn't want there to be a hierarchy. She wanted every listener to be treated equally and I respected that.

A knock at the door disrupts my moment of peace and I glance at myself in the mirror as I move to answer it. I don't have time to do anything more than run my hands through my curls, hoping it brings life back to them, before I take a deep breath and open the door. This is the moment everything begins, the moment I meet a member of Karma's team face to face.

A middle-aged man stands in the hallway.

It's unkind to think of him as middle-aged when really, there were probably only a few years between us, but I perpetually think of myself as still being twenty-three as opposed to the thirty-four-year-old woman I am. He furrows his eyebrows, which were too bushy for his face and regards me. Having always believed you should match the energy others give you, I return the favour.

So, for the two seconds he stands taking in my physical appearance I catalogue his. Of course there were the aforementioned eyebrows, that framed eyes so blue they looked unnatural. Like contact lenses a cosplayer might wear if they were at a Sailor Moon convention.

His hair was purposefully unkempt. I could see the remnants of the clay he'd used to style it so carefully in order to seem unbothered by his appearance. He wasn't an unattractive man physically, but there was something about his presence that made me feel uneasy. An ego about him that called out to my gut, warning me to be wary.

I felt the same way when I saw the photo next to his bland biography on the Foundation's website. Harry Smith - the Foundation and Karma's press officer.

But I wasn't about to give him the satisfaction of letting him know that I'd looked him up.

"Zoe?" he asks, as though there's a possibility he's knocked on the wrong room.

I'm not sure if I just look vastly different from the publicity head-shot on my website or if he's trying to unnerve me. It's true, my head-shot was a touch airbrushed but then again whose wasn't? And yes, I had spent two hours in the hairdresser's chair prior to the shoot making sure every curl shone with health (I couldn't run the risk of anyone pointing out my dry ends) but I didn't look that different - did I?

The urge to reach for my makeup strikes me, the desperate need to add another layer of concealer to the bags under my eyes but I decide against it. I hadn't been chosen for my looks, I'm not sure in truth why I was chosen, but I'm sure it wasn't for my looks. And the longer the man standing in front of me appraises me, the more I grow irritated by his presence.

"Who's asking?" I reply, not caring about the petulance in my tone. The chance to work with Karma was a once-in-a-lifetime opportunity, but if it meant spending time with people like this then I'm not sure I can hack two months of it. Maybe Jake had been right. Maybe I should have stayed home. All I can do is hope that this judgmental prick won't be travelling around with us the entire length of my contract.

"My name is Harry, I'm Karma Jones' press officer."

He holds out his hand and finally smiles at me, clearly pleased at having a reason to state his job title. With no other choice available to me I follow suit and we shake hands for a beat longer than necessary. Still sizing each other up.

"Pleased to meet you, Harry," I lie. "Is Miss Jones ready to meet?"

He nods and takes a step back from the door, raising an arm to guide me out into the corridor. I pause to slip my key card into my pocket and then follow his lead, the excitement in my stomach growing with every step. I am finally going to meet Karma in the flesh. The girl, no - woman, I'd learnt so much about. Even Harry's mouth breathing couldn't ruin this.

Chapter Five: Target #15

That morning started like any other in Jessica Lane's life.

She woke up after the third sound of her alarm, tied her dressing gown around her waist with its mismatched cord - she was always muddling them up - and plodded down the stairs cursing herself for leaving her slippers at the foot of them. She did it every night without fail because she didn't trust them not to trip her as she climbed the staircase to bed, but she regretted her decision every morning especially when the winter drafts found their way into the flat.

Upstairs she heard the familiar grunt of her husband and the small voice rousing him from slumber. Smiling to herself she allowed a feeling of contentment to wash over her, she never thought she'd be this happy and settled after everything that happened to her four years ago. But now, here she was, in their overpriced flat they'd be paying off until they were long past retirement age, with a man who loved her completely, who helped heal her wounds, allowed her to see joy in the world again, and a two-year-old daughter who made her laugh every day.

Life may have dealt her a shit hand at one point, but it had spent the years since trying to make it up to her.

She pulls the post from the letterbox and carries it absentmindedly towards the kitchen, ready to put the kettle on and start the day properly. It's a Saturday and she's been looking forward to a day off all week. The office has been working on overdrive due to seven project deadlines and she's barely had a minute to think let alone relax in the evenings - there are always emails to answer.

Now that everything has been submitted to the clients, she can truly enjoy the day. First of all, she's going to clean the flat top to bottom, and then maybe at lunchtime the three of them will test out the menu at the new family-friendly pub that's just opened up down the road. Yes, it will be the perfect lazy weekend she desperately needs.

As she waits for the kettle to boil, she heaps coffee into her mug and a tea bag into her husband's, and thumbs through the day's post. A bunch of leaflets and the local paper - all things she's asked the postman to stop delivering to them. With a sigh she picks the pile up and moves towards the bin to dispose of them when something catches her eye.

On the corner of one of the leaflets, she feels something that is embossed. Parting the pile of paperwork she pulls it loose, finding a flyer for an open day at the local museum. She can't think of anything worse than spending the day traipsing around exhibitions with a two-year-old, but there in the bottom right-hand corner of the leaflet is a branding she knows she can't ignore.

It's an intricate design of Medusa's head. Absent-mindedly, she rubs her thumb over it, feeling the detail of every individual snake's features as she tries to keep her mind in the present but it's no use. This one symbol has thrown her back into the past so viciously that it's not worth the energy to fight to stay in the present.

Jessica is four years younger now, a fresh-faced twenty-four-year-old. And she's been in a relationship with Jamie Fletcher for thirteen months.

Kind, reliable, respectable Jamie.

The man of her dreams and despite their ten-year age gap, he's her contemporary in every way. They like the same shows, share the same memes and both look forward to building a future together.

The imbalance between them started quietly, as it always does. An innocent comment about preferring her hair up in a high ponytail so he could see her beautiful smile easier, or a polite request to change her outfit into a dress he preferred so he could see the shape of her body - all tiny little requests that she abided by without questioning them. Because who wouldn't want to be attractive to their partner?

Next, it moved to concerned advice about who she should be spending her time with. Her friends' flaws were highlighted to her in technicolour and she couldn't argue with him. Everything he was saying was true. They did all drink too much, they weren't serious about their careers or their relationships. Not like she was. She was a grown-up now and to achieve all her dreams she needed to set herself apart from her past.

Then he pointed out that her job was below her. She was worth more than she was getting paid and had more brains than she was given credit for. Jessica was flattered by this observation, nobody had ever told her she was too smart for something before. So she handed in her notice the next day and spent the following months scouring recruitment websites, asking Jamie each time for his opinion on whether she should apply or not. She never did. All the jobs she suggested weren't worthy of her time, he said. She didn't believe in herself as much as he did, he said. It hurt him to see she thought so little of herself, he said.

Eventually, she stopped looking at the websites and settled into her daily routine, the right job would find her when it was ready. She knew it. Jamie knew it.

She was restless in their flat on her own, she found herself texting Jamie several times an hour, asking his opinion on everything from what she should watch to what she should have for lunch. He always replied and he was always there for her.

Kind, reliable, respectable Jamie.

He was the one who made a doctor's appointment to help her cope with her rising anxiety and insomnia. He was the one, who in the doctor's office, told the truth about the nights she spent pacing the floor worrying about their future. About how isolated she felt from the world. Jamie made sure the doctor took her seriously and paid for her prescription because she didn't have the £9.60 to pay for it herself. Jamie was so generous.

The sleeping pills helped, and after a week of taking them, she felt like herself again. She felt brighter and even had the energy to put on makeup when Jamie took her out for their anniversary dinner. He was pleased with the effort she made as he knew how much of her energy it would have taken, she'd even worn his favourite dress, the one he left lying out on the bed for her. It was so comforting to have somebody take care of her.

That night Jessica woke up with a start, still groggy from the sleeping pills she wasn't sure if she was dreaming or not. Jamie was on top of her, panting and thrusting, she could feel every inch of him inside of her.

Inside where he wasn't invited.
Kind, reliable, respectable Jamie.

He looked down at her face and with a start noticed her eyes were open. He flew away from her so quickly she was surprised he didn't break anything and then he lay on his side, under the covers, facing away from her, so still she would have been sure it had been a hallucination had it not been for the damp patch between her legs.

The sleeping tablets stole her away before she could react.

In the morning she awoke to Jamie placing a mug of coffee on her bedside table and she eyed him cooly.

"How did you sleep, love?" he asked, as he'd asked every morning for the last week.

"I know what you did," she replied firmly, shocked by her tone, a strength growing within her that she thought she'd lost long ago.

Jamie stands at the foot of the bed staring at her, all traces of affection wiped from his eyes and then he smiles at her. But it's not the smile she's used to. This one is cruel, detached from the rest of his features.

"I'm sorry I woke you," he replies, as though that's the apology she deserves. And for a moment she wants to accept it. Life is so much easier with Jamie making every decision for her, she never has to worry about what clothes to wear, what food to eat or how much she should weigh. He takes care of it all.

"How many times?" she asks, not wanting to hear the answer.

"Well, that was the first time you woke up," he replies, that smile never leaving his face. The kind of smile a wolf would flash to a lamb before it ripped its throat out.

Jessica can't help herself as she picks up the mug of coffee and hurls its boiling contents across the bed towards him. He yells out as the liquid touches his bare skin. She flies from the bed and throws her entire weight towards him, clawing, punching, and biting every inch of him she can find until eventually he pushes her away from him. How could he do this to her? How could her sweet Jamie do this to her?

The sobs that crawl up from her stomach render her paralysed on the floor and he gazes at her with disgust for a moment before leaving the room. She hears him slam the front door of their flat behind him and knows it's all over. He's left and it's all over.

With shaking limbs, she crawls across the floor towards her mobile phone and searches for her mother's number. It's been so long since she spoke to her mum, Jamie always said she was a negative woman so Jessica eventually stopped calling her.

Please pick up Mum. Please pick up.

Her mum answers the phone and between sobs, Jessica explains what happened. Her mum is at the flat within twenty minutes, holding her daughter in her arms, telling her everything will be okay.

It is her mother who holds her hand as they walk through the doors of the police station and report what Jamie has done to her. Her mother who waits outside the room as Jessica is examined. There is evidence she has had sex but there is no evidence of foul play. No bruising externally or internally. No evidence that it wasn't consensual. Jessica tells the officer her story but halfway through there is a knock at the door. Something new has come up that is related to Jessica's complaint.

Jamie has filed a restraining order against her. There are photos of the injuries she inflicted upon him. He's saying that her obsession with him had gotten too hard to live with and that she'd attacked him when he

told her it was over.
    Everybody but her mum believes him.
    Because he is kind, reliable, respectable Jamie.
    And she is a nutjob.

    Back in the present Jessica shouts upstairs to her husband and asks him to get their daughter ready for a day at the museum. They must attend this event. From open to close they will be witnessed by hundreds of people walking around the exhibitions, having lunch in the cafe, laughing together as a little unit on their walk home. This is important. They must all have a solid alibi. She lights a candle in her living room and tears the leaflet into small pieces, being sure to burn the Medusa branding as she was instructed. The rest of the paper she throws up into the air around her like confetti, laughing like a child as she does so. If her husband thinks she's acting out of character, he makes no mention of it as he kisses her good morning. He loves her and all her eccentricities.
    Jessica knows what's going to happen today, and she realises that this weekend is going to be the exact one she needs. The one she's needed for so many years.

    Across town, Jamie Fletcher flashes his award-winning smile at the barista who hands him his coffee. She's eighteen at best, but she's exactly his type, small and unassuming. Ready for the world but not quite sure how to take it on. He goes to introduce himself but she turns away at the last moment, busying herself with preparing her next order. Oh well, he thinks to himself. Her loss.
    What Jamie doesn't notice though is the bland-looking woman talking on her phone outside the cafe

ready to offer a confused stranger a helping hand into a waiting car.

As he takes two large gulps of his coffee he feels a small tingling sensation crawling down his throat. Little does he know that he just ingested his own death warrant.

Chapter Six: Zoe

I follow Harry through winding corridors, full of cookie cutter doorways and decor and down one flight of stairs until suddenly he stops walking. I'm so lost in my own thoughts that I nearly bump into him but thankfully manage to correct my path and instead just stumble over my own feet. I don't think that's a better outcome though, and neither does he if the roll of his eyes is to be understood.

He knocks on the door once, to announce his presence and then pulls out a key card before swiping it across the panel to the side. It's all so cloak and dagger that I have to stifle a giggle. I know Karma is a relatively big deal but it's not like anyone will be looking out for her here, in a hotel where rooms cost just £89 a night including breakfast.

Behind the door is a room not dissimilar to my own. All rooms in places like this are the same, it's what makes them such a safe and familiar bet to people who travel often. The town you're in might be different but the room still feels like home.

However in this room I can see that the bed has

been pushed up against the far wall to create a larger sitting area. There aren't any personal belongings lying around, unlike my hurricane of an existence in room 246, so I guess this must be what passes for an office space whilst Karma is on the road.

The woman sitting in the armchair, lost in her own world, was smaller than I'd imagined. I'm so used to seeing her standing on a stage, her presence projected across screens whilst being lit up by a thousand phones. But she is still, unmistakably, the Karma Jones.

Every inch of my brain longs to reach out to the woman, just four years my senior, to tell her she's become somewhat a personal hero of mine. Not necessarily because of what she'd survived, but because of how she turned a childhood that would have broken many into a fierce legacy.

She constantly lobbies for harsher punishments for rapists and more support for victims of domestic abuse. She leads war cries at vigils when another woman is murdered simply for walking home alone. Karma Jones is braver and stronger than anybody I have ever known, and all I wanted to do was to tell this woman how much she means to me.

It wasn't the best idea though, if Karma or her team saw me acting so unprofessionally, like a true fangirl, they might take me off the project. After all, there was an entire ocean of podcasters lined up ready to take my place.

Karma hasn't yet looked up from her phone to greet us and Harry impatiently clears his throat. Quick as a flash Karma looks up at him, and I'm struck by her beauty.

It wasn't that she necessarily had the most symmetrical face, but she was still beautiful in the way that Greek goddesses had once been painted.

Her jet black hair was swept away from her face,

tied back into a haphazard bun and many stray strands have escaped its grasp. Her fringe is parted in the middle, clearly it was in that irritating stage of regrowth. And her brown skin glowed, so much so that I wanted to ask her what moisturiser she used. But it was her eyes that startled me the most, such a dark brown that at first glance they appeared black. If eyes truly were the gateway to the soul then Karma's reflected all the pain she's lived through.

All the photographs and video footage I'd watched whilst learning about her had failed to capture the complexities of her presence in the flesh. I felt comforted and unnerved all at the same time as I drank her existence in. No wonder people were so willing to part with their money just to be in the same room as her.

"Sorry Harry, news update." She shrugs and places her phone face down on the side table next to her. Standing, with a smile now, she extends her hand out towards me.

"And you must be Zoe," she says and we shake hands. A brief shock jolts between us as our palms touch and I quickly apologise.

"Static shock. All the carpet," I explain with a shrug, trying to be nonchalant. I can feel my cheeks flushing warm despite trying my best not to appear embarrassed, because really, what did I have to be embarrassed about? These things happen. But trust my luck to make it happen in my first meeting with Karma.

"Quite a connection," laughs Karma who sits back down and gestures at the seat next to her. "It's a pleasure to meet you, Zoe."

Harry moves to join us when Karma tuts at him.

"Thank you, Harry, why don't you take the night off?" It was delivered as a question but was quite clearly an order.

"I think perhaps I ought to stay, make sure things get off to a smooth start." It was clear from the way his eyes flick over me once again that he doesn't trust me. Which is irritating. I am the one they had invited here, the one they'd decided to trust with this story and yet he has the audacity to act like I'm a gatecrashing nuisance. It was his email, his offer of this job that blew my life up. That was the final nail in the coffin for my feelings towards Harry.

"Zoe here is part of the inner circle for the next two months," Harry goes to protest and she holds up a hand to stop him. "She's under the same NDA as the rest of you, right? You signed the NDA, right?" She directs the question to me and I nod quickly. "Good. Then she knows the only information she can discuss publicly is what we talk about in the interviews. Everything else is background noise. I don't see what the problem is. You can go now Harry."

Reluctantly he does as he's told, letting the door close a little louder than necessary behind him.

Karma stands and moves to the mini-fridge that's seated on the dressing table. She pulls out two miniature bottles of white wine and shakes them at me inquisitively.

"That would be lovely, thank you." I hate every syllable falling from my mouth. Why am I talking as though I've got a stick up my arse? This isn't like me. I don't get tongue-tied or put on airs and graces.

"Hope mugs are okay," says Karma as she decants the bottles into two white porcelain mugs she lifts from the coffee tray.

"Wouldn't be the first time," I reply with a laugh, determined to relax and show Karma who I really am.

We sat together in silence for a moment, both sipping from our mugs of wine, both pretending that it was a comfortable silence that had formed between us.

"Sorry about Harry by the way. He's employed by the Foundation, therefore everything he does is with its reputation in mind. He doesn't mean anything by it."

"That's okay, I get it." I hold back on my true feelings toward Harry. If I'd been at home with one of my friends I would have described the paranoid rat exactly as I found him, but it was clear that in Karma's eyes, he was only doing his job. She probably doesn't even know what a judgemental prick he is.

"Doesn't mean he has to be such a judgemental prick about it though," Karma adds and I can't help the shocked laugh that barks from within my chest. Perhaps the next two months weren't going to be as hard as I'd thought when Harry first arrived at my door and appraised me. Karma was more on my wavelength than I thought.

Before I can compose myself enough to reply, a noise emits itself from my phone. Without making excuses I unlock it and read the latest e-mail, I can't help myself. Every time my phone makes this particular chime I have to look almost instantly, it's a compulsion. Because that noise means there's been another body found. That noise means there's been another death.

Jamie Fletcher, a 48 year old financial advisor, has been found dead in a side alley. He asphyxiated on his own vomit and had it not been for the two prong marks in his neck and the calling card on his chest, his death may have been dismissed as nothing more than intoxication.

"I'm sorry, I..." I go to explain myself, having remembered whose company I'm in and how important it is that I'm thought well of - my fingers are still hovering over my screen though.

"The Medusa Network?" Karma asks and I nod.

Jamie marks the fifteenth body found in as many weeks now, scattered all across the country. Each had died in the same manner, and each came with a calling card pinned neatly to their chest.

A white business card, with a pencil drawing of a Medusa and a single word. Guilty. And it wouldn't be long before the cause of Jamie's guilt was made known.

The truth always seemed to seep out by the time the body was buried, usually in the form of a dossier delivered somewhere random on the internet. Sometimes it was in message boards, sometimes in online chats on video games. The dossier could appear anywhere - it was Medusa's way of letting the world know she was always watching.

"I am sorry, I wouldn't normally be so rude but..."

"It's fine. You're not the only one who's obsessed with the case. Have they found out what he did yet?" Karma follows my lead, picks up her phone and tunes in to read the latest headlines.

"I'm hoping to do a series on the Medusa Network, once we're done with your show of course." I don't know why I've just confessed this to her, the person who's supposed to be the sole focus of my energy for the next two months but she doesn't seem to mind. In fact, she appears just as enthralled by the murder spree as I do. It was refreshing, sitting next to someone who shared my interests, however dark they may be at times.

I tried to talk to Jake once or twice about the case, to get his opinion on what was happening, but all he ever wanted to focus on was the person who died. Claiming that nobody deserved to die like that. He had a little too much empathy with the murder victims now I come to think about it.

He wanted to stop discussing the network altogether once light began to be shed on the so-called victims' crimes. He didn't understand the Network's drive for death, because Jake had never wanted to hurt anyone in his entire life. Innocent Jake had never felt the simmering violence of hate stew inside his veins.

But I had.

Sometimes I still do.

"What angle do you think you'll take?" asks Karma and again I'm struck by how odd it feels to have somebody actively engage with me in conversation about my passion project.

"I want to talk to the survivors, the ones we know about anyway. To see how they feel living without nightmares." I hadn't meant to say that. I hadn't meant to make it so painfully obvious that I felt no pity towards those the Network killed.

It wasn't the correct thing to say. It wasn't a nice thing to say.

But it was the truth.

There hadn't been a body yet that hadn't been linked to some crime they escaped punishment for. Rapists. Paedophiles. Abusers. All had walked away from their victims with barely a scratch on their reputation.

Yes, there is a little voice in my mind that likes to remind me from time to time that surely the Network couldn't be 100% certain of their guilt, but I pushed that part away from me more often than not, because it only confused my morality.

"And that's why I knew you were the right woman to tell my story." Karma raises her mug towards mind and we clink, the sound of china bouncing off each other ringing in the start of a healthy working relationship. Then, without pause, we both turned back to our phones to see if there were any updates.

An hour later and there was a knock at Karma's door. The gentle conversation between the two of us paused at the intrusion.

"That will be Harry, the car's probably waiting outside to pick me up," she explained. I felt a twinge of disappointment that our time together had come to an end, it had passed by so quickly, so easily, that I felt like I hadn't made the most of it.

"Thanks for the drink," I say as I move to the bathroom to swill out my mug. She follows me and we stand with our shoulders touching as the tap runs.

"Thanks for the company," she adds as we stare at each other in the mirror. Her hand brushes over mine as she pours the running water over her mug and it hovers there for a moment, the cold water running between our fingers as they lay millimetres from each other.

She holds my gaze in the mirror as she pulls her hand away, shakes the last few drops from the mug and places it on the table in front of the mirror. I'm about to say something, to ask her if she felt a moment pass between the two of us, when the door knocks again.

"Coming!" she cries out, and just like that, any intimacy that might have existed between us is broken. Did I imagine it? The air had felt loaded when her hand touched mine, but it could have been innocent.

Of course it was innocent.

We've only just met.

And yet I felt more of a connection to her in that hour than I had to Jake in the last few months, but still, I'm overthinking things. Longing for moments that never existed. I can admit to myself that I have a crush on Karma, but that doesn't mean she'd ever feel the same.

As I leave her room and wave goodbye to her and Harry, who are leaving earlier than I'm due to, I do feel a little guilty. The reason I'd been so keen to take on this job hadn't just been to tell her story, it had been to get to know a woman who fascinated me. Who attracted me. And maybe Jake had realised that but had been unable to verbalise it for fear I'd admit the truth.

I'd taken this job for professional, and personal reasons. I just had to remember to put professional first from now on.

Chapter Seven: Zoe

Laying in my bed the next morning I take a moment to take stock of the last twenty-four hours.

When my alarm had first sounded I'd hit snooze, as usual, and waited for Jake to sleepily snuggle into my back. Of course he didn't, and I'd been surprised by how much I missed his presence. Not that ending our relationship had been the wrong call, we were too different to ever make it last long-term, but he'd still made me laugh more often than not and it would have been nice to keep that in my life for a little while longer.

I haven't made a mistake coming here though, choosing this opportunity. I'm certain about that now.

I sat with Karma, in mostly comfortable silence, until we had to leave the hotel to attend the talk Karma had been booked to host.

After the moment I imagined between us in the bathroom, I had given myself half an hour to recenter before I called a taxi to take me to Karma's talk. I stood at the back of the room and marvelled at the atmosphere around me. Every single person was enraptured by the woman on stage before them. There were no small pockets of chatter or giggles of discontent. Every single person from the attendees through to the staff had stood with drawn breath, and listened to Karma and her words.

They sighed in sympathy at the appropriate moments, loudly agreed when she asked for their support and opened their wallets wide when the card machines came round. Karma may one day tire of the world, but the world was far from being tired of her.

All the while I watched the crowd in fascination, wondering how many of them would one day tune into my podcast. It was a selfish thought, but still it thrilled me to wonder. One day these people would be enthralled by my voice, by my story telling - it all seemed so far-fetched to imagine but one day soon it would be true. I would hypnotise audiences like these around the world, just as Karma does.

And it was Karma who had given me this chance. Karma who had hand picked me from all the applicants and who trusted me enough to share the next two months of her life with me.

After the talk we had stayed as long as was polite at the function before quickly ducking out of the room, grabbing a bag of chips from the kebab shop next door and retiring back to our hotel rooms for the night. Everything had just been so light and carefree, exactly what I needed to remind myself that the breakup with Jake was the right call.

I'd woken up and made a decision, after a fitful night's sleep, punctuated with lustful dreams about Karma, it was time to get my head on straight. No pun intended.

I have to remember that I am here for a reason.

I am here for work, and my first official on-the-record interview with Karma is scheduled to start in two hours. Thankfully I'm a prepper, so I already have my first batch of questions scribbled down in my notebook. Which is a good job because just as I am about to get out of my bed my phone chirps with the notification that always steals me away from the world.

There had been another murder.

Sinking back into my pillow, I pull the duvet up to my neck, push my arms out of the top, get comfortable, and open the news story.

Last night's chips gurgle in my stomach as I read the victim's name.

Graham Williams.

The most beloved teacher at my secondary school. The man who had been my mentor as I undertook my final exams, was the first person who encouraged me to lean into my interests and strengths.

It wasn't possible.

Mr. Williams was a good and kind soul. He rarely raised his voice and always tried to see the best in his students, even those that acted up. Every child in his class had passed their exams, even those the rest of the teachers had given up on. Graham Williams was a blessing to education. And the Medusa Network had left him to choke on his own vomit in a derelict building.

Is this how the other victims' loved ones felt when they were given the news?

Or were they unstartled, quick to believe that the person they'd cared about was a monster.

There must have been a mistake.

The Network had to have made a mistake.

His poor wife.

Oh god, his poor wife.

She was just as kind as he was. Always sending him into work with a box of cookies or cakes she'd baked the night before, never wanting a child to go without a sweet treat for the day. I pray that the press have yet to dig up their home address, that his widow could grieve in private at least for now.

So far, no dossier has been released on Mr

Williams. It had been six hours since his body was formally identified, which going by the usual time frame of the Network meant we could expect the information to be in the public domain by this evening. It usually took around twelve hours, give or take how rapidly the document spread around the internet.

By the time my day is finished, Medusa will have put their hands up and apologised for making a mistake. I know it.

Mr. Williams will be remembered as a tragic murder rather than an offender who deserved what was coming to him. The Network wasn't infallible, everybody eventually makes mistakes and they had made a mistake on this one. I only hope they are moral enough to own up to it and clear my beloved teacher's name.

With a shake of my head I put my phone down on the bed. This won't do.

I can't go into my first official interview with an angry mind.

If I do, then I run the risk of wasting this opportunity that fate had bestowed on me, I won't be as naturally present in the interview as I need to be. I would be letting the memory of Mr. Williams down.

He still commented on every one of my podcast episodes, telling me how proud he was of all I've achieved. He did that for a lot of his former students, wanting them to know he was still in their corner. His messages to us all were screen-shot and shared in countless group chats between long broken friendship groups and the reaction was always the same - Mr. Williams was still a legend.

No.

No.

I have to stop thinking about him. I can be sad later on, when I'm alone in my room with nothing that needs to be done. I can mourn him, and all he meant to me, once the Network had admitted they made a mistake.

With a sigh I lean over the side of the bed and pull my messenger bag towards me using my foot. I hook the strap and lift it up from the floor towards my chest. Unzipping the top I reach inside until my hands find what I'm looking for - my green notebook.

My tally of deaths as Jake took to calling it.

It is important research though, if I'm intending on one day investigating the Medusa Network on my podcast then it's vital I record the news as I digest it.

12) Naomi Stuart - Trafficker

13) Phil Stuart - Trafficker

14) Bobby Clint - Murderer

15) Jamie Fletcher - Sexual assault

16) Graham Williams - TBC - Mistake?

I underlined the word 'mistake' several times and then read back the full list to myself.

All fifteen of the other targets of the Medusa Network had undoubtedly committed crimes. They deserved to have justice delivered to them, but for the first time, now somebody I know has died by their hands, I'm wondering if they're going about it in the right way?

Clearly their research isn't as thorough as it should be when dealing out an execution. Why else would Mr. Williams have been targeted? And if the Network weren't making sure their targets were actually guilty of what they killed them for then what was to stop another innocent person from being caught up in their crusade?

So far, with a dark fascination, I'd been addicted to the coverage of each murder, refreshing my feed multiple times after a body was discovered until the dossier was released. Wanting to be amongst the first to digest the information. Desperate to read about the horrific crimes that deserved such a brutal punishment. But now I feel a little ashamed of myself and my interest in the Network. Now I can see the other side of their work. The side of the people left behind. Their grief. The unjust punishment loved ones had to live with after the news broke. They were innocent regardless of what crime the dead were guilty of.

The significant others and families of all the victims so far had gone into hiding. Most have had to move in order to escape the shadow of their former loved one's crimes. That wasn't right, was it?

Innocent people were having their lives torn apart, in the most public fashion, were being hounded because somebody they loved happened to be a monster. There has to be a better way to get justice for the people the victims had hurt. There just has to be.

If the Network could find out about the victims' crimes and publish their evidence globally then the general public assumed that anyone who associated with the deceased must also have known. After all, how could strangers in the virtual world know something that they hadn't realised when seeing the victim day in day out? In the eyes of the world the victims' families were just as guilty as they were. And that wasn't fair.

You could live with somebody every single day of your life and never see the side of them they wanted to keep hidden.

The loved ones of the victims should be swallowed up in empathy and offered support from all angles, but they were just left to rot because in most people's minds, the apple never fell far.

After putting my notebook back inside the privacy pocket of my bag, I finally force myself to get out of bed. A shower would help calm me, get me ready for my first proper interview with Karma. To throw away this opportunity would be wasteful, I can have my personal crisis once the work has been done.

Still, as the hot water cleanses my skin, it can't wash away the moral conscience that has gripped me. Am I as bad as the Network for being obsessed with their work? If the public stopped paying attention to their crimes, would the deaths stop? Would their glory fade? The more we spoke about them, the more power we gave them and only now am I questioning whether that power is being wielded correctly.

If the Network has made a mistake with Mr. Williams, which they had, how many more mistakes would they make along the way?

Chapter Eight: The Farm

The young girl's name, or at least the name she gave him was Erin. And Erin proved her worth when she brought three additional founders into the fold. Peter married her two days after they all moved in, in a ceremony he officiated because his words were God's words.

Erin, Owen, Ian and Paula were enthralled by Peter and the new world order he promised them. They trusted him because his word had provided them shelter, food and safety.

In return all they had to do was spread his word amongst the homeless and vulnerable, those who current societal ties had thrown aside. They weren't smart enough for the best jobs, or kind enough for traditional relationships or attractive enough for acceptance - or at least that's what they'd been told by the general populace.

And so Peter's new life society on his dead mother's land grew in size.

Day after day there appeared to be a new member

ready to sign in and take his word and teachings as gospel. He was King on his land and finally, Peter felt like he'd found the place he was always meant to be. Here, amongst his people, he could finally be the man God needed him to be.

The members of the congregation slept in their personal shacks, fifteen to twenty to an abode, although there were usually only about half of that number in occupancy at any time. The shacks were no more than some wood planks hastily nailed together, furnished with sleeping bags and the like. Meals were served en masse in the mess hall and there were communal showers and toilets, so there was very little need for their resting place to be more homely than that. Nobody complained. Why would they when everything they needed was available to them on tap?

Food. Water. Drugs. Company. Flesh. Anything you could ever want to indulge in was ready and waiting for you at The Farm. Father was a kind leader, unlike the lesser men who had once tried to make their mark on the world - he didn't keep his followers starved or sleep-deprived. He made sure everyone's bellies were full and that rest rotations were always adhered to.

He wanted his followers to stay with him because they believed in his cause. Not because they were malleable due to hunger or delirium. He was better than the leaders who had stooped to that level. He was greater than them. He understood that people needed a purpose in order to thrive, and so he made sure there were no idle hands in his congregation.

There was always something that needed doing on the settlement and each member had their own roles to keep the ecosystem of The Farm running. There were different levels for each member depending on their skill set and the level of trust they had earned in their time in the complex.

Level One was the most basic of levels. They were the physical labourers. They kept the livestock fed and healthy, the plants watered and fertilised, and the supplies for the congregation running to plan in general.

They were also in charge of repairs to the buildings, learning plumbing and other trades as they went. Thankfully, some of the earlier members had training in these areas and they passed these skills from person to person.

Level Two was where most members resided. Those who were a little longer in the tooth when it came to The Farm and their teachings. Their main job was to go out into the world, as quietly as possible and recruit new members. Those in charge of recruitment had to have a certain quality about them, a high level of charm but the appearance of low level ego. It wasn't a skill everybody could master, but those that succeeded in their tasks were rewarded highly. Given first picks at mealtime, mating time, and bathing time. Treated like Lords and Ladies amongst the rest of the congregation.

Father knew treating them in this manner created a hierarchy in his new world, which was something he didn't agree with, but it was a necessary evil. Those who were successfully growing his number of followers had to be rewarded above and beyond others in order to drive those who fell short to try harder. Besides, he reasoned with himself that this unfairness was only temporary. Once the rest of the world understood his methods and teachings there would be no need for this recruitment and the bonuses it brought with it.

Level Three workers were chosen for their position because they had a little more bite about them. Angry chips on their shoulders made them the perfect candidates to take care of the congregation's security. Not only did they make sure The Farm was kept from misunderstanding, prying eyes, they also went out into the world to send reminders for others to keep their distance when needed. Nothing that would bring the police to come sniffing around, but a well-timed broken window could send all sorts of messages to anyone who stuck their nose where it didn't belong.

And finally, there were the handful of recruits who belonged to Level Four. The closest level to the inner circle - because nobody new was ever invited into the actual inner circle. The founding members could trust nobody but themselves to make the decisions that benefited the new world order. Not that anyone other than Father got the deciding vote, but he at least liked to give the illusion to his closest companions that they had some level of influence over the world they were creating.

Level Four workers were the ones entrusted to uphold the values of The Farm. They ruled with an iron fist, stationed in every area of the congregation's lives. Always ready to step in should somebody be doing something they shouldn't. They were the founding members' eyes and ears across the settlement and they could be the difference between someone living or being put to death for a crime with just a few carefully selected words. Level Four recruits liked to believe they had a level of influence over Father. But he only paid attention when it suited him.

He read carefully curated passages from the Bible to his congregation and within the year the first generation of babies had been born on The Farm. A fresh start, a chance to keep minds unsullied from the pain and the sin the outside world could offer.
The mating rituals were an essential part of his new world order. If nobody knew who had conceived who, then nobody would value one child over another.

Everything had to be fair and so, after the mothers birthed their child, they were separated from them. All kept in the same nursery, the women never even being told the gender of the child they had held in their bodies for nine months. Of course, without medical intervention death during childbirth for both the mother and the child was an inevitability but Peter knew it was all God's plan. Only the strong survived. Only those with purpose survived.

Nobody was ever forced to partake in the nightly fornication sessions. Nobody who said no would be forced to carry on. He wasn't a monster. But Peter made sure there was plenty of home-brewed alcohol and hand-farmed mushrooms that someone saying no was never a problem. Everybody in The Farm agreed with its sole purpose - to create a better and fairer society.

The opinion of a child however very quickly lost its weight. Children didn't know any better. They didn't have the full picture of what they were trying to achieve and therefore couldn't make the decisions the society needed to thrive. It was agreed that once a child reached eighteen and could recite the manifesto in full without prompts that they were sensible enough to make the right decision. The decision that would benefit The Farm and their new world order.

Every night though, despite who he writhed around with, Peter fell asleep in the arms of Erin, his wife. Mother as she was known to the wider collective. Because he was a faithful and moral man. He told himself that he did what he had to do in order to please God, but that so long as he only fell asleep next to his wife, he was never breaking his vows.

Peter still felt unusual as the years rolled on and his society swelled in numbers. Even when Erin fell pregnant with what he knew, for certain, was his child, he still felt misplaced in the universe. He reasoned that it was because he wasn't from this universe. He was from a higher place. And until he was back at God's side he would always feel like an outsider in a world he was only meant to save.

Then one day, almost exactly to the date of their ten-year anniversary, Erin went into labour. As per his own rules, Peter excused himself for the duration, nobody other than the mother and the midwife were supposed to be at the birthing ceremony and he couldn't break the rules just because it was his own child that was being born.
Every child was equal on The Farm.
Even his.
Peter knew he wouldn't be able to keep his own rule though, not when he met his own child. And he'd known instinctively who that was as soon as he laid eyes on them. Of course he would. Because he was better than all of his followers. He was the chosen one and as such his child would be the next in line and it would be impossible for him not to feel that. He was certain.
Five children were born that day.
Five lives were brought into the world. And one was lost.
Erin.
Erin was lost to Peter. She died bringing a child into the world, as many women had since the start of The Farm, but Erin was different. Because she was Mother. And Mother wasn't supposed to die. That wasn't part of his divine plan.
God had made a mistake.
And Peter didn't appreciate mistakes.

Chapter Nine: Zoe

I listen as Karma fusses around in her bathroom.

I've just put the finishing touches to my portable recording booth, which despite its price tag, is a glorified box with sponges stuck to it, but hopefully it will do the job. This is the first job I've hired a professional editor for so I want to make sure the sound quality is as clear as possible to make their job easier. It's not that I doubt my own skills but it's time I learn to let go of my podcast a little. I don't have to control every aspect of it for it to be a success.

Okay, so it's not entirely about learning to be a more gracious person, I'm also painfully aware that this will be one of the top podcasts in the world the week it's released. My subscriber numbers are nearing a million now that Karma has officially posted on her socials about us working together. A simple selfie of the two of us relaxing in her room last night was all it took to confirm to everyone that she was ready to share her story, and that it was one they would want to hear.

Usually I'm a little shy when it comes to what I

post on social media, preferring to take shots of landscapes as I travel or arty shots of my studio, but I didn't hesitate for a minute when she turned to me and asked for a photo. It felt like the most natural thing in the world for that particular moment to be captured forever. Like it was always going to happen.

She placed her arm around my shoulder and pulled me in close for the shot, and her arm lingered there as she showed me the image before posting it.

Despite the heat from her body closing in around me, I still had goosebumps at her touch. She'd ignited something in me the moment I lay eyes on her. I was drawn to her, knew I had to get to know her - and not just for my career. But because if I didn't make the most of this opportunity, if I didn't get to know the layers of Karma, I knew I'd regret it for the rest of my life.

And now, we are about to begin our very first interview. I'd planned for the podcast to be made up of 'recorded as live' interviews, with minimal editing, a way to create an intimate atmosphere for the listeners. The rest of the airtime is going to be taken up with clips from other media channels over the years, intercepted with my research.

I am aiming to take the listener on a journey, making sure they left knowing the woman behind the trauma. Although, let's face it, a lot of people would only be tuning in to hear about the horrors she lived through. So it is my job, my main job, to make sure they stick around for the whole story. Only then would they realise how much a person could survive despite their very worst days.

The booth is a little smaller than I expected, and I place two chairs as far apart as I can on one side of the table, praying that the microphone will still pick us both up. Her words are the most important here, so I make sure to sit in the chair furthest away from the booth.

Karma reappears in the room, and stands in the open doorway of the bathroom regarding me. She's pulled her hair back into a ponytail, and has made an attempt to pin her growing fringe out of her eyes. I can see the ends of it escaping the clips, but on her it's an endearing style choice as opposed to an unfortunate hairstyle.

"Didn't want to be blowing it out of my face the whole time," she says. Crap, she noticed I was staring.

"You look great," I reassure her, choosing the word that my brain decided is the most professional. Radiant. Beautiful. Perfect. All are more apt to how I feel, but they aren't the right thing to say. And I try to always say the right thing.

She smiles slightly at my compliment, and I know I chose correctly. She must have people fawning all over her all the time, I don't want to be like those sycophants. I won't be like them.

Without asking any questions she scoots her chair closer to mine and reaches out to move the booth, before pausing in her actions and looking to me for my permission. I give a quick nod, hoping she doesn't knock any wires, and she moves it so it's facing both of us equally.

Our chairs are so close together that our shoulders are touching, and although I have faced my body towards the microphone I can tell that her attention is on me.

"It will be okay," I offer, sensing her nerves without her having to verbalise them.

"Every time I've spoken about this stuff before, people have turned away. So many families turned me away because I wanted to talk. I got used to not sharing."

"I won't turn away, Karma," I say, moving my head so I can look at her. Hoping that I can relay the depths of my truth in just a glance.

She looks at me for a moment, matching my eye contact until eventually she breaks it. There's an air of sadness around her, and I'm struck by the fact she doesn't believe me. She doesn't believe that her story won't scare me away, just as it has so many people in her life growing up.

I see another layer to Karma now. The one that exists behind the proud public speaker, beneath the megaphone at political rallies and beyond the smile on the photos taken for the Foundation's website.

She's afraid. She's truly afraid of revealing her secrets to the world.

And who can blame her?

So many people abandoned her because of them. I've read about how many foster homes she went through. I'd assumed she'd been a problem child (and who could blame her), but now I know the truth.

She went through so many families because they couldn't handle the trauma that came alongside the little girl they'd promised to care for. They didn't listen to her when she needed them to. Putting their own comfortable view of the world above anything else.

And I'm so angry for her. So angry for that little girl that felt so lost and unheard growing up. She must have been made to feel so inherently monstrous because of crimes that were heaped upon her. She grew up believing it was better to be silent than to be heard.

I can relate to that. In a way.

I knew what it was like to choose the easier life of silence when I should have shouted from the rooftops. I knew how it felt to have the decisions of another affect your life.

"Karma," I take her hand, "I promise you I'm not going anywhere. If you don't want to do this anymore, if at any point you want to pull the plug on this project you just say the word and I'll delete everything. You are in control here. It's your story and if you want to tell it then I'll sit here, right by your side and listen. I won't turn away. And if you don't want to tell it then we can just, I don't know, drink wine from mugs together. Whatever you want."

Her fingers wrap themselves around my palm and she gives it a gentle squeeze.

"Thank you," is all she says in reply, and yet she's spoken volumes.

"Whenever you're ready, just let me know. We don't even have to start today, we've got weeks -"

"I'm ready," she replies, finally turning her body towards the booth.

I click the icon on my laptop that starts the microphone recording, and put on my most professional voice as I introduce us both. All the while my heart is racing in the knowledge her hand is still in mine.

Chapter Ten: Zoe

Z: So, I thought we'd kick things off with a few personal questions if that's okay?
K: Sure, why not.
Z: There's something I've always wanted to ask you - why your name?
K: It was the name I was given at birth by someone, I'm not quite sure who. I decided to keep it, because it's who I am. But I respect the decision of my siblings who chose not to.
Z: We'll circle back to that point, but no, I meant why Karma Ann Jones? Why that middle and last name?
K: (pauses) I guess it was to remind me that I wasn't alone.
Z: Is it in honour of Joanne Klein? The woman who helped you on the night you escaped?
K: It wouldn't be a stretch to assume that.
Z: Speaking of your siblings, do you speak to any of them?
K: Most of them actually, at least sporadically. It was hard, you see, to find them all. We were housed all around the country for our safety. And most of them changed their identity when given the option, but they

knew where I was and over the years they've all gotten in touch. You can't grow up the way we did and not still need each other, they're my family, in whatever twisted way it happened.

Z: You were the oldest, weren't you?

K: I just managed to survive the longest, is all. There were older children than me, once upon a time, but they either disappeared from the congregation or aged up into The Farm. Things were better for you once you turned eighteen. People were less…interested…in you.

Z: I know you've spoken many times about the abuse you suffered.

K: Yes.

Z: And of course you have agreed to cover it again for this podcast, but I don't want to get into that yet. I want the listeners to have a chance to get to know you away from all of that, to see that you're more than what happened to you when you were young. Would that be okay?

K: That would be perfect.

I pull the headphones from my ears and sigh.

As much as I'm happy with how the first interview went, I can't concentrate on creating the transcript. Every few minutes I find myself Googling the name of my teacher, waiting to see if the dossier justifying his death has been published yet.

Now I've cleared my head a little of emotions, I've decided to trust in the Network. They must have had a solid reason for dishing out their punishment. As much as it pains me to admit it, everyone has secrets and Mr. Williams clearly had some that were darker than I could ever have imagined. All I have to do is wait for the Network to speak out and his death will make sense.

I've decided though that regardless of what the

dossier says, I'm still going to reach out to his widow to offer my support, she has done nothing wrong. When I cover the Network on my podcast I've decided I'm going to highlight our treatment of the families of the deceased, and how we should be supporting them rather than hounding them.

I only hope people take notice.

But the dossier still hasn't been published.

It's nearly 8 p.m. and my phone battery is on its last legs after spending the last two hours lurking on forums, hoping for a hint as to why he had to die.

A knock at my door serves as a welcome distraction and I bounce towards it, happy to be taken out of my own mind and spiralling thoughts - with every hour the Network stays silent I become more and more certain that they've made a mistake. Why couldn't they own up to it? Don't they realise the harassment his widow would be facing without them clearing his name?

"Do you fancy joining me for dinner?" asks Karma as soon as the door opens. There are no empty pleasantries, no beating about the bush, just a simple request for my company. It is refreshing - and surprising. I thought she'd be sick of me after our three-hour interview earlier.

"Sounds lovely, just give me five minutes." I step backwards into my room and hold the door open for her. A shiver runs down my spine as Karma crosses the threshold to my private dwellings, and I immediately curse myself for being such a slob. There were half drunk mugs of tea and dirty clothes strewn around the place. I should have asked her to wait for me in the lobby, why did I invite her in? What on earth had possessed me to do that?

It is simple. Karma possessed me.

There is something about this woman, something beyond hero worship that causes me to act without thinking. In the very short time we've spent together she's shown more genuine interest in me, in my habits and my work than anybody has in years. It's like she wants to get to know the real me and I know she won't turn away from the less attractive bits like Jake did. Because she'll understand the darkest parts of my mind, and I imagine to her they'll seem light compared to her own.

During our interview, I felt like I was in the hot seat once or twice as she bounced questions back toward me, until eventually, the session had become more of a natural conversation than a Q&A.

It had been nice, I'd never had that kind of discourse with someone in an interview before. She valued getting to know me as much as I valued getting to know her - and I was already coming to think of her as a friend rather than a subject. Something I had to keep reminding myself to steer away from, I couldn't risk reading more into our interactions than there was. She is my client, and she is only showing an interest in me to make herself more comfortable with sharing her secrets. I have to remember that.

"Harry has arranged a private dining area at the restaurant down the street, and I remembered you saying you liked sushi so I thought you might want to join me before we set off for the night." Karma fills the silence as I pull my hair back into a ponytail and pinch my cheeks. This would have to do, I can hardly start applying fresh makeup with Karma standing just behind me. It would add weight to this dinner that I am not sure is needed.

We walk down to the lobby together, easy conversation flowing between us just as it had the night before the interview.

The interview itself, well that had been a bit of a different atmosphere at points. I had found Karma a little guarded at first, her answers were clipped and overthought. But thankfully by turning the conversation around to Karma herself rather than the crimes of The Farm, it had thawed a little, and I had learnt some interesting truths about the woman I so admire.

She worked hard at school, earning herself top grades in every subject despite none of them really holding her attention.

Her various foster families had all cared for her as much as they were able to but shortly after Karma tried to open up to them about what she'd lived through the situation had always changed.

She had six sets of parents and each had lasted for about twelve months. Eventually, Karma learnt to stop trying to confide in the adults that were supposed to raise her and instead turned to the online community that turned her into the speaker she is today.

On forums she found kinship, people who had survived similar things to her. Horrible things. People who didn't shy away from her or become awkward after she told them about being Father's 'special one', and all that entailed. She was accepted. She was supported. She healed. If it hadn't been for those forums then she might never have made it to adulthood.

Which is why, when she turned twenty-one, she started up The Foundation. She wanted to support survivors of assault in the way she'd been supported by strangers across the globe. The Foundation was all the family she needed.

Karma had never married, never had children and never been linked to anybody significant publicly. Her opinion on the matter was well-publicised:

"I spent the first decade of my life being held somewhere I didn't want to be, I don't wish to repeat the process."

A quote that was used by surly teenagers up and

down the country as though they could understand the meaning behind her words. As though being grounded was the equivalent of what Karma had lived through. Still, they didn't know the ignorance of their feelings; when you're young everything is dialled up to eleven.

Karma sits down at the table in the restaurant and orders a bottle of wine for the two of us to share, a waiter appears, takes our order and finally we're permitted to relax.

We smile at each other, in the way two people do when they're comfortable in the company they're keeping, and I'm looking forward to a nice meal with a woman I'd love to get to know more about. Just keep it professional Zoe, I tell myself, remember she's your subject not your friend.

"Did you hear about the latest case?" asks Karma, pulling out her mobile phone, ready to engage in the same manner in which we had the other night. Bonding over a mutual interest. But things were different now, I feel differently now I have a personal connection to one of the victims.

"He was my old teacher," I begin, hoping that my connection to him will quell the conversation before it becomes too much for me to bear. Any minute now the Network would apologise for his death. Any minute.

"Sheesh. You probably had a lucky escape," replies Karma, a soft smile on her face. She feels for me, wants to make sure I know that I'm in a safe space where I can express my feelings at my supposed near miss.

"He wasn't like that. Besides they haven't published the dossier yet," I bristle. I can't help myself. Deep down I know Karma means no malice with her comment, but it still stings. Innocent until proven guilty. That's how the world is supposed to work.

"Still, there must be something…"

"Let's wait and see before we condemn him any

further, shall we?" I don't mean to sound so abrupt but I've spent all day swirling around in my own thoughts about Mr. Williams and what crimes he might have committed. And then I'd felt guilty about having such treacherous thoughts about a man who up until recently had been one of my biggest supporters.

The rest of our meal together is punctuated with awkward chats about nothing of substance and the entire time a slow sense of regret washes through my stomach.

I shouldn't have snapped at Karma like that.

The woman, for all intents and purposes, is currently my employer, and could end our contract at a moment's notice. It had been foolish of me to have spoken to her like that, to have shut down the thread of friendship growing between us. We'd spent most of the prior night pouring over the internet together, sharing new information about the Network and bonding over it. I've been unfair to Karma, she'd only been trying to connect with me.

And yet my tongue feels too fat to apologise.

I know I ought to. It's owed to her and yet I can't. Because that would mean acknowledging that I stepped out of line.

Karma pays our bill and we both stand. Now is the time to apologise, before it's too late. Before it ruins the flicker of friendship between us because I don't want this to just be a professional relationship. If I'm to tell her story then I need to know the whole of her. The real her. The kind I'll only get to know if we bond outside of the interviews.

"Karma, I'm sorry. I shouldn't have snapped at you like that."

"Don't worry about it. I get it. It must be hard knowing somebody involved." Karma places a hand on my shoulder and gives it a gentle squeeze. "Don't give it a second thought."

We both smile at each other and I sigh with relief.

"Have you been worrying about that the whole meal?" Karma asks and I nod. "Oh you daft thing. I've been spoken to much worse than that, believe me!" She laughs and shakes her head.

I'm so lucky she's such a forgiving person. I tend to speak without thinking, although I do care about the weight my words wield. I must be quite unlike Harry or the people who book her services. You know the kind of people I mean. The ones who always seem to think two sentences ahead of themselves, every word calculated for maximum impact.

"Still, I am sorry. It put a bit of a damper on the evening."

"We could always stay for another drink?" she suggests and I'm happy to take this as a sign that she'd like to speak with me properly, for the two of us to hang out and enjoy each other's company. I'm about to agree when I make the mistake of glancing at my watch.

"Shit, we're supposed to leave in twenty minutes," I can imagine Harry waiting for us impatiently in the lobby. Clucking his tongue and shaking his head with every minute that passes. The drivers of our cars are surely enjoying their extra-long break before the night drive begins.

We're driving to the other end of the country tonight ready for Karma's next engagement. It would have made more sense, at least to me, to have left directly after our interview and had dinner in our next hotel. But Karma viewed the hours she spent sleeping as wasted so thought they were best put to use whilst she was travelling between locations. Besides, it allowed her time to explore the cities she was passing through in between engagements, because what's the point in travelling the country if you never get to see it?

I'd been quite touched that she'd explained the reasoning behind it to me when I'd asked the question. Most people I've worked with have never felt the need to clue me into the logic behind their plans.

"Did you want to travel with me? My van is really comfortable, the seats recline all the way." Despite her being the one to make the suggestion, Karma still looks shocked by the words. As though she is rarely so open about wanting to spend time in somebody's company.

I guess when you've been through all she has, friendship is hard to put a finger on. "Plus, then we can carry on this evening?" If I didn't know any better I'd take her expression now as flirtatious, but that's the problem with being as charismatic as Karma - everybody mistakes your interest for lust.

I'd been due to travel in the small car, the same as Harry's, only able to rest in a vaguely reclined position.

"If you're sure? That would be great," I reply before she can change her mind, and the deal is done.

Chapter Eleven: Target #23

Thomas Jenkins had been only eight-years-old the first time he met Savanna Scott. She was sixteen and he was enthralled by her.

They met one day as she walked past his house, on her way to pick up groceries for her ailing father, and the two of them had started talking about superheroes. She noticed his Avengers t-shirt and struck up a conversation with him.

Savanna's favourite superhero was Batman she said, and so that became Thomas' as well. He took to playing in the front garden more often, keeping his eyes out for the older girl who fascinated him. She was like a grown-up, but one he understood. All the other grownups in his life talked too loudly or pretended he wasn't there when they had to make their big important telephone calls. But Savanna always made time to stop and chat with him.

For his ninth birthday, she gifted him a comic book and said it was no big deal, she already had a copy at home in her collection. It was the most important gift Thomas had ever received and he cherished it, reading it continuously until it was held together by more sticky tape than staples. Savanna was impressed with his knowledge of the story, she told him so after he recounted the action for her - making sure to include the special superhero moves he'd spent so long practising in his room. He felt so proud under her gaze, and nothing made him happier than seeing her smile.

One afternoon, not a particularly special one, Thomas was playing in the front garden as usual whilst his mother and father milled around the house getting dinner together. They were having friends over later. He saw them blowing up balloons, but he was not interested in helping them decorate. Thomas had been left to his own devices, Savanna strolled down the sidewalk, watching Thomas.

"Hey Thomas, you're looking a little bored," she said casually, leaning her elbows on the fence and placing her face in her hands.

"My parents are doing dumb stuff and I'm stuck here," he replied, keeping one eye on her and the other on his house.

"Well," she said slyly," when you're Batman, you're never really stuck are you? How about you come over to my house and we can go through my comic book collection."

His face flushed. He can't believe his luck.

There have been so many times over the past year when he'd squeezed his eyes together and wished for just this. Savanna has so many cool superhero comics and figurines and he's practically dreamt about what wonders her room contains. He'd even used up his birthday wish on this as he blew out the candles on the cake his mother had made him. It had been a Batman-themed one of course. He had wanted to invite Savanna to his birthday party, which had made his mother laugh. A teenage girl didn't want to come to a child's party, she said. So he never mentioned it to Savanna, too afraid it would make her laugh at him as well.

He knows she would have come though. Savanna is one of his best friends. She would definitely have wanted to come to his party.

"I only live around the corner. They won't even notice you're gone. Come on, I'll even let you have one if you want, if you promise to take care of it." She opens the gate to the fence and takes his small hand in hers.

Thomas makes the most promising promise he has ever made in his short life. "I will guard the comic with my life!" he tells her as the two of them walk away from his front garden and towards her home.

Nerves start setting in as he notices his driveway getting further and further away. Savanna doesn't live quite as nearby as she said, maybe she's rubbish at geography. He knows he is, always getting his capital cities and continents muddled up. He probably should have told his mum and dad where he was going, they would worry if they looked out the window and he was gone.

Just as he was about to voice his concern to his friend, she stopped outside a front door, he watched as she fished around in her pockets for keys. One day he'd have his own house keys, and he'd be a grown-up like Savanna too. He noticed the Batman logo on one of her keychains and smiled to himself, he'd make sure to get a matching one of those when he was older.

The inside of Savanna's house was old. He didn't quite know how to explain it but that's the sense he got from the yellowing walls through to the sticky floor. He didn't feel comfortable here and for a moment he wished he'd stayed home and helped stick balloons to the walls with his dad. Still, the promise of comics loomed over his head, he could always help his parents when he got home.

A man's voice called out to the two of them, it sounded echoey and far away.

"That's my dad," explained Savanna as she gestured towards a door. "He's in the basement building me new shelves for my comics."

Thomas did not want to follow Savanna into the basement. Sweat began to bead at his lips as an instinct inside of him told him to run far, far away from this place. To keep himself as far from the keeper of that voice.

"Are you coming?" she asked, holding the basement door open. Thomas shook his head briefly. One fluid movement that summed up the aching panic inside of him.

Savanna looked upset. Her shoulders sagged and she looked down at the floor. He didn't want to upset his friend, but he didn't want to go into the basement.

"You didn't really like the comic I gave you, did you?" she asked, looking hurt. He wanted to explain to her that that wasn't the case, that the comic she gave him was his most treasured possession. He wanted to tell her all of these things but his tongue felt fat in his mouth with feelings he was too young to verbalise.

"It's fine. I get it. None of my friends like comics like I do." She goes to walk down the stairs towards her collection in the basement and Thomas takes a step towards her. She called him her friend. He knew they were friends and now she'd just confirmed it. And his mother taught him that he must always be kind. He'd just pop down the stairs, look at her comics and then run all the way home. Everything would be fine.

Except it wasn't.

Savanna locked the door behind him as he stepped through.

The room was pitch black and Thomas screamed. Hands were on his body. Hands that had no reason to be on his body.

He didn't like the way they touched him. The way they made him feel.

A camera flashlight blinded him as his top was pulled up.

And then.

And then.

He heard the click as the basement door unlocked and flung himself up the stairs. Savanna stood at the doorway, a wicked smile across her face.

Six months later, Thomas saw Savanna again. This time across a courtroom as she gave evidence against her father. She said he used to beat her, threaten her and forced her to bring Thomas and others to him. They moved often, but this time they were not quick enough, expecting shame to keep the young boy's mouth shut. Instead Thomas had run home and told his parents exactly what had happened and his dad had subsequently been arrested for the beating he inflicted on Savanna's father.

They hadn't moved fast enough and his father's knuckles still hadn't fully healed. Thomas was glad.

He watched as Savanna's entire body shook with emotion as she told the tale of the abuse she'd suffered at the hands of her own father. How he'd hit her, beat her, molested her.

Thomas knew none of it was true.

Because Thomas would never forget the way she'd smiled at him when he finally escaped the basement.

Twenty years later, Savanna, now living under a different name, made her way through the city streets.

Her father had died recently in prison and she mourned him. She cried for the life they had together, for the way they understood each other. She'd called up her best girlfriends and asked to meet for a drink under the guise of having 'had a bad day at work', but really she just needed their voices to wash away the sadness in her heart.

There was an ache inside of her that she could never openly name. She'd walk past playgrounds and long to pinch a child's wobbling thighs, or to trip one of them up so they'd fall face-first onto the ground; she just wanted the rush so she could feel alive. But she could never act on her impulses. Her father had saved her from prison with his lies. By allowing her to speak of the terrible crimes he never inflicted on her he had shown her how much he truly loved her. But he'd told her not to waste her chance. He'd made her promise.

She arrived at the bar twenty minutes ahead of schedule, as she always did and ordered a shot of tequila, as she always did - to calm her nerves. It was so exhausting always pretending to be someone else, to act like she didn't have the urges to inflict pain that she did. She could never show that part of herself to her friends, they would never understand. The tequila helped numb the fatigue that was constantly lurking around her.

So she'd kept that promise every day for the last twenty years.

Almost every day.

There had been a few occasions over the last two decades where the compulsion had gotten too much for her to handle. Her ex had thrown her out of his house after his daughter confessed to the little punches Savanna threw her way. Never enough to leave a bruise, just enough to elicit a cry. Thankfully, he'd put it down to jealousy and never reported it.

She made a habit of dating single dads. Because

they always came with a miniature human-sized benefit. The younger, the better. A baby can't tell tales after all.

As she was taking a walk down memory lane Savanna noticed that she felt drowsy, her head was spinning. That must have been a really strong tequila. She goes to ask the bartender what brand she's been served but finds herself alone at the bar, the staff member has disappeared.

"Are you okay?' asks a kind voice, but Savanna can only slur out a response.

"Let me get you a car," offers the voice and Savanna takes the stranger's arm gratefully. She'll message her friends when she gets home and let them know she wasn't feeling well.

As she crawls into the backseat of a waiting car she notices the doors lock behind her. Panic begins to fill her stomach but she's unable to move or to talk. The driver doesn't turn to look at her but even from here, she can make out the faint lace line of a wig and her heart beats wildly. She'd read the news reports, heard about all the murdered victims and the crimes they were posthumously linked to. But she hadn't for a moment been worried, at least not up until she heard the door locks click.

Medusa had come for her.

Chapter Twelve: Zoe

As I climb into the waiting car, Karma is busy moving pillows and bags into the back seats to make space for me. I'm relieved as I spent the time whilst packing worrying that she'd changed her mind about travelling together. I would have been perfectly happy sitting alongside the driver if that's what she'd wanted, but it's a welcome sight to see that she wants me to ride alongside her. Clearly my overstep at dinner really had been blown out of proportion in my mind.

She pauses mid-shift, with a duffel bag in her hands, "Sorry it will just take me a second, unless you'd prefer to sit separately?" There's a knot of uncertainty sitting between her eyebrows and she's worried she's assumed I'd like to sit together. That perhaps I'd appreciate some solitude as we drove through the night. She couldn't be more wrong.

"This is perfect, thank you again." I'd already texted her three times before meeting her tonight and had somehow found a way to thank her in each message as she informed me of our plans.

"Honestly, you can stop thanking me. It will be nice to have some company."

I can feel my cheeks colour, I'd been too keen and it had been noted. I need to play it cooler, like all the subjects of my podcasts want me to get this involved in their lives. Like they all treat me as friends. Like they're all as interesting as Karma Ann Jones.

My crush on her is growing with every second I spend in her presence. But that's all it is. A crush. A silly school girl crush that won't, and should not, lead to anything more.

I am a professional.

I am a professional.

I am a professional.

But Christ, how can a person look this good after a full day of work?

She's wearing what appears to be a very comfy pair of jogging trousers and a black vest top, her face has clearly been scrubbed of makeup - I can see a fleck of moisturiser she's missed rubbing in - and yet she's still as radiant as she was when we met for dinner.

Time has been kinder to Karma than fate ever was, she's aging with a grace and a slowness that women our age would kill for.

"Right, belts on," she smiles at me as she clips her seat belt into place and I follow suit, "and let's go!"

The driver, on instruction, starts the engine and the privacy panel between compartments slowly winds itself up automatically. Karma watches it with a dispassionate gaze until it finally clicks into place and then she turns to me.

"So, how shall we fill these hours?"

"I was thinking, if it was alright with you, that we could talk for a while." I move to pull out my phone, ready to record our conversation.

"Do you mind if we just chat, I don't really feel like working on the podcast right now."

Without her noticing, I let my phone slide back into my bag and instead rummage around until I pull out some gum, as though that's what I'd been rooting around for all along. Of course she doesn't want to work right now, I'd been stupid to assume that she would. Everyone needs downtime now and again. Besides, anything I learn about her I can use to paint a picture to my audience. It doesn't need to all be in her voice.

"How long do you think it will take to get to Lincoln?" I ask, despite having googled the journey time myself before heading down to meet her.

"Well, it's the other end of the country so with the drivers' rest stops, probably most of the night."

"Have you been there before?" My questions are so bland that I hate myself a little. I've never been good at small talk, don't see the point in it. Words are important and they should be treated as such.

She sighs, and it's clear I'm boring her. "Where haven't I been? I feel like a walking talking guide to cities in England sometimes."

An awkward silence descends between us, and it's clear we've both realised that travelling together was a mistake. Without the work of the podcast we really have very little to talk about.

"God, I hate small talk," she says, "words are important and shouldn't be wasted on discussing the weather."

Rather than being stung by her words, I'm warmed. She's on my wavelength and it's clear she isn't judging me for the stilted conversation we've just had.

"I couldn't agree more. It doesn't help that I'm

rubbish at it either."

She laughs and pride flushes through me. I love the sound and I love that I'm the one who's brought it past her lips. Those amazing lips.

"Tell me a secret," she turns to me with a wicked grin on her face. "One nobody else knows."

The secret races through my mind.

I like you.

I really like you.

I would like nothing more than to fill the space between us and kiss you.

"I cheated on my A'Levels."

She leans back and looks at me with admiration.

I've never told anyone, not even Jake, about that. It's one of the leading causes of my impostor syndrome because it was thanks to that passing grade that I was able to attend the university of my choice, the one that led to me learning the skills I needed to start this podcast. It led to the job I had before this became a full-time career. It led me to this very moment, sitting in the back of a car with the woman whose story everyone is salivating to hear.

And it was all because of the test answers stuck to my water bottle label.

"Well, I never," she replies, that wicked smile still on her face. The kind of smile that sends tingles of attraction down into the pit of your stomach.

"Okay, your turn," I say, wanting to keep this interaction going. Wanting to strengthen the bond growing between us.

Her smile falters and I can see thoughts running through her mind as she weighs up what to share with me. Her lips open and close, as though there are words stuck there that she knows she shouldn't get out and the knot reappears between her eyebrows.

Karma wants to tell me a secret. A real secret. One

she knows she shouldn't share. Perhaps one that isn't truly hers.

But she decides against it.

I can see the moment she pushes it from her mind and picks something else to tell me.

I've always been good at reading people. Always been good at getting them to open up to me.

But it appears my talents are lost on Karma. She still has a layer around her that I'm not permitted to see behind. And although it hurts to realise that, I have to accept it. She's my client and she only has to share with me what she wishes. There should be parts of her that she doesn't share with the world. I just wish she trusted me enough to share them with me.

"I take a memento from every function I attend."

"What? Like a placecard?"

"Placecard, cutlery, Christmas ornaments…" She admits the last one with a shy shrug of her shoulders.

"Are you telling me you have a stash of Christmas ornaments somewhere?"

"Enough to decorate my entire house twice over!"

It's an endearing secret. A harmless one. One we've all been guilty of once or twice.

My university flat was littered with glasses swiped from pub gardens.

I laugh alongside her and she pulls out her phone to show me a photo of her Christmas tree from last year. It looks as though Santa himself vomited up the clashing decorations of various sizes and shapes, nothing matches and a lot of it has logos of companies or hotels upon it.

"It's my dirty little secret!" She laughs again and I allow myself to bask in it.

Karma might not be ready to share everything about herself with me, and I get it. Her whole childhood was full of well-meaning adults turning away from her because of her past. Of people asking her to hide the worst parts of herself. And scars like that don't disappear overnight.

    I thought we'd broken down the barrier at the start of our first interview when I reassured her that no matter what I wouldn't turn away. But it is clear that I still have more work to do in order to prove myself to her. I am more than happy to put the time and effort into it, because Karma Jones is a woman worth getting to know.

Chapter Thirteen: Karma

Karma leant back in her seat and glanced across at Zoe who was already asleep.

She noticed that her friend's blanket had slipped down and reached across the interior of the car to pull it back up towards Zoe's chin and then paused.

What was it about this woman that was bringing out this nurturing side in her? She'd spent so many years looking out for others growing up that she'd thought she'd lost that part of herself after she fled The Farm and yet here she was, worried about a virtual stranger's comfort as she slept.

She needed to save her compassion for those who truly needed it, the people she was helping through the support groups. She couldn't give a toss about the many faces she had to smile towards at her conferences and black tie events, as long as she knew she was making a difference to the world of those who mattered, she would be happy. And nobody could deny that Karma Jones was making her mark on the world.

Yet Zoe brought something out in her she thought Father had destroyed. A flame within her that he had extinguished through his relentless attention and cruelty. For the first time, in a long time, Karma cared about somebody new. Really cared about them.

There was nothing particularly special about Zoe.

She was beautiful, yes, but not in the way that would launch ships.

It wasn't solely a physical drive that Karma felt as she watched the woman sleep, it was something deeper.

There hadn't been another runner in the race the moment she hit play on Zoe's podcast entry. Her voice soothed Karma's soul in a way that therapy had never been able to touch, and she'd laughed alongside the host as she managed to insert her dry sense of humour into the worst stories about humanity.

She was the breath of fresh air Karma had been waiting for.

And now she was here in the flesh, and for the time being at least, all Karma could do was sit next to her and breathe her in.

The back and forth between them in the restaurant was regrettable. She should have dropped the conversation as soon as Zoe made it known that the victim was somebody she'd once been close to. But Karma couldn't do that, could she? She had to keep pushing. She was always pushing. Always running. Always turning away from thoughts that were too dark to remember.

She knew she could trust Zoe with those thoughts though. She knew that over the next two months all of her truths would be revealed. She just hoped by then the bond between the two of them would have grown strong enough to be able to withstand it. That she wouldn't be judged too harshly by the woman before her. If things went the way she hoped then perhaps after that she could explore her feelings towards Zoe a bit more, but not right now, not when there was so much at stake. She had to stay laser-focused for the next eight weeks.

Zoe stirred in her sleep and Karma turned her attention back outside the car, watching the road whiz past them. It would do her no good to be caught in a daydream, she needed to keep her head in the game and wait for the pieces to fall.

There were seven bodies discovered an hour ago. Six were dumped in Bristol outside the home of the ex Avon & Somerset's Police and Crime's commissioner. The man who had overseen an investigation into human trafficking in his geography and declared that it didn't exist. Each of the six bodies was a known trafficker. Each of their deaths was a reminder to him that he had made the wrong call. Crime was rampant across the country and the Medusa Network were doing their best to clean up.

The seventh victim had just been identified, a woman who used to go by Savanna Scott before she was given a government provided alias after her father's trial for child abuse. The dossier on her had yet to be published but it wasn't a far stretch of the imagination to think she knew more about her father's crimes than she let on.

Karma wondered if she ought to share the latest updates with Zoe. Prior to the death of her teacher, the two of them had a shared interest in the Network and had a mutual morbid curiosity about their campaign. But now things felt a little different. Hopefully Zoe would bring it up first and they'd be able to converse as easily as they had the first night they'd met.

She'd been foolish to touch Zoe's hand as they were washing the mugs, and she hoped the moment had gone unnoticed. But she hadn't been able to resist the physical draw she felt to her. She spent months listening to Zoe's entire back catalogue of podcast episodes, wondering what it would be like to meet her in real life, as opposed to her dreams. And now she has. And the connection she'd felt when only listening to her voice had increased tenfold.

Zoe spoke without thinking, which was refreshing to Karma, how she herself preferred to live. And Zoe had a fire within her, something unexplainable that drew you in. Perhaps extending the contract to her had been a mistake. A rash decision based on animal instinct. There were others, who were much more suitable to tell her story, a fact that Harry had drilled home to her everyday during the application process. But she had her heart set on Zoe, and would not be swayed.

Karma really should be focused on her goals right now rather than fantasising about somebody she'd just met. And yet...

Reclining fully in her seat now she decided the time for sleep had come. It was one of the few things in life she'd never had a problem with - falling asleep. Not even on The Farm on the worst nights, those where Father would come for her and punish those he thought less of. She was always able to switch off from their terrified sobs as they tended to their wounds in the same way she was able to float outside of her body whenever Father was near her.

If he never touched the real her then she would always be okay.

That's how she'd survived the torture the adults inflicted on her - by taking herself away from it all as best she could. That and knowing that one day the world would punish them for what they'd done.

That hadn't happened though, not in a court of law as it should have done. Because the adults at the centre of The Farm had disappeared into thin air. Never to be seen from or heard from again.

That was why she kept making her talks and kept

her face in the public domain. They were out there somewhere and she wanted them to live with the constant reminder of her existence, to be terrified that one day they would be found.

Even now, as an adult who was mostly healed, she could simply switch her brain off to outside influences and achieve a peaceful night's sleep. Some may say that the ability to do that was slightly sociopathic but she knew it was just a trait of a survivor.

But, for the first time, she found herself too distracted to drift into nothingness.

It was because Zoe was here.

For the first time, in a long time, Karma wanted something and she didn't know how she was going to get it.

Chapter Fourteen: The Farm

After the loss of his beloved wife, Peter began to unravel. His sermons took on a darker tone, now reflecting the resentment he felt towards the God he'd once revered.

God had made a mistake in letting Erin die.

God was fallible - Peter was not.

Therefore, he began to wonder if perhaps his true purpose when he finally ascended to the Heavens was to take the top role from someone who clearly didn't deserve it.

Whilst on Earth it was his destiny to show mankind a better, kinder way to live. A world in which everyone was equal. It's why it was so vital that Peter kept reminding himself that all the children born on The Farm belonged to the community. But it was harder than he imagined.

After Erin's death, he couldn't bring himself to visit the children's house where his baby would be. In fact, he steered clear of all the children, regardless of their age, for seven weeks until the rage inside of him had begun to dull. He was certain the youngest members of his congregation had missed his presence and was disappointed when he saw the clouds fall across their faces on the day he finally decided to visit them.

How dare they look at him like that. With fear in their eyes. As if he was some kind of monster that had crawled out from under their beds.

He was Father to them all and they did not appreciate all he was building for them. Ungrateful brats.

If the children had been frightened of Father before Erin died it was nothing compared to what he became after. He'd dole out daily beatings upon them based on nothing more than a whim. His nightly visits to their rooms became more frequent and less sacred. He knew what he wanted and no longer tried to explain to them why it was important that they saw the bigger picture. They were children. What did they know of the new world?

One day, when they came of age, they themselves would continue this glorious cycle and help raise the numbers of the congregation. And one day they would all grow to change the world. Perhaps on that day they would finally look at him with gratitude. Perhaps then they would appreciate just how hard he worked to make their world a better place.

They weren't all wastes of space to Peter though.

There was one child.

One girl.

Karma. She was special.

He'd felt it from the moment he finally allowed himself to lay eyes upon her. Of course, there was no way to know for certain that she was his heir but it was blindingly obvious to Peter.

She had Erin's deep chestnut complexion. Her eyes. Her lips. He could practically see his wife standing over the girl, calling out to him that Karma was their child.

Karma became Peter's chosen one.

She was by his side more often than not. Privy to conversations between him and the founding members, there was no part of Father's life that he kept from his special little girl. One day, when he finally met his higher purpose, she would be the one to carry on his legacy. And he had to make sure the congregation recognised her importance.

However, he couldn't outright tell everyone that she was his daughter. It went against his teachings, his morals. Every child on The Farm was born equal and treated as such. Nobody knew who had spawned who and that kept things on an even keel.

So no. Peter couldn't very well tell his followers that he was above his own rules. He had to be seen to be on the same level as them, even though clearly he was not. But it was important to keep up appearances, you catch more bees with honey after all.

Instead Peter made it obvious by his actions, and his affections, that Karma was precious to him. He told the waiting crowds that God had spoken to him once again, how God had guided him to Karma's crib after Erin's death and how he had seen the ghost of his wife place a blessing on the babe's head.

She was Mother reborn.

And Mother belonged to Father.

Chapter Fifteen: Zoe

I wake up before Karma, just as the driver is taking the turn off the motorway and into the town that would be our home for the next twenty-four hours.

Stretching my back out as best I can I'm surprised to find I haven't woken up with numerous kinks and knots in my muscles. I'm sure I would have if I'd travelled in the car Harry had arranged for me.

I smile to myself, though I know it's unkind, as I imagine what an uncomfortable night's rest he must have gotten. Perhaps a bad back is why he's been so off-putting towards me. Still, today is a new day and hopefully I'll be able to thaw the ice a little. I've usually always been able to make people laugh, and if you make people laugh then they like you - life can be as simple as that. So I vow to myself that I'll at least elicit a smile from his miserable face today. I still have two months to spend in his company and it would be nicer to have at least a slightly positive working relationship with him.

Looking across I regard Karma as she sleeps.

She looks so peaceful. Blissful even. If I had lived through what she had I don't think I'd ever stop having nightmares so I'm happy for her that she can at least escape The Farm in her dreams.

Her hair has come loose from the bun she's had it in since we had dinner and it's tangled around her head from where she's clearly been tossing and turning. Perhaps she isn't sleeping as peacefully as she looks.

I'm about to straighten her blanket to keep the breeze from the driver's window away. He's had it cracked for half an hour now - clearly trying to keep himself awake after driving us through the night. But something stops me in my tracks. And it isn't the intimacy of the gesture, no, to look after Karma feels natural to me.

What stops me is the tiny tattoo I can now see, nestled just behind her ear lobe.

A Medusa.

A beautiful, intricate, perfect Medusa. One that is eerily similar to the one the Network leaves on their calling cards.

This has to be a coincidence right? The tattoo doesn't look fresh so she couldn't have gotten it done recently. A lot of people have Medusa tattoos, I'm sure. In fact, I can remember Instagram grids being flooded with them as a symbol of survivorship against sexual assault. And Karma deserves to wear that symbol more than anybody I've ever heard of.

But still.

Something about seeing it in the flesh, on her flesh, chills me.

There's no way Karma is involved in the Network.

She's an interested outsider, just like me. It's just not plausible that she could be involved. Not her. Not Karma. She's too good a person to be doling out bloody justice and besides, she's one of the busiest women in the country. She doesn't have time to oversee a network of murders. Because that's what the Medusa Network is.

Murderers. I can see that now. Now that their actions have affected me, even in such a small way.

What they are doing is not the correct way to bring about justice for the victims. And I don't deny that those that have been killed have victims. I believe every single person who has spoken out against the dead since it was safe for them to do so. But still, it's been nearly twenty-four hours and no dossier has been released on Mr. Williams. They killed him for no reason and that isn't right. None of this is right.

Seven bodies have been discovered since I was last awake.

Seven dossiers were published.

Seven families torn apart.

Seven lives ended.

Immeasurable people left behind to be affected by the fallout.

It's not right.

There has to be a better way.

Karma lets out a soft snore and I turn away from her, finally able to tear my gaze from the Medusa on her skin.

No. Karma is not involved with the Network. I'd know. We've spent the best part of twenty-four hours together now and at no point has she disappeared to make a mysterious phone call or exchanged an envelope with a cloaked man in the hotel lobby. All things that I'm sure would be happening in the Network because that's what television shows have taught me. When somebody is trying hard to hide something they inevitably make it obvious that they have something to hide.

A shift of an eyeline. A smile that's just a little too wide. A lie that has no place in reality.

Karma has done none of those things. She's been nothing but friendly and receptive towards me and if she were a criminal mastermind with blood all over her hands, then she'd hardly invite a stranger into her life for the next two months. It would be too risky. She'd be a fool.

Now I've talked myself out of my paranoid thought spiral. I try to turn my attention back to the world outside the car. Spotting a magpie I give a little salute, something my Great Nan always taught me to do. A way to ward off the sorrow a single bird can bring. She was always teaching me little things like that.

Saluting at magpies. Holding your collar when you see blue flashing lights to give the first responders luck. Crossing a baby's palm with silver to bring good fortune. Seeing a penny and picking it up. Never putting new shoes on the table or giving a knife as a gift. A lifetime's worth of superstitions all with the same aim - to bring in good luck and force out bad. Humans will do anything to feel like we have control over the world.

I don't know if any of it works, but I still do it all religiously. You know, just in case.

The driver indicates.

I listen to the hypnotic sound of the clicks and wait to see where we're turning. A service station. To be fair, I could do with a rest break. Despite having more room than I'd expected I'd still like to stretch my legs.

"Karma?" I say to her, hoping to rouse her calmly, wanting to make sure she can step out for some fresh air if she needs to.

She makes some form of noise at me that sounds halfway between a yes and a fuck off and I smile to myself. Clearly she's not someone who likes to be woken.

"We're pulling in for a rest stop if you need one."

I watch as she opens one eye and peers across at me, startled by my presence. She must be so used to being alone on these journeys and has probably forgotten she invited me.

"Could you grab me a coffee?" she croaks out the question through a voice that hasn't quite caught up to her brain. Maybe I should have let her sleep a little longer. When we get to the hotel I could take a nap if I wanted, our interview isn't scheduled until this evening before she attends a charity gala. She, on the other hand, has a whole day of engagements ahead of her.

I'm not planning on napping though, I want to attend as many of Karma's functions as I'm permitted to. It's the only way I'll get to see the full picture of her, to be able to verbalise the juxtaposition between the person she shows the world and the person she is behind the scenes. I need to make sure my podcast shows her in all of her glory, she deserves that.

"Of course," I reply and reach for the door handle. Letting myself out I take a moment to stretch out my back and shake the sleep from my toes. We have at least another twelve night journeys over the next eight weeks, whilst it would be presumptuous to think Karma might invite me to share her lift again, a girl can hope.

And maybe if I pick her up a pastry to go with her coffee, that might help sweeten the deal.

As I'm waiting at the counter, bank card in hand ready to pay, I notice a snake tattoo wrapping itself around my barista's wrist.

I stare at it as she works on the coffee machine, getting my order ready, and her sleeve slips up slightly revealing the full magnificence of the artwork on her skin. The snake curls down from her middle finger, which makes me smile, around her wrist until it reaches what looks like the start of a head on her forearm. I'd place a hefty bet that it ended in a Medusa.

See. I have nothing to worry about.

Lots of people have Medusa tattoos.

And Karma is just one of them.

Yet.

Yet there is a crinkle of doubt in the corner of my mind.

Whispers through my veins that I need to be wary. That I should keep my wits about me.

Chapter Sixteen: Zoe

The interview this afternoon got off to a better start than it had the first time. Conversation flowed more naturally between us and Karma even answered some of my more probing questions.

She hadn't had a best friend by the time she left The Farm, which is unusual for a young child, usually everybody and anybody is a friend after five minutes of company. But it was a dog eat dog world inside the compound and she quickly realised that caring about others meant more pain for her, at least emotionally speaking.

Once or twice she'd tried to talk Father out of delivering punishment against one of her siblings, but he'd never listened to her pleading and it usually resulted in harsher beatings for whoever she was trying to save so eventually she gave up.

You can't negotiate with a maniac.

She alluded to one time Father took his punishment too far, but she didn't divulge any further information and I could sense it wasn't something I should push for. She'll share that story when she's ready.

There had been a few of her siblings she'd cared

for, at least privately. Father didn't like her to give her attention to anyone other than him because she was his special girl. So it wasn't like she could play with them or even talk to them too often. But she used to slip them some of her rations at dinner time, or tell a joke to distract the adults whilst they made themselves scarce. Karma did all she was able to protect her siblings, and she carries immense guilt that she couldn't do more.

She also acknowledges that whilst she refers to all forty-nine of the children rescued from The Farm as her siblings, she doesn't actually know if any are actual blood relatives. It would be simple to find out, a quick DNA test but she's never pushed them for it because it isn't something she's interested in. Her family was built by surviving trauma and a blood test wouldn't change that.

None of the survivors of The Farm know who their parents were. After some of the tales she told me today I'd be surprised if any of the adults knew either. Drug fuelled orgies resulted in pregnancies and no one ever stepped forward to parent any of the children. They were raised by a rotating group of volunteers, although given how they treated the children in their care, it seems it was viewed as more of a punishment than a good deed.

At no point did she gloss over the details of what she'd lived through, she shared every nightmarish thing she'd witnessed in full technicolour citing the fact that if she had to live with the memories then so should anyone who was interested in her life. There were a few times I wanted to stop the interview, when the truth became too hard for me to hear, but it wasn't my place to police her story. I promised her that I would never turn away from her truths, and I had to stick by that oath. She was the one who had lived it all, I thankfully only had to listen to it.

Now, rather than typing up my transcript, I'm busy trying to get ready for the charity gala Karma is booked to attend tonight. Quite out of the blue, at the end of our interview, she asked if I'd like to attend as her plus one I jumped at the chance. Then I quickly panicked about what I was going to wear. Thanks to a quick trip to a local department store though that issue was dealt with and now all I have to worry about is my growing social anxiety.

Fingering the delicate beading around the neckline of the black dress I purchased, because black is always the safest bet when it comes to a formal dress, I find myself wondering what's in store for us tonight.

Karma is due to introduce the main auction of the night, the part of the event that raises the most money for charity. She was a bit flimsy on what the charity actually was, she gets booked into so many of these functions it all merges into one for her, but she assured me it would be on 'brand' which most likely means victims of sexual assault.

I wonder if she ever finds it weird that the darkest crimes are considered 'on brand' for her. If at any point whilst living on The Farm she imagined she would become the national poster child for rape...

That's a harsh way to put it.

But it's fair.

I spritz my setting spray over my makeup and quickly jot down 'poster child for rape' in my notebook, that's definitely a question worth exploring with her. How it makes her feel. What pressure it comes with. Whether she ever gets tired of being forever linked to the crimes of adults who should have known better.

Isn't that what I'm doing as well though?

By making this podcast and telling her life story I too am feeding into the Karma as a victim train of thought. I need to make sure each episode focuses more on her survival and less on the crimes. That's the only way to show her as the true woman she's become and to free her from the preconceived notions society holds about her.

Harry knocks on my door to collect me. Standing there in his three-piece suit he certainly looks the part and for the first time since we've met he smiles sincerely at me.

"Don't we scrub up well?" he asks with a chuckle.

I'm not sure what I've done to cause this change in character but for now I'll be grateful for it. Getting on with Harry will make my life and job infinitely easier. He offers me his arm and with a brief hesitation I hook my hand through it. If he wants to play the part of a gentleman then it would only damage our relationship if I were to refuse.

He makes pleasant small talk on the walk down to the lobby and I respond where I can.

Something about him seems off, but I can hardly accuse the man of being too nice. That's not exactly something to be suspicious of, and yet suspicious I am.

He asks me about my life back home, how the podcast is shaping up, all sorts of innocent questions with the aim of getting to know me better. And my responses are clipped but polite. Something is going on with Harry. I'm just not sure what yet.

Karma is waiting in the lobby for us and she looks beautiful.

Beyond beautiful.

Her dress is a floor-length emerald green, with a split up the side. On her feet, she wears a pair of heels with a strap that ties up past her ankle, like a formal gladiator. Her hair is a nest of curls piled up high on top, and her makeup is dramatic with dark eyes and red lips. She looks like she's stepped out of a history book, like one of the great beauties that the Gods used to start wars over.

"Zoe, you look amazing," she says, reaching forward to give my hand a squeeze. A shiver runs down my spine at her compliment. It's so hard to stay professional when I melt like this under her attention.

"You look beautiful, Karma," I say in response and Harry stands next to us waiting for his turn on the compliment train.

"And I'm the luckiest man as tonight I get to accompany you both," he says with a grin, standing in the middle of us and offering us both an arm.

"Harry, you look dashing," offers Karma with a smile as she takes his arm.

I follow suit and the three of us walk out into the frosty night air and into a waiting town car. If she's noticed a change in Harry's demeanour she's making no show of it. Perhaps he usually reserves his charming side for her company, maybe that's the only reason he's shining it on me tonight too. A way to score brownie points with his employer.

There's something more to it though. I know there is.

I can see it in the way he watches Karma as we drive to the venue, as though he's trying to read her phone screen over her shoulder. The way he quickly averts his gaze from it when she looks up at us, as though he's simply been taking in the passing view of the roads as we drive.

But I saw it.

I noted his interest in the messages she was typing. I saw the cloud that passed in his eyes as he managed to catch sight of something that perhaps he shouldn't have.

Harry is up to no good.

Chapter Seventeen: Zoe

Walking into the function room, I've never felt like such a fish out of water. Everywhere I look there are people. And not just people, people dressed up to the nines, tens and even elevens. Suddenly the dress I'd felt so elegant in back at the hotel seemed immature and cheap when surrounded by miles and miles of satin, lace, and velvet.

Karma fits right in though. She's welcomed with open arms and a small smattering of applause, whilst me and Harry lurk awkwardly in the background.

"Do you fancy a drink?" he asks as we watch Karma get swept into the well meaning crowd. Everyone is desperate for their pound of flesh.

"Never needed one more," I reply dryly. A tickle of envy tightening my throat.

I am not jealous of Karma, nobody in their right mind would ever be jealous of her. She's only who she is because of what she's been through and how hard she's fought to carve out a name for herself.

I'm envious of the crowd. The way they get to openly fawn over her, whereas I have to keep my admiration for her in check. Not once have I been able to tell her how much I admire her, or anything close to that, because that would be unprofessional. And I must remain professional.

That's all. I'm just envious that they can be honest with her.

It's definitely not the way she's laughing in their presence.

Or the hand that just swept the small of her back.

Not any of that.

She catches my eye across the room and holds my gaze until I look away. Could it be that she's watching out for me, too?

I follow Harry towards the bar and we order our drinks, his shoulders relax a little as we wait for them to be poured.

"She really is something, isn't she?" he says, aiming the words in my direction but not taking his eyes from Karma as she works the room.

"Incredible." There's no other word to describe her and the effect she's having on the populace of this event. Yet each time I glance over, she's looking in my direction. Like she only has eyes for me.

I'm imagining it, though, she's doing what she does best and making those around her feel special. That's what she's doing for the crowd and what I'm beginning to suspect she's doing for me.

The late-night chats, the offer to share her car, the moment in her bathroom on that first night - will all mean far less to her than it does to me because all she's doing is shining her light on me. It's what she does. What she's paid to do. And she does it so well that for a moment, I allowed myself to believe that she's falling for me in the way I am for her.

Shit.

I'm falling for her.

"It's like she turns into someone completely

different at these events, isn't it? Like she's two different sides of the same coin." He thanks the barman and guides us to a small table in the corner of the room.

It isn't admiration in his voice when he talks. It's mistrust.

"I guess it's a skill," I reply, trying to stay diplomatic. He isn't wrong, though. The woman practically gliding around the room, shaking hands and laughing at anecdotes is not the same woman who sits across from me in a hotel room and bares her soul. That isn't the woman I'm interested in getting to know, and yet it still irks me that I have to share her tonight.

I don't trust Harry, not after I caught him trying to look at her phone. He has some kind of motive here and I want no part in it.

"I'm sorry we didn't get off on the right foot. It's the Foundation you see, my one job is to look out for its and therefore Karma's reputation. And this podcast idea of hers could really cause trouble if she says something she shouldn't."

"She hasn't spoken about the Foundation at all if that's what you're worried about." If he's fishing for tidbits of our conversations so far he'll have to cast a heavier bait than that.

"Karma is the Foundation, and the Foundation is Karma. They're symbiotic. And it's my job to look out for them both so I hope you'll forgive me for being a bit wary of your presence." He's looking deep into my eyes now, his fingers nervously grasping around his whiskey glass as he waits for me to accept his apology. It's a believable performance, but it is just that. A performance. I know people better than Harry thinks I do and I know a lie when I hear one.

He isn't sorry for how he treated me. And he doesn't give a rat's ass about whether Karma talks about the foundation on my podcast. He's just concerned with making sure she doesn't say anything that will turn public opinion against her. Anything that will stop the donations that pay his salary from dripping in daily. Harry is only concerned about one thing here. His paycheck.

"Of course, I completely understand." If we're going to sit here shooting lies at each other then I'm more than happy to play the game. "And trust me, Karma would never want to harm the Foundation. The work it does with the support groups and legal aid is so important to her."

She's never told me that. We've truthfully never spoken about the Foundation or the work it does across the country to help survivors of sexual assault and crimes, but I know she cares about it. Because it's her legacy.

An announcement from the stage draws a halt to our game of bluff.

"Ladies and gentlemen, if you could please take your seats. The first course is about to be served." A stout man, whom I recognise from a reality television show, with a microphone, blinks in the stage lights, smiling widely at an audience he can't see. So he's to be the host for the evening. It could be worse, I suppose, they could have asked a politician to keep us entertained. This man at least has a few humorous catchphrases to pepper the evening with.

Harry guides me to our table and to my pleasure and his disappointment, I am seated next to Karma. He is seated opposite us, wedged between two strangers who I can already tell love talking about themselves. Harry is in for an interesting night.

Karma smiles at me and reaches for my wine glass to fill. She's so attentive but soon her attention is stolen away from me, before I can even thank her, by the person sitting to the right. She's still working, always working. I feel for her, it must be exhausting to have to always be 'on' when you're out and about. To always have to consider the implications of your actions when you wear a crown of such heavy responsibility.

To entertain myself, I scan the room quickly, making up silly backstories for the guests in attendance, trying to guess their occupation based on their attire.

Then it happens.

I see someone I recognise moving across the room, just out of sight so I can't make out their features for definite. But their build is the same. Their height is the same. The hair colour is the same. It has to be him.

My breath catches in the back of my throat and my chest tightens.

It can't be him. He can't be here. It's impossible.

I need to leave.

I need to get up and get back to the hotel. The hotel is safe. I can lock my door and I will be safe.

Just as I'm about to make my excuses, the server lays down a small bowl of soup in front of me and on autopilot I pick up my spoon. Service has begun. It would be virtually impossible to try and push my way through the staff members as they start up their first waltz of table service for the night. It would draw too much attention to me. Then he would notice me.

I pluck up the courage to peer back across the room, to see where he is, to count the distance between us. If I'm unable to move from my seat then it should be the same for him.

But it's not him.

I can see that now. Yes the man I'd spotted bears a resemblance to the man from my nightmares but it isn't him. The man I'm watching is a complete stranger.

Completely innocent.

I wish I could say that all scars fade.

But they don't.

They might become less visible, you might forget that they are even there until you're confronted by their ugliness one non-descript day.

Just out one evening with your friends, in the same restaurant you meet up in every Friday, ready to order the same dish you always do. And it will happen. Something seemingly inconsequential will happen, the opening notes of a song on the restaurant's jukebox, a passing comment from a friend's lips, or the shape of a stranger's head from behind and suddenly you'll feel like your skin is on fire with a thousand cuts of history upon it.

In just a split second, you're transported back to the night the scars were inflicted. And you can't escape. You're stuck there, in the moment you lost all your strength. When it was taken from you. When it was forced from you.

I didn't say yes.

But I didn't say no.

Was it all my fault?

A question I'd long forgotten to ask myself daily. One I thought I'd moved on from.

But I never do. Not really. The question is always there, waiting in the shadows of my mind, ready to rear up and sink its fangs into me and ruin a perfectly lovely moment.

The wine tastes metallic in my mouth. I was drinking white the night it happened. Suddenly, I am wishing Karma had poured me something other than my favourite. Because that night he took everything from me, he may as well have taken my love of white wine too.

No.

No.

I'm not going to fall down this hole.

I've worked too hard, been too strong, grown too

much to fall down this hole once again. That's what I tell myself every time the scars become visible again. I am not that person anymore. He made sure I could never be that person again. I could never be that free and trusting.

I was drunk.

I should have been able to be drunk and safe with the person I loved. I should have been safe.

But I wasn't.

Was it rape?

I still don't know.

I didn't say yes.

I didn't say no.

Concentrate on the here and now, Zoe. Stay in the room. In for four, out for eight. In for four, he's not here, he's years behind you, you are safe, you are happy, out for eight.

My hands are shaking and I can barely hold my cutlery. The smell of his deodorant. lingering in the air around me might only be in my mind but it's choking me. The tears I spilled that night are resurfacing from my stomach where I've kept them long buried.

He'd stayed out all night, long enough for me to worry, to drink a bottle of wine by myself. Returning triumphant from a night with his friends, twelve missed calls not acknowledged. It was all about power and control. I see that now. I didn't then.

So grateful he came home to me.

Didn't put up a fight.

Never said no.

But I didn't want to say yes.

No. No. NO.

He will not ruin this evening. He will not ruin another minute of my life.

Was it all my fault?

Was it rape?

The two questions that plagued me every day that followed that night. Didn't confide in anybody, after all,

I wasn't even sure what I had to confide.

I didn't say yes.

I couldn't say yes.

I was so drunk I was slurring.

Still.

I didn't say no.

Karma's hand reaches across the table and sits on top of mine. She brings me back to the present and I blink away all memory of the man who ruined years of my life. Left me with scars that shadowed all following relationships. He doesn't matter anymore. He is nothing to me anymore.

She doesn't make a move to speak; can see I'm somewhere my mind doesn't want to be so instead she threads her fingers through mine and holds my hand in silence. Lending me her strength when I have none left of my own.

She's what I need in this moment.

She's exactly what I need.

I concentrate on the feeling of her hand in mine. Of the warmth of her fingers and the smell of her perfume. I am here with her. I am not back there. Those questions do not matter anymore. Karma is here for me and that's all I need to come through this moment unscathed.

The past is in the past.

It can't hurt me anymore.

"Let's go outside" she casually suggests and I nod numbly. We walk out of the benefit hand in hand, into the night and I drink down the fresh air to cure the suffocation those thoughts caused.

"Shall we get out of here?" Karma asks me, after waiting patiently for calm to restore itself upon me. There is nothing I would like to do more at this moment, but I should leave alone. She's here representing the foundation and my panic attack is not as important as that.

"I'll be fine honestly. I'll just hop in a taxi. You stay, enjoy the rest of the night."

"Absolutely not. We were supposed to enjoy tonight together, besides I've worked the room already and disappearing into the night will only add to my mystique." She chuckles as she acknowledges the public's fascination with her, it's the first time she's done that and I'm relieved to hear that she doesn't have an ego about her importance.

"Should we go back and get Harry? He'll want to know you've left."

"What he wants to know and what he knows are two very different things. Come on, let's ditch him." She grabs hold of my hand again, and I'm surprised by how natural it feels, and pulls me towards a waiting taxi.

"It would be a shame to end tonight so early though, do you fancy going to get another drink? Somewhere a little more…us." The way she pauses before she speaks that final word causes my heart to flutter and I nod without giving it any further thought.

Honestly, all I want to do is go back to my room, scrub my face clear of my layers of makeup and disappear under my duvet until morning.

But Karma Jones wants me to join her for a drink.

So that's what I'm going to do against all my better judgement. Because she made me feel better when I was sinking to my worst. She calmed me when panic had me in its jaws and she made everything feel right again.

Chapter Eighteen: Zoe

Karma is true to her word. The bar she leads us to is definitely more my scene than the gala had been. It doesn't make me feel any more comfortable though, funnily enough we are the only two women wearing formal wear to stand inside of it.

Heads swivel when we walk in, and had this been a movie the music would have scratched to a stop but of course it doesn't. Digital tracks don't tend to screech to announce the arrival of strangers. Karma doesn't let any of the attention we've drawn to ourselves bother her though, instead she saunters directly towards the bar and places our order whilst I scurry alongside behind her.

Losing Harry had been a bit more difficult than I'd imagined.

He emerged from the gala's doors just as we had gotten into our taxi and his arm quickly shot into the air to hail one himself. I could imagine him jotting down the license plate of our vehicle to make sure he didn't lose sight of us. Karma had slid the driver a few notes to make sure he took the scenic route and lost our tail. To be honest, I know Harry is a bit of a buzz kill, but I didn't think it warranted all the drama. What would have been the harm if he had joined us?

God. Am I softening towards Harry?

No. I still don't trust the man. I'm just not sure why Karma clearly doesn't either. Perhaps she'd spotted him trying to snoop on her private messages in the car earlier? I make a mental note to ask her about it later.

She turns to me, places a drink in my hand, and smiles.

"Here's to a well-deserved night," she says and though on cue one of my favourite songs starts to play. Music has always been like therapy to me, I have a playlist for every possible mood or situation. There's something about certain melodies that can tune into whatever feelings I can't speak about that heals me.

I can't help tapping my foot along with the beat and it isn't long until Karma has convinced me to move towards the small dance floor at the back of the bar. All memories of my earlier panic attack, my slide down memory lane, evaporate as she takes me once again by the hand and twirls me around the dance floor.

All eyes feel like they're upon us as we laugh and chat loudly, all the while moving our hips to the rhythm of the music. For the first time in a long time, I feel alive and free. I can't remember the last time I had fun like this, even with Jake. We met in a nightclub and that had been the first and last time we ever danced together. He was too self conscious to let loose like this, the polar opposite of Karma who didn't care about bringing any looks of derision her way as she dramatically pulls out her air guitar and begins strumming along to the track.

This is it.

This is the real Karma Jones.

Not a survivor. Not a victim. Not a philanthropist. But a woman.

One who dances. Who laughs. Who doesn't care

what anybody thinks of her.

This is the Karma the world deserves to know.

Then, just as I am growing used to basking in her light, it dims slightly. The smile on her face flickers as though she's been rebooted and I turn around to see what had caused it.

A man, an old man, easily in his mid-sixties, is sitting alone at a table on the edge of the dance floor. Pint glass suspended mid-air on its journey to his mouth as he stares straight through me and at Karma. His eyes are wide, just like in the cartoons I used to watch as a child, if he had been a character in one of them they would have shot out from his face on their stalks.

Quickly, I turn to look at Karma. She's staring straight at him, as though there's nobody else in the room, as though it's just the two of them facing off against each other. A slow smile tugs at the corners of her mouth and I'm reminded of the Cheshire Cat, such is the pride on her face.

"Who's that?" I ask her but she ignores me, not wanting to tear her gaze away from the man, not wanting to be the one who breaks their staring competition.

"No idea," she says. I know it's a lie. She knows it's a lie. But right now I doubt I have any hope of being given the truth.

"Shall we leave?" I ask, wondering if his presence is making her uncomfortable. Perhaps she caught him letching over us as we danced. Some men do have a habit of sexualising any close female interactions.

"No. Let's not let him ruin our night," she replies and snaps back to the Karma she had just been. With a quick shake of her hair and a flick of her wrists she's dancing again, perfectly on rhythm and once again I am drawn into her atmosphere. Although I am uncomfortable at what just passed between the two of them, I know I am safe. Because I'm with her.

Karma spins me around so I'm no longer looking at the man who disturbed her happy bubble, but not before I see a woman approaching him from the shadows.

I try to turn my head to watch what's happening but every time I do Karma pulls my attention back to her, which isn't a difficult feat as she's mesmerising.

"Tell me the truth Karma, who is he?" I ask between the beats of the latest track and she stops dancing and looks directly at me. She appears smaller now somehow. There's less of a gentle glittering sparkle around her, she feels more like a powder keg.

There's something simmering beneath the surface and I want to say it's vulnerability but I can't be certain. It's an emotion I can't put into words, one I've never witnessed before. Something powerful and raw.

"An old friend," she replies and I know there's a level of honesty in her words. I know it in the way I know I have to breathe to live. It's instinctual in my brain to believe her. Because she's offering me a truth she'd rather keep hidden.

The next track is slower than the one we've just been dancing to, and I'm grateful for the pause, the ability to catch my breath. I turn towards the bar, ready to take a break and have another drink when Karma's hand snakes along my hip.

The fabric of my dress is so thin that I know she can feel the outline of my underwear, and for a split second I could swear her fingers run absentmindedly along the waistband. Before I can be sure though she pulls me closer towards her, her hands now resting respectfully in the small of my back.

"One more dance and let's call it a night?" she asks and I don't know if she means a night together or just a return to our separate rooms. And I'm not sure I want to ask for clarification.

I want to live forever in this moment. Where this woman I admire so completely, desires me in a way I've never been desired before. Because if I stay in this moment then reality can't crush it. She can't tell me she isn't interested in me that way. I won't fall for her and have my heart broken. All the many various endings for us and our relationship will never happen if I just stay on this dance floor and keep my mouth shut.

There's a part of me, and I'm very certain I know exactly what part, that wants to pull her close to me. To press my body up against hers as we dance to the sultry track. To feel her curves brush against mine. But the larger part of me is screaming out at me. Telling me I'm acting recklessly. That I'm getting ahead of myself. That I need to be professional and keep my distance.

I wish that part of me would just shut up.

I'm filled with the need to be selfish and reckless. To act in the moment without worrying about tomorrow's consequences, and so I inch a little closer, close enough for her perfume to swim up my nose and cause the synapses in my brain to fire. I want this woman so badly I ache. But I can't have this woman. I shouldn't have her. It will ruin everything.

But she's leaning in closer towards me.

Her breath on my skin causes goosebumps.

Her lips look delicious and are parted invitingly.

Kiss her.

I need to kiss her.

I need to feel her skin on mine. To have her hands run themselves along my skin. To pull her hair and kiss her neck.

I need her.

A flash of movement over her shoulder breaks the spell of seduction that is washing over me.

The old man, a man who should be sitting at home

reading a paper instead of nursing a drink in a seedy bar, is stumbling around. He crashes into a booth and I watch as he tries to apologise to the patrons whose order he has just knocked onto the floor. They stare at him in disgust and bewilderment. He shouldn't be here. He doesn't belong here.

Karma is calling my name softly but I take a step away from her. Someone really has to help the old guy out, he's drunk and making a fool of himself.

She grabs my hand and tries to pull me back towards her and I stand frozen as a woman approaches the man, who is now trying to walk out of the bar, one hand gripping onto the wall for support. She takes his other arm and whispers something to him and I watch as he nods.

Looks like I don't need to be the good Samaritan tonight.

But something isn't right here. The air feels charged with danger.

Maybe I should still offer my help, she's only a small thing and might struggle to keep him moving once they run out of wall.

I'm taking a step forward to do just that when Karma yanks my arm so hard it forces me to turn around and look at her.

She blinks twice, almost surprised that she's managed to awaken me from my daydream.

"Harry is here," she says and nods her head towards the bar.

Sure enough her minder - sorry, the Foundation's press officer, is standing at the bar, watching us both like a disappointed father. He taps his watch and then makes a gesture that I think means it's time for us to wind up our dancing and leave for the night.

"At least we had fun whilst it lasted," she adds as she walks towards him, head hung slightly in an apology

I know she doesn't mean.

Once again I'm struck by how exhausting it must be for her to always consider her every action and word. Knowing that there are people like Harry in her life whose sole job it is to hold her accountable. To remind her that she's so much more than just Karma Ann Jones. She's an entire movement.

As I follow her off the dance floor, away from the passion that had gripped me and the worries I'd felt, I glance behind me at where I'd seen the kind woman helping the old man. The two of them have vanished now and that makes me feel a little more comfortable. He will get home okay, he will wake up with a very sore head, but he will get home safely.

Thank God there are still kind people in this world.

Chapter Nineteen: Target #25

As the young woman held his arm and led him from the bar the old man did not worry.

He felt calm, as though he'd been preparing for this moment his whole life.

And in a way, he had.

Ever since whispers of the Medusa network had begun he knew his name would be on the list. That his days were numbered. There were no two ways about it.

He was exactly the kind of person they were hunting.

It was almost a relief now that the moment was finally here. Now he no longer had to worry about when the gavel would drop and he would be called forward to answer for his crimes.

In all the nightmares he had, and there had been plenty, where they sought him out none had ever occurred in the bar. Not once had even his subconscious mind imagined that they might hunt him in his home away from home. If this had happened years ago he would have thought it cruel, but back then he was still blind to the evil of his actions. Back then he'd still believed he had done nothing wrong.

Time changed all men though.

Or at least it should.

How dreadful would it be to be facing his death in his sixtieth year with the same mindset he'd had when he was nineteen? To have lived for so many years, seen society evolve around him and yet still hold onto the misguided views and actions of his youth.

No.

He was better than that.

He'd proved himself better than that.

Sometime around his fortieth birthday he had seen the errors of his ways. And that's when he set about trying to make amends for them in whatever small ways he could.

A charitable donation here and there.

Helping a stranger carry their shopping back to their car.

Hosting free holiday meals at his business for those in need.

A hundred tiny good deeds would surely outweigh the misjudgements he had made when he'd been young and easily swayed.

Surely.

Soon he would know. Soon all of his thoughts, his worries, his guilt would cease to exist and he would know what fate awaited him in the afterlife.

The young woman was impossibly gentle with him, as though she could sense his lack of fight. As though she knew he was ready for what lay ahead. There was no firm grip on his arm, nor a wayward punch sent to his ribs to keep him in line as they walked towards a waiting car. She was almost kind to him, making sure he didn't hit his head as he climbed into the backseat.

Perhaps she didn't know who he truly was, what he had done.

She was just following orders.

Medusa had called for his name and she had simply delivered him.

There was no reason to suspect she knew of his crimes. In fact, he was certain that her mind was innocent of them because if she had even the inkling of the devastation he'd partaken in, hatred would burn in her eyes as she watched him drive away.

The last kind face he would ever see would be that of the stranger who delivered him to his death.

His vision was growing softer with each passing moment. Soon he would be asleep and then awoken for sentencing. It was inevitable that they would wake him. They would want him to suffer for what he had done.

As his eyes grew heavier he tried to keep his mind on his good years. His better years. The ones where he'd changed into the man he was now. But the tug of the past was too strong and his final lucid thought was of a memory of a crying child, begging him to leave them alone as he loomed over them.

Chapter Twenty: The Farm

On Karma's eighth birthday, she rebelled.
She refused to sleep in the same bed as Father.
It was supposed to be a birthday treat for her, a way to show her how special she was to him because after all, Peter still never slept next to anyone after losing Erin. He kept that vow to her for eight years after she died, and Karma was the only person he was willing to break that vow for.

Of course he had lay with other women since Erin passed. He'd laid with them whilst she'd been alive and he wasn't about to change the way he operated anytime soon. Especially not when it was for the better good of The Farm. The more children he and the congregation created the better and more stable their new world would be when it came to fruition.

But Karma was becoming an issue.

As much as Peter knew she was the rightful heir to take over when he ascended, she was a lot more wilful than he expected. If she was the chosen one surely she should be obedient, quiet and grateful. Instead she was rebellious, outspoken and irritable. She hadn't always been that way, when she was younger she'd grown to appreciate his attention. Flourished under it even. But something was changing in her as she grew older, there was an outside influence causing her to pull away from him.

Peter's first attempt to change this had been to isolate her from everybody else. He had insisted that she be kept locked in a room in his home, far away from everybody else. The sound of the outside world robbed from her via foam on the window panes. Meals delivered only by him.

When he visited with her evening meal that first night she screamed at him. Scratching out at him, she tried to reach his eyeballs. It had almost been adorable the way she'd tried to clamber up his body to reach his face, so small and angry but still he'd had to punish her. She had to learn that he was in charge. She may have been Mother reborn but he was still Father and that always ranked higher.

So he'd hit her. He hadn't enjoyed it in the way he enjoyed it with the others. She was precious after all. But it had needed to be done, and so with a heavy heart he struck her upon the face. Twice.

It had stung him more than it had her. She had to know that. To see the eyes of the wife he'd loved so much, tearing up because of something he'd done. But he pushed through the pain it caused him because the child had to learn. If she was going to lead the congregation into a better world then she had to be a leader they could respect.

Thankfully the next day she was less aggressive. She simply ignored his presence. Tried to pretend he didn't exist. Like the smell of the delicious meal he'd handpicked for her hadn't made its way to her nostrils and ignited her taste buds.

Peter took a different tactic that night. He sat on the floor, with her meal in front of her, until it went cold and the sauce congealed. It was ruined and still she ignored him.

After throwing the plate across the room, ensuring it missed her by an inch, he stalked from the room and vowed that in some way he would get through to her. He would get his special little girl back if it was the last thing he did.

When after seven days of isolation did nothing to change her attitude towards him, Father moved onto another plan.

If isolating her from others physically didn't make any difference to her attitude then perhaps doing it emotionally would.

He moved onto targeting those she seemed to be close to. Those she showed kindness to, shared her food with. Those she put her arm around after one of the nightly parties held in the children's home. Eventually even those she looked at for a moment too long.

It worked.

Eventually she stopped answering back. She fell in line, smiled as she sat by his side during his daily sermons and held his hand whenever he reached for her. And it was that way for three good years until she began to revert back to her dark self again. Until she started shying away from his touch, questioning his teachings and pushing away from his ideals.

On the night of her eighth birthday, when she refused to sleep next to him, she stubbornly lay on the floor at the foot of the bed. No matter how many times Father picked her up and put her back into his bed she would wait a beat and return to the floor. No shouting. No protests. Just movement.

Her silence was more infuriating than any words she could throw his way.

Father couldn't stand for the disrespect. He couldn't.

All he wanted to do was love Karma.

All he wanted was for her to love him back.
Just as Erin had.
Just as Mother had.

Chapter Twenty-One: Zoe

I wake up in my own bed.

Alone, unfortunately.

Harry's arrival poured a bucket of ice over any lust that had been simmering in my veins after my dance with Karma. He walked each of us to our bedrooms under the guise of being gentlemanly, when really we both knew it was because he wanted to be certain we didn't cause any damage to Karma or the Foundation's reputation.

We're grown adults though, and there had been nothing stopping us from sneaking back out once he left, and yet we didn't. There were no text messages exchanged between the two of us. Lord knows I sat with my phone for a good twenty minutes trying to write one, but I couldn't find the right words to say and eventually, I gave up and went to bed.

The first thing I do, as always, is reach across to my bedside table and unplug my phone. With a few swipes and my passcode I'm dialled back into the online world I love so much. I click through to my favourite newsite, one of the liberal ones that tries to pass itself off as independent despite its board of directors, and I'm shocked by the headline.

Karma Jones abandons Foundation.

Surely there's been some kind of mistake?

I quickly scan the article. Some two bit journalist seems to believe Karma has stepped down as Chairperson of the Foundation. He'll be sued to oblivion by lunchtime I'm sure.

I click through to a different news site just to see a similar story.

And another.

And another.

The news is everywhere, on every site and every forum. And yet the Foundation itself has yet to publicly speak out. Surely if this were true then Karma herself, or one of her colleagues would have spoken out to explain the decision?

And if it isn't true then they should be firefighting by releasing a statement reiterating Karma's loyalty to her Foundation. Because it is her Foundation. Everything they are able to do is because of her and how hard she's worked for the last three decades. How dare they not come to her aid when the internet is ripping her apart?

I quickly dial her number, desperate to hear the news from the horse's mouth but it rings out. I try again and I'm sent to voicemail. This has to be a mistake.

Pulling on a nearby hoodie and jogging bottoms I move towards the door of my room, not caring about my morning breath or last night's makeup smeared across my eyes. This is more important than my vanity.

If she hasn't stood down, she must be feeling abandoned by those she dedicated her life to.

If she has stood down, it has to be a decision that was out of her hand. She's given too much of herself to that place to just walk away.

Harry.

I bet this is bloody Harry's doing.

I'm full of rage as I open my door, and unfortunately for Harry he's standing on the other side of it. Hand raised ready to knock.

"What the fuck have you done?" I ask him, not bothering to contain my anger, to dress it underneath the veil of femininity we're supposed to adhere to. I didn't give a shit if he saw me as an emotional woman right now, because I am, and I have every right to be.

"I came to explain. I knew you'd see the news eventually but hoped I'd get here first." His face reads as honest but still I don't trust him. There is too much about Harry that I mistrust.

"What did you do?" I ask him again, this time with less venom. He's disarmed me with his show of concern, but I have to keep in mind that it's just a show. Harry doesn't care about me, he made that much clear the first time we met and a few forced moments of civility doesn't change that.

"I didn't do anything, in fact I advised Karma against it."

"What do you mean?" I'm painfully aware that we're having this conversation in a hotel hallway and the sound of our voices are probably carrying through to every room. All it would take is someone with a social media account to start posting our words and this situation would be made ten times worse.

"Shall we meet downstairs for a coffee? Somewhere we can talk more privately?" He glances around us, showing that he has the same fears I do. Always concerned with how he might be perceived.

I nod in agreement but close the door in his face before he can say anything else. I need to calm down if I'm going to sit face to face across from the man and get genuine answers from him. He'll be more likely to confide in me if he thinks I'm on his side.

Moving to the bathroom now I take a large handful

of cold water and splash it across my face.

Doesn't work, I'm still angry.

I repeat the process until my skin tingles from the change in temperature and whilst I may not be calmer, I'm certainly more awake.

Pulling my trainers on, I try Karma's phone one last time. Straight to voicemail again. I guess I have no choice but to go down to the hotel restaurant and meet with Harry. At the very least he should be able to tell me what room she's staying in so I can go check on her in person.

Just as I close the door behind me my phone sounds with an alert that once used to bring me joy, but now brings me mild stress. There's been another murder. Or perhaps they've finally published the dossier on Graham Williams. Mr Williams. Perhaps the Network is finally ready to tell the world why he deserved to die, or better yet perhaps they are finally ready to own up to their mistake and give his widow some peace.

But no.

I don't have that kind of luck.

There is no update on my school teacher. No clearing of his name, or damnation of his soul. The Network seems more than comfortable with the murder of an innocent man, and they don't even have the decency to clear his name and admit they got it wrong. I thought they were better than this. I thought the work they were doing was better than this.

Instead this is an update on a new death. A new murder.

Strange how I never really thought of the Network as being murderers until they took somebody I knew. And you know what, if they'd had a solid reason for doing so I would have accepted it. I would have kept supporting them from the sidelines, happily indulging in my dark interest in their work. Now though it all feels a little tawdry. How do I truly know that those they've killed deserved it? That they were actually guilty of the crimes they were accused of?

No.

I musn't start questioning the methods behind their work, even if I am questioning the way in which they are going about it. I believe every victim, every survivor who has corroborated the Network's dossiers. Hand on my heart I do.

But Mr. Williams' death changed something in me.

It showed me what life might be like for those left behind.

With a sigh, I don't delay the inevitable. I was always going to read the latest headlines, no matter what moral quandary they bring up in me now.

I squint at my screen, using my fingers to zoom in on the picture of the latest victim.

Impossible.

There's no way.

It looks similar to the old man I saw stumbling around the bar last night.

Eerily similar.

The man who Karma had described as being an old friend.

The one who looked as though he'd seen a ghost the second their eyes met across the room.

My stomach feels cold. Heavy. Like the contents inside of it have instantly rotted.

I walk down to the hotel bar feeling like I'm not quite in the room. Like I'm hovering above myself, watching everything occurring around me with a displaced stare.

Harry is already sitting at a table. Two mugs settled in front of him. The steam from them rising, meeting the version of me that's floating through the air. He looks tired, like he's been up for most of the night. There's a pair of glasses perched on his face that I've never seen him wear before. I guess his eyes are too tired to put his contact lenses in this morning.

Is Karma part of the Network?

That's the question on repeat in my mind, the one that's kept me company on the long walk down to the lobby.

It's not possible. She was with me the entire night, up until Harry escorted us home. And even then she wouldn't have had time to sneak out and kill a man, much less get back to the hotel unnoticed.

Her face is recognisable, a staff member would have spotted her, she'd be on CCTV sneaking out of the doors - all of these things would have made it impossible for her to leave and murder somebody.

And yet there is no denying that the Medusa network is far-reaching. She could be involved in his death without ever having spilt his blood.

No.

No.

I'm being paranoid. Thinking like a crazy woman. I need to focus on finding out why she stepped down from the Foundation. I need to get answers that only Harry can give me.

"Thank you," he says as he pushes my coffee towards me and this strikes me as odd. What does he have to thank me for?

"You're welcome," I reply out of British courtesy. I might not understand his thanks but he felt the need to give it and I was raised to be polite.

"Karma handed in her notice last night." He speaks quickly, as though his words are on a timer and might expire. "I asked her not to, told her it was too hasty but she wouldn't listen."

"Why would she do that?"

"Because the police want to come and speak to her. They called me about four hours after I brought you home last night. They want to speak to both of you in fact."

"What?" Even though I know I've done nothing to be concerned about, I still am. The police wanting to speak to me is not something I've ever experienced before.

"Don't worry. You haven't done anything wrong. They just want to speak to everyone who was at the bar last night. I'm sure you've seen the news?" he offers me his phone but I turn it away, of course I've read the latest headlines, Harry knows of my interest in the Network.

"Yes. I have. Okay, so it's just a routine inquiry then, so why would she do something so drastic?"

"This isn't the first time they've been out to speak to her. She's adamant that the task force has her in their headlights and she doesn't want the reputation of the Foundation to be tarnished whilst they hound her."

"But if she's innocent, she doesn't have anything to worry about."

"That's what I said to her. But she was so sure of her decision, I couldn't talk her round. Trust me, I tried." He takes a sip from his mug and winces at the heat of the liquid.

"Has she consulted with a lawyer? If she's so sure the police are out to get her then she needs to be prepared." Even now, even with my earlier worries about Karma and her involvement in the Network, I want to make sure she's doing all she can to protect herself. That woman has been through too much in this life to let a group of police officers ruin her reputation.

"If it comes to it, she has one on retainer. But she doesn't want to call him yet."

"That's ridiculous," I scoff. She is being stubborn.

Being a martyr.

"It's just a routine Q&A session. If she lawyers up, it will just give them more ammunition." Harry seems completely deflated.

"When was she questioned before?" I can't help but latch onto the fact that Karma has been interviewed before in relation to the Network, and yet she didn't mention it to me when we were exchanging our mutual interest in their work. What an odd thing to leave out of conversation.

"She's been questioned a few times. Whenever we happen to be in the same town as a murder. Whenever one of the victims had links to one of her support groups. Pretty much any time they can find an excuse to speak to her, they do. And she complies every time."

"Jesus. They really are out to get her, aren't they?" I shake my head at the thought. "And those are such ridiculous reasons, just coincidences, they can't link her to anything or she'd be arrested. She really ought to put in a complaint."

Harry pauses and stares at me for a moment. Weighing up his next words before he speaks them.

"Unless she's guilty."

He leaves the words hanging in the air between us as he takes another sip of his coffee, this time being sure to blow on it beforehand.

A thousand responses blow through my mind. Most of them are full of irritation at his lack of loyalty to Karma. But none of them make their way to my tongue.

Because he's only verbalised what I'm worried about.

Chapter Twenty-Two: Zoe

Harry leads me to a small meeting room where Karma is already waiting. I take a step towards her, and go to speak, before I notice the presence of two strangers standing just to the side of the door. Clearly we aren't to be left alone before we're interviewed. Sensible I suppose, to stop us from colluding in our stories, but unnecessary if we're innocent because we only have the truth to tell.

The first officer steps forward. So, he's leading the show.

This is most likely the person heading up the investigation into the Network, the one Harry told me has spoken to Karma multiple times. The one who is hounding her despite having no evidence to do so.

He's taller than I imagined, younger too. I'd drawn a picture of an inspector approaching retirement, back broken from years of desk work, determined to get one last big win before he left the force. Instead I'm greeted by a man who is probably only in his early forties, not much older than me, and with a posture the King would fawn over.

"Inspector Sandways, so nice to see you again." Karma forces a smile onto her face, although I can see the frustration behind it. I'm sure he can too.

"Apologies for the early call, especially after you had such an eventful night." He sits down on the other side of the banquet table that's been dragged in here. It looks ridiculous in this little room, its size overpowering all of us, but if he feels it is necessary then so be it. He's the one directing this ridiculous witch hunt.

The hotel is probably abuzz with gossip by now. No doubt forums are already full of candid snaps of the rooms set up, Karma walking towards it and now images of Harry leading me to the door.

God, I hope no one I know sees them. I can't be doing with the attention and won't respond to any enquiries for information. This is someone's life, Karma's life, not a sideshow for people's entertainment.

"Please, there's no need for apologies, this was practically a lie-in by your standards." Karma retorts and it's the confirmation I need of what Harry told me in the cafe. Inspector Sandways has spoken to Karma before, she's on his radar and she's bored of his attention.

"True, true."

He's not making any show of being affected by her barbed response. Playing his cards close to his chest.

"And I believe you're Zoe Lewis, yes?"

I nod my head and move to join them around the table. Might as well get this farce over with and then I'll be able to speak to Karma properly, to find out how she really feels about stepping down from the Foundation.

"I'll cut to the chase. You both know that a body was found last night, another victim of the Medusa network. You've been called in today as you were both seen on CCTV at the victim's last known location. This is just a routine interview, we'll ask a few questions and be on our way."

The second officer in the room steps forward and places a dictaphone on the table between us, then without a word being exchanged between them sinks back to the shadows. I guess this is their good cop, scary cop routine.

"You're certainly going to have a busy day talking to all the patrons from last night. The place was packed." Karma replies, her tone sympathetic but her face ice cold.

"You are talking to everyone, aren't you?" I ask, unable to help my attitude. We've done nothing wrong and they're treating us like suspects. Burying us away in this dark room, recording our answers just in case we fall over our words. I don't like any part of this and if I find out that they aren't talking to every single person who stepped foot in the bar last night, I'll be sure to kick up a stink.

"Of course, patrons and staff will all be interviewed in turn." Inspector Sandways replies, casting a curious glance at me. I guess I've got more bark about me than he expected.

"We're just the lucky ones who got picked first?" It's asked as a question but Karma knows it's a fact. There's no way she wasn't top of Sandways' list of people to speak to. The tension in the air is only increasing in volume. I'm stuck in a game of cat and mouse and I'm only just certain that Sandways is the predator in this situation.

"You were nearest to our office, so it made sense. Plus with your busy schedule, we can never be sure where you'll be off to next." he replies, giving an explanation that's most likely drenched in accusation but we can't point that out without looking like we're hiding something.

He turns his attention back to Karma, staring at her unblinking with a smile tugging at the corner of his mouth.

"Did you know the victim?" he asks her.

"No," she replies, without shaking her head.

I know this is a lie though; she told me he had been an old friend. And even if she hadn't told me, it was obvious they had history from the way they stared at each other across the dance floor. Why would she lie to the police? And if she lied about that, what else has she lied to them about in the many times they've spoken?

"And you, Miss Lewis, did you know the deceased?" He now directs the question to me but I know my answer is unimportant. He's just following routine.

"No," I reply, knowing that I'm the only one out of the two of us on this side of the table speaking the truth. I should interject here, tell Sandways that Karma knew the man. Tell him what she told me.

But I don't.

Because I have to believe that Karma has a good reason for her omission from the conversation, and I'll be able to ask her about it when we're alone. Karma isn't a liar. She's just chosen not to tell the truth. There is a difference.

Isn't there?

"That's strange you see, because we have the two of you exchanging quite the look across the dance floor." His colleague steps forward again, this time to place a folder of photographs onto the table. Inspector Sandways opens it with a flourish and takes his time placing each photograph in front of Karma until she's presented with an entire gallery of images.

Each shows either her face, or the victims staring unmistakably at each other.

"The video footage captures about one minute of, what I have to say, is very intense eye contact between the two of you. Care to explain?"

"I guess I thought it was a bit strange to see a man of his age in a bar like that."

"You guess?" Sandways asks.

"You might find it unbelievable, Inspector, but I don't have a conscious decision behind every movement of my eyes."

"A minute is a very long time,"

"Is it? Can't say I've given it much thought. I was probably away with the fairies. Alcohol can have that effect, you know?"

Like a game of tennis, their responses are being knocked back and forth and I'm sitting in between them like an unwilling spectator.

"Would you say you were very drunk last night?"

"I had a drink or three, as I often do at social functions. A way to cope with the anxiety, you know."

"You don't strike me as an anxious person."

"Appearances can be deceiving."

"They certainly can," he replies, each of them staring into the other's soul.

A pause between them as they weigh up each other's words and the insinuations behind them. I'm pretty sure my head is spinning like a character in a cartoon, my eyes out on stalks at the underlying anger between the two of them. Where I'd once been sure that Sandways was the cat, I'm beginning to feel like he's nothing more than a mouse Karma is toying with.

"Do you have any more questions for us, Inspector?" I ask, wanting this back-and-forth to end.

"I do have one for you actually, Miss Lewis. You appeared to be watching the victim leave the pub, unfortunately, the cameras didn't catch a clear image of the woman who aided him. Would you be able to give a description?"

Can I?

Can I remember the woman in enough detail to give a reliable description?

And if so, do I want to?

Describing the woman would take the heat off

Karma. It would prove that she didn't know the stranger who led the man to his death.

Describing the woman would draw an obvious line in the sand on where I stand on the Network and its actions. And as much as I've been questioning my feelings towards them since Mr. Williams died, I'm not sure I'm ready to partake in the unpicking of them.

"I'm afraid not. It was very dark, all I can say is that she seemed kind. I thought she was just helping a drunk get home safely." I tell as much of the truth as I can. Because try as I might, I can't conjure up an image of the woman to share with Inspector Sandways. She was just so normal. Nothing about her stood out, or called attention to her.

"Honestly, she looked just like any other woman you might walk past on the street. And I was on the other side of the dance floor," I shrug to show there's no real end to my sentence. Could you perfectly describe a stranger you saw on the other side of a bar? Because I'm certain I could not. And it certainly isn't some deep-seeded need to protect the Network preventing my memory from painting a picture for the Inspector. Certainly not.

"Right." He draws the single word out with far more flair than is required. It's clear that he suspects the both of us now, but there's nothing further he can use to prod us with.

"Will that be all?" Karma asks.

"For now," he sweeps the photos back into the folder and stands. Taking the time to offer his hand to each of us. I shake it and Karma offers him the limpest grip I've ever seen. I'm not surprised, she must be sick of the man by now.

"I'll see you out Inspector," offers Harry. His words and expression are tight, it's clear he's enjoyed this little charade as much as we have.

The three of them leave the room and finally, I am alone with Karma.

"Are you okay?" I ask. She sighs in response and runs her hands through her hair. What once had been a magnificent crown of curls on her head last night now resembled road kill. As though she knows what I'm thinking, she pulls it back into a ponytail.

"That man is incessant," she finally replies, looking absolutely exhausted.

"Harry did mention that he's spoken to you before."

"Ten times. Ten times he has brought me to a room like this and asked me questions. Questions about my life, my work, my social habits. Any excuse he can find to knock on my door, he takes. I could be on the other side of the country when the Network strikes and still he'd find a reason to speak to me."

"Have you thought about putting in a complaint?"

"What's the point? He's doing his job. But every alibi I have ever given him is solid and I have no direct links to the targets. I'm starting to think the Inspector just enjoys my company." She gives a wry laugh at her own sense of humour and it lights up her eyes, removing the frustration from within them.

"Why did you lie though? About not knowing the victim? You told me he was an old friend?"

Karma looks at me, a glimmer of shock in her eyes, has she forgotten what she'd said to me last night? Or is she surprised I have the stones to ask her that question?

"Because Sandways will use any excuse at his disposal to hound me. The man won't be happy until there are cuffs on my wrists."

It's an excuse, yes. But not necessarily the best one.

"You didn't correct me though Zoe, tell me why you didn't do that? Why lie to the Inspector?" There's a glint to her tone now that I don't like. Her words are loaded with a danger that brings goosebumps to my skin.

"Because I could see he had an axe to grind, and if I'd told him you'd lied then he'd never stop." I think I've chosen my answer carefully enough because with a blink of her eyes Karma is back to the woman I was growing to know. All the threat evaporates from her as though it had never existed.

Had I imagined it?

Perhaps the stress of the last few hours is affecting my logical thinking. I am seeing emotions that aren't there. Karma has shown me nothing but kindness since we met. And last night, something had flitted between us on the dance floor, I know it had. She means me no harm. I'm just overthinking things.

"Imagine if I'd lied and you were part of the Network, I'd look like a right twat." I attempt a small joke, chuckling at my own expense.

"Imagine if you'd lied and I was the Network," she replies with a smile. Before I can think too hard about her words, she stands and leaves the room.

I sit at the banquet table alone, but not without the feeling of eyes upon my skin.

Chapter Twenty-Three: Zoe

Just as I've composed myself enough to follow her, I hear a heated exchange from the corridor just beyond the meeting room.

"Inspector Sandways, back so soon?" Karma asks as I stride towards her, ready to defend her against this rabid dog.

"Karma Ann Jones, I am placing you under arrest for the suspicion of murder." He replies, pulling handcuffs from his belt with a victorious flourish.

"What the fuck?" I gasp, turning the corner and stepping fully into the scene.

Harry stands to the side of the two of them, speaking in a low whisper to the Inspector's colleague. His head is hung low as he listens with the occasional nod. There is no shock in his expression though, he believes whatever he's being told.

"I think there's been a misunderstanding," Karma says as she steps away from the Inspector and his cuffs. But it's no use, he's quicker than her, more prepared for this moment and relishing in it. Before I know what's happened there's a soft click and my friend is being led away from me.

"Zoe, this is a set up. Whatever they think they've

got on me they don't. Call my lawyer." She issues instructions with each footstep and I follow behind like an obedient lamb.

The reception area is full of wide eyes and phone screens and I want to knock each of them onto the floor and stamp on them.

How dare they treat her like fodder after all she's done for society?

Have they forgotten the good work she's painfully undertaken? The support groups. The rallies. The never ending campaigning.

All forgotten in a moment because of two metal bracelets.

"What the hell happened?" I ask Harry as the two of us stand side by side watching Karma being loaded into the back of a waiting vehicle.

"They found her brooch at the scene of the crime. Her fingerprints were all over it."

It isn't possible.

This can't be happening.

Karma isn't a murderer.

Chapter Twenty-Four: Zoe

The public have not reacted kindly to Karma's arrest.

It appears that society has not forgotten all the good she has done despite the gawking faces that surrounded her as she was led off this morning. I misjudged the general public, assuming that they'd burn her at the stake just as quickly as they built her up as a saviour.

The news of her incarceration spread like wildfire, and I'm not ashamed to admit that I helped light the match. A few anonymous posts on forums, brief emails to gossip sites and the online world was ablaze with rage at the way she is being treated.

Talks have already begun of organising rallies outside the station she is being held in, with plans to shout loud and proud so she'd know that the world still supported her. I hope that Karma hears their chants, and that it brings her comfort but I have the feeling that Inspector Sandways will do all he can to keep the noise locked away from her. To keep her as isolated as possible so she feels abandoned. Vulnerable.

Right, that's it.

Time to try and do something productive about

this. Laying on my bed constantly refreshing news feeds isn't helping me or Karma. Especially now that the online trolls have come out to play. The ones who think she's guilty until proven innocent.

They don't care that she's been harassed by the police for months, they believe blindly in the law enforcement of this country and can't bring themselves to entertain the idea that sometimes they make mistakes. Sometimes they have their own goals in mind.

I need to get out of this hotel room. The walls are closing in on me and I feel very claustrophobic. Fresh air will help clear my mind, stop me from arguing with the trolls on forums who are desperate to bring a strong woman down.

Thankfully, the corridor is empty as I make my way downstairs towards the hotel's entrance. The press have all moved on now, they had little choice after Harry reminded the manager about the NDA he'd signed when the booking for our rooms had been made.

Staff were quickly ushered away from journalists and told to keep their heads down and get on with their jobs. Without the chance of any sound bites, the bottom feeders had moved location; they're probably all lurking outside the station now, ready to capture photos of the protests.

There's a bench just to the left of the hotel's archways and I make a beeline for it. I'm not sure where my final destination is going to be, I'm just happy to be out of my room, and a bit of people watching might help clear my mind.

So I sit and I gaze out at the world around me, allowing my brain to disassociate slightly, to give me the feeling that I'm just watching rather than participating in life at the moment. It's easier to feel that way sometimes. Makes reality a little more palatable.

Just as I'm beginning to enjoy the quiet in my mind

something catches my eye.

Harry.

The fact that he's outside shouldn't be that big of a deal, I am also outside. We can't be expected to hide in our hotel rooms as spare parts whilst our employer sits in an interview room.

So it isn't the fact that he's out enjoying the early afternoon sunshine that intrigues me.

It's the way he's moving.

He's trying to hurry but being desperately self-conscious about it. As though he doesn't want people to notice.

Whenever someone is trying their best to look innocent, that's when they seem most guilty.

And Harry is guilty of something. I'm just not sure of what yet.

I watch as he makes his way further away from the hotel, pausing occasionally to look at his phone, until eventually he comes to a stop by a public bin.

Bizarre.

What's even more bizarre is the envelope he pulls out from his jacket pocket, running it between his fingers for a moment whilst staring intently at it. As though it's a love letter he isn't quite ready to get rid of yet.

He shakes his head slightly, as though arguing with himself and very carefully places the envelope into the bin. This is some of the most abnormal behaviour I've seen a man display.

Then, as though to intrigue me further, he pulls the envelope back out. He shakes off some dirt from its surface and goes to put it back in his pocket, but pauses.

Something, or rather someone has caught his eye. They're out of my line of vision but it's quite clear from Harry's stance that their appearance changes matters. With a visible sigh he folds the envelope in half and puts it back in the bin he just pulled it from.

Without a second glance back, he walks away, following the street as it winds around the hotel and I watch until I can no longer see him.

I'm about to stand up and move towards the bin hoping to grab the envelope for myself when a new player enters the stage.

It's a man. I can tell that much from their build and clothing, but frustratingly his back is turned to me and I can't make out his face. I watch, with drawn breath, as he reaches into the bin and pulls out the envelope Harry has just deposited.

Am I watching a drug drop?

A blackmail pay off?

Whatever it is, it's clear nobody is supposed to be paying the level of attention that I am to this exchange. What the hell has Harry got himself involved in? Does he need help? Should I offer? Or should I duck my head and keep myself out of it?

My decision is made for me when the man finally turns to check behind him and I catch a glimpse of his face.

Inspector Sandways is the man rooting through the bin for Harry's envelope.

Unfortunately for me he notices me at the same time I become aware of his identity, and there's no hiding the gormless look of shock on my face. I'm pretty sure my mouth is hanging open wide enough that he can see the fillings in my teeth, even from this distance.

Now turning his whole body round to face me, he slowly places the envelope into his inside jacket pocket and begins to stride towards me.

I have to get out of here.

Panicking I stand, tripping over my own feet as I make my way back into the sanctuary of the hotel lobby.

Diving onto an armchair behind a potted plant, I stoop down, trying to make myself as small as possible in the hopes the plastic leaves will protect me.

Inspector Sandways walks into the lobby.

He pauses in front of the reception desk and scans the area, looking for me, seeking me out.

My back aches from the curve I'm forcing into my spine. I have to stay hidden. I don't want to talk to this man. I don't want to hear his excuses or threats. I want him to give up, forget it ever happened and leave.

Out of childlike instinct, I pull my eyes tightly closed, because if I can't see him then he can't see me - right?

Wrong.

His footsteps are soft as they approach me, trying to convey a sense of nonchalance. Not wanting me to know how desperate he is to talk to me. To explain what I'd witnessed.

"Miss Lewis," he says and I give thought to keeping my eyes closed. Maybe he'll leave if I refuse to acknowledge him.

Sadly that's not how the world works and I know that. Nothing can stop a man with a woman in his sights. It's a story we've heard so many times.

It's why sometimes it's easier to just give in to politeness. To give someone your number and then block it when you're safely home. To create a fictitious boyfriend as a reason why you can't accept a drink. To stay quiet in a meeting when you know their answers are wrong. To open your eyes and accept their lies as truths, so you can safely sleep at night.

"Inspector Sandways, what brings you here?"

"You ran inside awfully fast, I just wanted to check everything was okay?" he asks, when what he means is he just wants to check what I've seen.

"The sun has given me a terrible headache; it's a lot brighter out there than I expected," I reply, hoping that this excuse also explains why he came across me in a hotel lobby with my eyes closed.

"You really ought to wear sunglasses if it bothers you that much. Eyesight is such an important thing, you'd be wise to protect it."

"You're right. I should have thought about it." Make yourself small. Make yourself kind. Make yourself malleable.

"Did you see anything interesting before your headache struck?" I suppose I should be grateful for this question; at least Inspector Sandways doesn't beat around the bush.

"Not really. I'd been playing on my phone for most of the time, and then I spotted you."

"And you ran away?" he asks, trying to trip me up in my story. It's true, the timing of my sun-induced headache was quite a coincidence in terms of his appearance.

"I was worried you were going to give me bad news about Karma," I reply, putting a tremor into my voice and averting my gaze from his at the last two words. As though I'm an injured animal, worried about the farmer's gun.

He considers my response, and looking back up at him, I can see the moment he chooses to believe me. Because he thinks he's smarter than me. Too smart for a woman like me to have caught him in the act.

Quite what the act is I'm not sure yet.

"If there are any updates, I'll send them through Harry. You don't need to worry yourself. We are looking after Ms. Jones as best we're able." I smile at him as he finishes talking, grateful for the care he's showing my friend despite her supposed crime.

It's the biggest bit of bullshit that's ever stemmed from my face.

Inspector Sandways and Harry are up to something. And I need to work out what.

Chapter Twenty-Five: Karma

"I bumped into your friend this morning," begins Inspector Sandways, waiting for a response from Karma. She's handcuffed to a bar on the table in an interrogation room. Her makeup from the night before is long gone, her hair is limp in its ponytail and she requested a jumper an hour ago that he has yet to bring her.

He prefers her like this.
Broken.
Honest.
Raw.

For so long he's waited to get her into this position. Because she's guilty. He knows she is. It's written all over her body language, even if her words still protest the impossibility.

The brooch was covered in fingerprints.
And now her hair had been found at the scene.
All he needs is a confession and he would have closed the biggest case in the country in a decade.

It was all coming together.

"I imagine she was pleased to see you," Karma finally replies. Goosebumps raised on her arms but she hasn't inquired about the jumper again. She doesn't want to give him the satisfaction of knowing how much she wants it.

Her lawyer sits next to her and she knows if she mentioned it to him it would be on her person within ten minutes. But she doesn't want to go running to her lawyer. She wants Sandways to do it out of human decency. But it's becoming clear that he has none.

Her brooch could not have been found at the crime scene. Because up until she was interviewed at the hotel, it had been on the side table in her room. There was no way it could have been in two places at once.

Of course, it has her fingerprints on it.

It is hers.

Until it wasn't.

"Let's revisit what we discussed earlier, shall we?" he asks as though she has a choice about the direction of their conversation. Her lawyer goes to interrupt, to point out that they are moving around in circles. She silences him with a look. She will not be accused of not cooperating with the police; that would be seen as a point against her.

She never wanted to bring a lawyer into this situation; it had the potential of getting too messy but Sandways had left her little choice when he marched her from the hotel in handcuffs. At least with the lawyer here she has another witness to any words she decided to share. Someone to prevent them from being twisted, or to agree with the meaning behind them.

"Quite a few of the murder victims have been linked to attendees at your support programmes as you know, do you have any new thoughts about this?"

"I think if you looked hard enough in your life, Inspector, you'd find someone who's been to one of the support groups my foundation offers. Or one similar. It's really not as unusual as you seem to believe."

"And yet I still believe it." He shuts her down once

again, still refusing to buy into the fact she was sharing with him.

Because they are facts.

Seventy thousand adults, aged sixteen and over, are raped a year in this country.

Seventy thousand.

Seventy thousand lives interrupted. Destroyed. Changed forever.

Seventy thousand people forced to survive the worst humanity can offer.

And those are just the ones who are technically raped. There are so many other things you can force onto a person that isn't classed as rape.

Those are just the ones who make reports or complaints. There are many more who keep what they've survived to themselves.

Because it's safer that way. It's almost easier, as though anything about that situation could be considered easy.

If you keep quiet, then you never have to confront your abuser. Never have to face the calls that say you're lying or that you somehow brought it on yourself.

"Did you know Inspector Sandways, that only 1.3% of reported rapes result in conviction?" Karma asks him, rage beginning to override her logic. Who does this man think he was, to sit opposite her and try to pretend like support groups aren't attended up and down the country. Like he can't possibly know someone who draws comfort from them.

The fact that the people who had been killed had tenuous links to attendees of her support groups is no reason to hound her relentlessly. Is no reason for her to be sitting before him in handcuffs.

And she's had enough of his games.

"Tell me, why are you so busy speaking to me instead of doing your best to raise those rates? To deal with real criminals. Real monsters. Is it not on the checklist for this quarter? Will it not bring you as much acclaim as sentencing a woman who had a brooch stolen for a crime you're incapable of solving?"

Her lawyer clears his throat, trying to warn her to calm down. To remember that she'd have more luck in this situation should she remain agreeable. But Karma has reached the point of no return.

She is done with the Inspector and his accusations.

She is done pretending she didn't have the emotions and anger she does.

"Stolen? Are you trying to suggest that you've been framed, Ms. Jones?" He may have been able to keep a straight face when he delivered this line, but Karma can see the smile inside his eyes.

He's done this.

He's stolen her brooch and placed it at the crime scene.

Carefully plucked discarded hairs from her hairbrush and arranged them around the corpse to give himself a reason to arrest her.

He has orchestrated it all.

And Karma was through.

"No comment," she replies, stonewalling him.

Retreating into the safe space in her mind she'd built when she was a child. The one that let her switch her emotions off and view the world as nothing more than a television show. Something fake. Something she doesn't have to deal with.

"Ms. Jones, can you please clarify what you meant?" He is pushing her now, hoping he can irritate her enough into saying something she shouldn't.

"No comment," she replied once again, defiantly looking across at him.

Karma will not be broken by this man.

Worse men have tried and failed in that regard.

Justice would take care of Sandways.
She is certain of it.

Chapter Twenty-Six: The Farm

Father had spent the last year trying to reason with Karma, since the night of her eighth birthday, when she'd refused his offer to sleep next to him. He'd tried at least once a week to get her to see the error of her ways.

Sometimes he was kind. Sometimes he was cruel.

When he had to be cruel, he told himself it was just a different way of being kind. A higher way of being kind. A predetermined way of being kind.

Because it was all predetermined.

This was all part of fate's plan. It had all been decided for Father on the day he had been born. All of it had been planned out, and he was merely following the path that had been chosen for him.

His father's affairs. His mother's death. Meeting Erin. The birth of their child. The death of Mother. Her rebirth.

It was all written in the stars the day Father had been sent to Earth. That's what he believed. What he knew to be true. Peter had been special, but Father was something more. He had become something more.

His congregation swelled in numbers every week. Waifs and strays always arriving at their door, seeking the salvation that only he could offer. Willing to do what was required to earn their place in the better world that was coming. Father should be satisfied. He was satisfied, for the most part.

The one thorn in his side was Karma.

Bloody Karma and her constant need to fight him and all that they stood for. If he were a lesser man, he might call it a day on her. Find another heir, a more suitable one. One who would listen to his teachings and take them to heart. Who he could trust, one hundred percent, to carry on his good work.

But he couldn't quit her.

There was something about the girl. Even at just nine years old, there was a quality, a draw about her that people already couldn't ignore. A charisma that couldn't be denied, or resisted. And she wasn't aware of her power over everyone that came into her orbit, but Father was aware of it. And Father knew it had to be harnessed, because it could be used. It could be used to power his movement further, to achieve great and wonderful aims; all he had to do was get her on side and he could tap into it.

She had been sent to him. She had been destined for him.

It was the only plausible reason for Erin's death. The only one Father could accept.

Karma had been sent to replace Erin. He had accepted that the moment he laid eyes on the girl. The all-encompassing grief he'd felt clawing at his brain since the day he lost his wife had vanished the moment he walked into the nursery and saw the baby for the first time. As much as he had never been able to confirm it, he knew instinctively that she was a part of him. The best part of him. And it was his duty, his responsibility to make sure she achieved all she was meant to.

He just had to get the girl to understand.

Once she did, he could concentrate on his ascension, knowing that she would continue his good work.

Chapter Twenty-Seven: Target #30

Phillip Smith walked into the party with an air of confidence that money can't buy.

Here he was important, he was king. People fell over themselves to befriend him. Sure, he knew their admiration was mostly down to the wares he could acquire for them but still there was no harm in making the most of the situation. And Phillip knew exactly how to make the most of this situation.

The party was in full swing and it was nearing midnight. The perfect time to hunt. Before he began enjoying his extracurricular though, business had to be concluded.

Moving his way through the sweating bodies, thriving around to some god-awful techno music, he thought about how much he pitied them. With their simple existence, content to spend the night dancing and drinking until the sun came out when they'd finally sleep, ready to do it all again when twilight came around. What kind of life was that? Where was the risk? The adventure? If you always partied with the same people then you always had the same problems.

Phillip easily located his buyer, the man who had foolishly invited him tonight, and exchanged drugs for notes. A simple, straightforward transaction, one they had partaken in several times over the last two weeks. He'd never known someone to get through so much cocaine, then again, he'd never known someone who threw fourteen-day-long house parties. His buyer was most likely a school jock in a prior life, he certainly carried himself with the ego of someone who was desperately trying to cling to their glory days.

The last time Phillip had been here, he had spotted a redhead that caught his attention. She had sharp angular features which resulted in her looking a little like a Picasso painting. All face and no body. The kind of girl who didn't attract attention, even when she's parading around half-naked.

Exactly his type.

He'd been disappointed to see her draped on the arm of his buyer, she looked classier than that to him. Better than that. Still, at least it showed she was simply desperate for male company. It certainly wasn't his buyer's personality she was hanging around for. The man could bore paint from the wall.

He tried to catch her eye the last night he was here, and engage her in conversation so she might notice she was wasting her time with a mediocre chad when she could have a man like Phillip. But it had failed. His every attempt to interact with her had gone down like a lead balloon. He knew it wasn't a problem with him, after all, he was always surrounded by a crowd of people who laughed loudly at his every quip. It was her problem. She was the problem if she couldn't see what a catch he was.

That happened sometimes to Phillip. He set his heart on someone who didn't see his worth. He always got them in the end, though. One way or another. He'd been sure to bring something special for her tonight, a little gift to loosen her up. She was too stuck up for her own good, and he was the one who had to remedy that. Soon she'd be putty in his hands.

He rooted through the kitchen cupboards until he found a clean glass, and then located a bottle of red wine - he'd seen her drinking it the last time he'd been here - before finally sprinkling some powder into the liquid as he poured a large glass. It quickly disappeared into the wine, just as it had many times before.

Phillip knew he was an intelligent man; how else would he be able to take what he wants from life and walk away unscathed? In the morning, she wouldn't remember her groans of pleasure, but she would feel the shadow of him inside of her, she'd never forget it. Never forget him.

Looking around the room, he tried to locate his target again. The need to have her was beginning to take him over and the situation wasn't helped as he watched her kiss his buyer. He'd have to make sure she rinsed her mouth out before he took her later. He didn't want to share saliva with that peon.

Just as he locked eyes on her and was making his move across the room, somebody jolted into his side causing him to spill red wine all down his shirt and upon the floor. Phillip was furious and not just because of the mess. He barely had any of his special little powder left over to start the process again, and if he didn't have enough then his prey would just become messy rather than unconscious and he'd never be able to have his fun if that was the case.

He whipped his head up, tearing his gaze away from the tannin-soaked carpet at his feet, ready to throw vicious words and threats in the direction of the one who knocked into him.

The words died on his tongue.
His intent on violence took on a new colour.
Because it was a woman.

And not just any woman. The kind of woman he'd fantasise about at night when he was alone, his duvet growing warm with his movements. The kind of woman that defined beauty, and here she was, standing before him, smiling nervously.

"Shit, I'm so sorry," she said. Phillip noted her soft Scottish accent, it was a shame but still nobody could be perfect. In his opinion, any regional accent should be trained out of the populace's dialect so everybody could sound the same as each other.

"That's okay, honestly, don't worry."

"At least let me help you clean up," she smiled at him now and fireworks exploded inside Phillip's head. Did this woman actually want to stay in his company? She could have just apologised and then disappeared and yet here she was, offering to accompany him to the kitchen to sort himself out. This had to be more than guilt at causing the spill, this had to be an attraction.

The two of them walked together back across the room, and he noted the way her shoulder kept brushing against him. She wanted to walk as close to him as possible, this was happening, this wasn't his imagination. This woman was clearly interested in him and he hadn't had to resort to inducing it in her.

She handed Phillip the towel she'd quickly run under the tap and he knelt down, starting with his shoes first. These had been brand new trainers, brought just yesterday and pulled on this evening with hope in mind.

He didn't mind sacrificing them to the wine though. If she'd never bumped into him then he would have wasted his night on someone who wouldn't even remember him in the morning.

Still. It had been a while since Phillip had been with a woman who'd been present. Conscious. Perhaps he had just enough powder left to make her a little drowsy, a little more pliable. He was too nervous to go through with the deed knowing she'd be cataloging his every move.

"Here, I made you a drink," she said, passing him a glass of red wine. He could hardly turn her down given that was the drink she'd spilled down him. If he did, if he had to explain that actually he rarely drank, then he'd have to come up with a lie as to why he'd been holding a glass in the first place. It was just easier all round to drink the damn wine and be done with it. Besides, it might give him the confidence boost he needed.

She was smiling at him again now, this time over the rim of her own glass. Phillip took a large gulp of the wine and within minutes the world began to feel fuzzy.

She took him by the arm.
She guided him unseen out of the house.
She walked him down the front path.
She put him in a waiting car.
She signed his death warrant.
She was vengeance.
She was Medusa.

Chapter Twenty-Eight: Zoe

I wake up to a new alert on my phone.
There's been another murder.
I punch the air in celebration. Not because somebody has died, or that's not quite the reason anyway, but because this surely proves that Karma is innocent. Inspector Sandways will have no reasonable justification for keeping her under arrest anymore. She has the best alibi in the entire world - the Inspector himself. Even he won't be able to argue against that.

I check the news headlines but there's nothing about her release. Strange. The murder was announced six hours ago whilst I slept, that's more than enough time for Karma's lawyer to have demanded she be allowed out. More than enough time for the wheels to have been set in motion.

Hopping onto one of the forums I posted the news of her arrest on, I see a new video link has been posted in the last hour. The thumbnail is quite clearly the rally outside the police station, and so I click play and watch.

Rage at the unfairness of the situation swells inside of me at every minute of the footage.

According to the main campaigner, who claims to have inside knowledge, the police are going to continue to hold Karma. They don't see the latest work by the Network as proving anything because to them, she could still be the mastermind behind the whole thing. They're saying that this just goes to show the extent of her reach.

It's ridiculous.

Utterly ridiculous.

They're holding her on trumped-up charges and circumstantial evidence.

A brooch doesn't make you guilty of murder. I very much doubt her fingerprints were found on the body or on the scene itself because I'm certain that news would have trickled into the public hemisphere by now. All they have is a bit of costume jewellery and they intend to hang her from it.

Not on my watch.

Inspector Sandways is not a good officer. I very much doubt that he's a good person. The way he's hounded Karma and his weird bin diving prove that. And if he's harassing an innocent woman right now, there's a good chance he's done this before.

Unfortunately for Inspector Sandways, I'm rather good at my job and the research it entails so I set myself a deadline and start to uncover everything I can about the man.

I start with the obvious information - finding his personal social media accounts, which isn't as difficult as you'd imagine, despite him using a false surname online. Very sensible I must admit, but not infallible.

Most people let their guard down eventually, they'll like a post or join a local community group and then all I have to do is trawl through faces until I find the one I want.

Within an hour I know the names of his family members (one sister, two nephews), have pictures of his closest friends (taken at a barbeque last year and helpfully tagged with all attendees), that he had his phone repaired at a local shop and was very pleased with the service (left a public review on the stores shop front). I also know he leans right politically based on the memes he's publicly shared or interacted with.

All that information is interesting, but it's not groundbreaking.

Next, with a quick swipe of my credit card, I have his home address. And although it's tempting to go and put a brick through his window, I resist the urge.

A Google search of his name and job role brings up various cases he's been involved in and I scroll through the news articles until I find one that interests me.

Karma's case isn't the first 'miraculous' case he's managed to solve.

In fact, the Inspector has a history of solving the unsolvable with evidence others missed.

There was one case, a trafficking ring in Scotland, that had perplexed the local authorities for months. Within seven weeks of joining the task force, Sandways had found evidence that linked a local school teacher to the gang.

The schoolteacher is now serving life in prison and still to this day protests his innocence. The man even turned down the offer of a lesser sentence if he admitted his guilt and showed remorse.

Why would a guilty man not take that deal?

And, if the evidence was as solid as Sandways claimed, why were there still pockets of people in his local community who were pushing for a review into his case?

On a whim, I open the messenger icon on my social account and contact a family member of the man in question.

Hi.

You don't know me but my name is Zoe Lewis, I'm friends with Karma Jones and I'm concerned about how her case is being handled. I can see that Inspector Sandways also worked on your uncle's case before he was sentenced - do you think I have anything to worry about?

I don't have the time to compose a more vague message, or to pick words that might not come round to bite me in the ass. If my message is screen-shotted and posted on forums, then I'll be thrown into the limelight alongside Karma, and the Inspector will certainly put a target on my back for doubting his work. It could even result in my podcast being targeted by trolls who blindly support law officials.

But it's worth it if I get an answer.

Stretching my arms above my head, I'm about to get up from my bed and take a break when a flashing icon pulls me back in.

It's a response to my message. Already.

Inspector Sandways is a lying bastard. My uncle never even met the man who testified against him. Your friend is in trouble.

Shit.

So not only does the Inspector have a history of lightning bolt evidence arriving on the scene when he was present, but now he has an accusation of witness tampering against him.

Why haven't you brought this to the Ombudsman?

Because there has to be a complaints process for the police to answer to, surely?

We did. They threw the case out. Ironically, not enough evidence.

What should I do?

Do I believe this stranger on the internet? Somebody who is emotionally invested in their family member being innocent? For all I know, their uncle is guilty and I wouldn't blame them for desperately clutching at straws to prove he's not.

Then again, I've seen firsthand that the Inspector is up to something. I don't know what yet but I'm certain it's not ethical, and most likely not legal.

Harry left the envelope in the bin.

Sandways picked it up.

The two of them are in cahoots about something. And the only common link they share is Karma.

It's time I had a conversation with Harry.

Chapter Twenty-Nine: Zoe

I march through the hotel's corridors like a woman possessed, until I realise that I'm wasting energy because I don't know which room Harry is staying in. I can't be everywhere at once, no matter how fast I pace the floors, and for all I know he might not even be in this damn place anymore.

Looking through my phone contacts and emails I realise that I don't have his personal number, probably not an oversight on his part. Joke's on him though, as it means he's left me with only one option. One he definitely won't be pleased I've taken.

I call the Foundation.

The woman who answers the phone is kind and patient, but she won't give me Harry's contact number because of some kind of safeguarding nonsense. I explain to her that I've all but been abandoned in a hotel when it was the Foundation's employee, Harry, who hired me for this project making sure to tell her that he hasn't reached out to me to check on my well-being or to update me on my employment. I make sure to sound a little lost as I describe the ways in which he's been lacking as a host and I can tell from the sympathetic way she tuts that the news will be round their staff coffee room before lunch is over.

Harry will hate that I've done this. That I've led his place of work to believe he's lacking professionally but screw him. He's just lucky I didn't tell her about my suspicions about him and Inspector Sandways.

The receptionist ends the call with an empathetic promise to pass my message along to Harry and a personal guarantee that she will make sure I know what's going on by the end of the day. I almost feel bad for manipulating her, but nothing I've told her is a lie. I don't know what's become of my contract, I don't know what happens when my booking at this hotel runs out and Harry hasn't done a damn thing to make sure I'm okay.

Within five minutes my mobile is ringing with a number I don't recognise.

Harry.

So predictable.

"Zoe, I understand you've been trying to reach me?" he asks, cracks of his annoyance seeping through his professional tone.

"Can I have five minutes of your time?"

"The foundation will honour the full fee agreed in your contract, and your hotel room is yours for as long as you need it. We weren't sure if you had anywhere else to go and whether you had travel arrangements to return home." He doesn't bother responding to my request, much less acknowledging that I'd even spoken. All pretence of friendship between us, the pretence he'd introduced the night of the Gala, has vanished. I guess Harry has no use for me anymore.

Pity.

Because I still have a use for him.

"Harry, we need to talk." I try again, this time adding a stern inflection to my words. He won't weasel out of my questions; I've got answers from harder stones than him.

There was the episode about the shoe shop killer, where his family had refused all offers of interviews. But they spoke to me.

Or the one about Ariana Smith, who'd gone missing at fifteen only to reappear at her place of work three years later with no recollection of the time she'd lost. She hadn't wanted to dive into those memories with anyone. But she spoke to me.

I have a way with people.

There's a certain part of my personality that makes them want to talk to me. To confide in me. To trust me. I wish I knew exactly what it was, as I could make a fortune teaching others to do the same, but it's always been that way.

At school, I was everyone's agony aunt. The bullies only bothered me when they had something to talk about. Lunch ladies filled me in on school politics I didn't quite have a grasp on.

My whole life people have been telling me their secrets and worries, and that's what makes me so good at my job. That's what's made my podcast grow in success with each new installment - not only do I get the viewpoints others haven't but I take the time to really know the backstory of each tale I tell. It becomes my entire life until I'm satisfied I know all there is to know. And it's that passion, that tenacity that my listeners enjoy.

That's what Harry should be worried about.

One way or another, this man is going to meet with me, and he is going to give me the truth.

What I do after that is undecided, but I'm certain I'll make the right choice when it shows itself.

"Are you at the hotel?" he asks.

"Yes, I can be downstairs in five minutes," I reply, turning on my heel and heading for the lift.

"Meet me in the lobby, I have a few minutes between calls."

He hangs up, a way to try and yank the power back in his favour. By letting me know that he's squeezing me into his calendar, he's reminding me that he's important. That he's granting me the small favour of his time. But I'll take as much of his time as I need. If he is involved with Inspector Sandways, if he did help procure Karma's brooch for the man, then I'm certain he'll be able to make time for that conversation. Liars can always find time if it means avoiding the truth.

I make sure to be sitting calmly waiting for him, two coffees already ordered cooling off in front of me - just as he had done on the morning of our interview with Inspector Sandways. I see now that it was all a pretence, a way to get me on side - show me kindness and I wouldn't suspect the truth.

The truth being that he's in cahoots with Sandways and the two of them have somehow arranged for Karma's arrest.

"Zoe, how are you?" he asks as he takes the seat opposite me, his face giving nothing away. I knew I should have trusted my gut when it came to Harry, he made my skin crawl the first time we met and I should never have let him try to win me round. If I'd been smarter I could have seen this coming, I could have done something to prevent it.

"I've been thinking a lot about Karma's arrest," I begin, not bothering to exchange pleasantries. If this offends him, he doesn't show it.

"Terrible, isn't it? I was shocked when the Inspector explained to me what was going on. To think, she was orchestrating all of that right under our noses." He gives a visual shudder as though the truth has walked over his grave.

"But there's been another murder since her arrest,

that's what I can't understand. Surely they should have stopped now?"

"I wondered that myself, to be honest. But we just have to trust that the Inspector knows what he's doing. The evidence against her is pretty solid."

"Is it? A brooch and a few strands of hair?"

"That and the links to each of the murder victims through her support groups or appearances. Now it makes sense as to why the Inspector insisted on speaking to her so many times, and he was right to." He takes a sip of his coffee and looks away from me, watching a family check out of the hotel. They aren't that interesting so I know he's just trying to avoid the intensity of my gaze.

"I need your help, Harry," I say and this takes him by surprise. He places his mug back down and leans his elbows on the table, a sign that he's giving me his full attention. God, this man is good at pretending.

"Anything Zoe, like I've said, the Foundation will make sure you don't leave empty-handed. If you don't have anywhere to stay, I'll be happy to book you accommodation back in your hometown." He sounds so sincere and kind but he's just trying to get me to leave. Because I'm the only loose end to their sham of an investigation. I'm sure that the Inspector confided in him about what I may or may not have witnessed between the two of them yesterday morning.

"That's very good of you Harry, but it won't be necessary. I'm happy to stay here until Karma gets released."

He looks at me with pity, as though she doesn't have a hope in hell. And maybe she won't unless I intervene. An idea is beginning to form in my mind, a way to cause enough uproar that the charges against her will be dropped, at least for now. But it's a stupid idea, a reckless one. Still, any idea is better than no idea.

"It's sweet that you still think so highly of her, but you have to accept the fact that she's most likely guilty. The police don't make mistakes like that, especially not in the face of such public scrutiny."

Thinking that referencing the public outcry, the rally outside the station, will get me on side is a mistake. All it's doing is adding weight to my idea, because if I talk about Karma then people will listen. And they might just listen well enough to make a difference.

"I suppose you're right. I just keep thinking about how strange it is though."

"How strange what is?" he asks.

"That she wasn't wearing the brooch on the night of the Gala and yet it was found at the crime scene." For a moment, some of the colour drains from Harry's face and that's the moment when I know my suspicions are true.

"She must have come back to the hotel and put it on."

"It just seems a little odd to me. That she'd get changed into something that would make her unrecognisable, as the press are quoting from the Inspector's conference, and put on a brooch to accessorise it. Personally, if I were on my way to commit murder, I wouldn't stop to make my outfit a touch more fashionable - would you?"

"Who knows how her mind works, now if you must excuse me I have a call to make." He pushes himself up from the table but before he can leave I reach out and grab his arm.

"I'd say it's much more likely that somebody else put that brooch there. Somebody who had easy access to her belongings, maybe even her hairbrush, don't you think?"

"You're being ridiculous," he replies, trying to twist his arm from my grasp. I don't let go though, and I'm banking on Harry being too concerned with his reputation to make a scene.

"Am I Harry? Or am I right on the mark? The Inspector has a track record of discovering last-minute evidence, doesn't he? In fact, I've already reached out to a few family members of people he's incarcerated and they all tell me the same thing. Don't trust Inspector Sandways. Now, what you have to think about, and I mean really think about, is whether or not what he's offered you is better than what I'm about to offer you."

Finally, Harry sits back down, his facade broken as he nervously chews on his lip.

"What do you want?" he asks.

"I want you to make an anonymous tip-off to the station, letting them know that somebody was seen entering Karma's room the night of the Gala. You do that and I'll keep your name out of it."

"Out of what?" he asks as he considers my offer. He knows he's out of options though, if he sticks with the Inspector he'll lose everything else.

"That's not your concern. And if you breathe a word of this conversation to anyone I won't hesitate to report you to the police myself for stealing Karma's belongings and for helping to falsify evidence."

"Fine. I'll call them in a minute."

"Smart man." I go to stand, to leave him to wallow in his own guilt and stupidity.

"Why are you helping me though?"

"I'm not helping you Harry. I would never help you. I'm just not condemning you."

With those as my parting words I leave the hotel lobby and head back up to my room.

I didn't owe Harry this small grace, not after the way he'd treated me during our time working together, but I did owe it to Karma. If this scandal emerged the Foundation's name would forever be linked to

Sandways and his crimes, and I wasn't about to be the person who destroyed all that she worked for.

It's time to do what I do best.

To talk. To tell the truth. And to let the cards fall where they may.

Chapter Thirty: Target #31

Annie took extra care as she wrapped the vial and popped it into the crossbody bag looped across her chest. She'd undertaken this work so many times, but finally this particular vial was destined for the name she'd put forward to the Network.

It was destined for Stewart.

She'd waited patiently as the Network undertook their due diligence, making sure that her claim was true. As far as she could tell this involved a lot of background work on the target, given all the information she'd had to supply about him, and she had no doubt in her mind that along their journey they would have uncovered other victims of his. And now the moment she'd waited eight months for was finally here.

Eight months.

Nearly the amount of time she'd grown her precious daughter in her body.

Rose had been her pride and joy from the moment she'd seen the positive symbol on the pregnancy test, and that love had only grown when the midwife finally handed her the baby. She was a gorgeous infant, everyone agreed, and she grew in beauty and personality every year.

Even now, if she tried hard enough, she could still remember the feel of Rose's tiny five-year-old hand in hers. The warmth of her teenage tears on her shoulder as she helped guide her daughter through puberty and all the drama that came with it. The light in Rose's eyes that she never thought she'd see fade.

But Stewart had robbed that light. Piece by piece over a course of two months she'd watched as her fabulous, bubbly, charismatic daughter faded into herself. And she'd been clueless as to what had brought about the change.

It hadn't been until after Rose's funeral that she'd found her daughter's diaries.

Outlining her relationship with her college professor thirteen years her senior.

It was clear, as a detached party, that the man had been grooming her child from the day they first met. And then he swept her up in a whirlwind romance, before things took a darker turn. The things he made Rose do in order to prove her love to him still turned Annie's stomach, even after all these years.

He forced her into physical relationships with other men for his own sexual gratification. Plying her with alcohol, and his special pills, telling her that if she truly felt for him what he did for her then she wouldn't complain. That she'd be his good girl. His special one.

Rose had been seventeen when it started.

Seventeen.

And she was dead by eighteen.

Yet Stewart still lived.

He'd even attended the funeral. Had the nerve to offer Annie his condolences, resting a gentle hand on her shoulder as she sobbed out her pain.

The man wasn't just a predator, he was a psychopath as well.

Annie had marched straight down to the college

the day after she finished the diary, staying up all night sobbing in her daughter's bed, and confronted him.

Security had sadly intervened after she'd knocked Stewart to the floor with a single punch in front of a shocked classroom and yet even with the diary as her evidence - nobody believed her.

Rose had killed herself because she couldn't bring the 'fantasies' she'd written about to life. That's what she'd been told by one tired officer after weeks of hounding the station. That's what everybody believed because Stewart had been clever. He'd made sure to confide in several colleagues about Rose's 'obsession' with him, how he kept her at arms length during the working day for his own safety.

The man was a liar.

Annie knew that with her whole heart. That man had taken her daughter and destroyed her and then had the gall to attend her funeral without so much as a twinge of guilt on his face.

Everything Rose had written was true. Her daughter didn't lie. And she had seen first hand the gradual decline it had brought to Rose's personality.

She hadn't been unwell. She hadn't been crazy. She had been trapped in a predatory relationship and couldn't see any way out when Stewart had eventually tired of her.

She would never forgive herself for her daughter's death, she should have seen it coming. That's what she told herself every day despite all the grief counselling she'd undertaken. She wished, with everything she had, that she would wake up on that morning again. She would run to Rose's room and tell her that it was a bad day, not a bad life. She would stay by her daughter's side and they would ride out the wave of depression together.

But wishes don't come true. All she could do was

seek justice for her daughter.

And the Medusa Network offered that justice.

She'd been approached at a grief session by a woman who had passed her a business card. It had a date and a time printed on it, and on schedule her mobile phone had rang. She poured out Rose's story to the caller and promised to do whatever was needed to get justice for her daughter.

That's how she found herself in this position today, heading out for another dog walk, to undertake another exchange. But this one was personal.

She'd spent the last few days lurking on the book forum that the Network used to send messages to the runners like her. They each had a book title they had to keep an eye out for, and one they had to post about. Her's was The Islander's by Caroline Mitchell and the second she saw a post, from the name she'd been told to watch out for, she knew it was time to put the lead on Bella and take her out of town for a walk.

Just finished the islanders, pic for attention, desperately need to go for a dog walk to blow away the shock at the twist!

The woman who posted was located a half-hour drive from Annie, up by Windermere lakes.

Nobody ever batted an eyelid at a dog walker going out of town with their pup. Why would they? Over half the country did it. Dogs were a part of the family and deserved fresh scenery just as much as anybody else.

She'd picked up the vial two days ago, at a beach local to her, from an elderly gentleman with a chocolate Labrador. The two of them had stopped, as if by chance, and exchanged pleasantries about the weather and their dogs. She'd bent down to pet his lab and removed the vial from the dog's bandana collar, slipping it into her bag whilst still crouching down making a fuss. It was always that easy.

Nobody paid attention to middle aged women or the elderly. Especially not on busy summer days when everyone was too preoccupied with their own lives. If anyone had noticed their exchange it would have seemed so non-descript they probably wouldn't have been able to describe either of them if they were pushed.

But they never were.

Nobody in the runner circle had ever even been questioned by the police in relation to any of the deaths. It was too ridiculous an idea for them to have even thought of it. A deadly poison, being shifted round the country, by a series of dog walkers. Implausible.

She wanted to ask the elderly man his story, find out who he had on the list and why, but she didn't. She never pried because that would be a risk, and not one worth taking.

And finally, finally she'd been in possession of the vial that would end Stewart's life.

There was a spring in her step as she strapped Bella to the backseat, letting her know that she was a good dog.

Over the next couple of weeks she would watch the news with intent, waiting for news of the man's death, and on that day she would drink an entire bottle of champagne knowing that Rose had finally been avenged.

Chapter Thirty-One: Karma

Karma rolled her eyes as she was marched to the interview room once again. Inspector Sandways was a thorn in her side that she'd never been able to shake and now she was trapped here, subject to his every whim.

It was a surprise then to see a new face waiting for her in the room. The officer who had been present when she was interviewed at the hotel with Zoe. The one who had never spoken. She'd barely even glanced in his direction that day, now she had no choice but to notice him.

He was an attractive man that couldn't be denied despite where Karma's preferences lay. If she had to date a member of the opposite sex it would most likely be one as aesthetically pleasing as this specimen. The deep red flecks in his dark beard caught the sun that was fighting its way through the grime on the windows and his eyes were crinkled ever so slightly at the corners - a sign of having lived an enjoyable life. Yes, thought Karma to herself, he was definitely an attractive man.

"Good afternoon, Ms. Jones," he began as he poured her a cup of water. She took it gratefully. Sandways had always waited until she asked to allow her a drink, enjoying the mini power trip it gave him.

"Good afternoon -" she began, waiting for him to fill in the blanks.

"Detective Moore," he finished, reaching across to shake her hand. The sound of the handcuffs rubbing against each other as they shook was jarring to her senses. He smiled at her kindly and fished a set of keys from his pocket.

Was this Detective mad? Inspector Sandways would have his badge for this.

She'd overheard him giving every staff member possible the instruction that she was to be kept cuffed at all times because of the danger she posed. An absolute lie, but one her lawyer had been unable to overturn.

"Where's Inspector Sandways?" she asked as she flexed her hands, happy to be free of the metal that had been laced around them a size too tight. Something she was certain Sandways had orchestrated.

"The Inspector has been suspended pending an internal investigation. I'll be able to explain more once your lawyer arrives."

As though he'd been waiting in the wings for his cue, her lawyer came bustling into the room, bringing with him an irritated energy. One that Karma could do without. What on earth did this man have to be irritated by? He's not the one who's spent days locked in a cell and questioned by a rat.

"What's going on?" Karma asked, directing her question to the Detective as opposed to the man hired to supposedly aid her. He'd been useless in all of her interviews thus far, failing to produce a single legal argument that would convince Sandways to free her. He hadn't even pointed out the coincidence of the evidence that had been found until Karma herself pulled him up on it. She was beginning to suspect that this lawyer didn't have her best interests at heart.

After all, there was a lot of notoriety to defending a

high profile client in a court of law. That's how the Kardashians had been created after all. She wouldn't blame him entirely if he'd been trying to prolong her incarceration to elongate his five minutes of fame. Sadly Karma had grown used to people aligning themselves to her for their own benefit. It had happened when she was a child with Father's interest in her and it continued to happen as she aged.

It's why she rarely trusted anybody in her life, and why she was so surprised about the instant connection she'd felt with Zoe. It was safer to keep people at arms length, or if that wasn't possible it was safer to always assume they had the worst intentions.

So no. Her lawyer wasn't a terrible person for not fighting her corner more viciously - he was just a person with all the faults and foibles that came along with it.

"The evidence that Sandways used to arrest you has been called into question. As it has been in a few of his previous cases. I'm sure your lawyer will fill you in on all that's happened, but for me to do so would be engaging in gossip. All I can tell you is the official party line."

Karma pauses and lets the weight of Detective Moore's words sink in. She's free. Somehow she's about to walk out of this station a free woman, despite all the odds stacked against her.

"We're going to sue every officer involved in your case Ms Jones," the sniveling voice of her legal adviser pipes up.

"I have no interest in suing anybody. The force has enough problems to deal with, and less money isn't going to solve that."

Besides, Karma wasn't prepared to pay this man any further fees once she walked from the station. As much as she accepted his weakness for celebrity, she wasn't going to continue to fund it. The more attention she drew to herself the harder life would become.

Karma smiled at Detective Moore, who looks relieved to hear her opinion. There's no doubt she would have an iron clad case if she chose to drag them over the coals but money has never interested Karma. And a lawsuit is the last thing she needs right now.

"Can we leave now?" She looks at the Detective for a final confirmation, sure that this is some kind of test. Some final torture dreamt up by Sandways. Detective Moore nods and without wanting to waste anymore of her life in an interview room, she walks out, her lawyer scurrying along behind her.

Satisfied that he was telling the truth and she was free to go, she takes a deep breath of air upon leaving the station. Finally, the nightmare is over. She always knew she'd get out, the evidence that they had against her was a farce, she just wasn't sure how she could prove it. Thankfully the universe had been looking out for her. It was the least it owed her after all.

As she moves through the waiting crowd, the group of people who have been chanting for her innocence for the last few days, she thanks each person she comes across. A member of the press shoves a camera in her face and tries to elicit a sound bite but her lawyer, for once, does his job and puts a stop to it.

A driver holds the door to a nearby car open, and she gratefully slides inside. As much as she'd grown to hate the solitude of the cell, diving straight from that into a ravenous crowd was a culture shock. She needed time to adjust before she undertook any more engagements.

Her lawyer takes his seat next to her on the backseat and as the engine starts up she finally decides to look into his eyes as she talks.

"So, what happened?" she asks and the man wilts under her gaze. Worried she'll be able to see through his professional veneer and see the man underneath. The man who had already signed on for a live TV interview with a national news station should his client have been found guilty. Karma Ann Jones would have been the making of a lucrative side hustle, and he was almost ashamed at his lacklustre handling of her case. But he had bills to pay.

"It turns out your friend Miss Lewis is rather resourceful. She released a podcast episode about Sandways and the rumours about him. It gained quite a lot of traction before it was removed. Clever girl, she'll be in a lot of trouble now though. My colleagues have already been discussing what grounds he could use to go after her."

"He'd have to prove what she's said isn't true though, and I doubt that's possible."

"I am, of course, happy to make some recommendations on legal counsel should you wish to pass my information across to -,"

"I think we'll be okay, thank you," interrupts Karma, not wanting to plant false hope in the man. Once this car journey is over, so is their professional relationship. The last thing she wants him to do is hitch himself to Zoe's coattails in any potential libel case. Quite why Harry and the Foundation recommended him she didn't know.

"Right, yes, of course," he fell over his words, all too aware that he'd made a mistake. He never should have allowed an opportunity for himself to overrule his duty to his client.

"I assume I've been booked into a new hotel?" she asked and the lawyer nodded. "And Miss Lewis?" again he responded with a simple nod.

Having received all the information she needed from the man, Karma turned her attention to the outside world, watching the street whizz past as they drove to their final destination.

What Zoe had done for her could not be underestimated.

She used her platform, risked her platform, to shed light on Inspector Sandways and prove that the evidence against Karma was false. There would no doubt be some pushback against Zoe now, both online and off, and Karma knew she would do whatever she could to help her friend weather the storm.

Her friend.

The thought was almost unnatural to Karma.

Father had beaten the idea of friendship from her psyche at such a young age. If she cared for someone she put them at risk, so she learnt to hide her empathy and need for kinship. Learnt to turn away from those who showed a genuine interest in her. Because it never ended well for them.

Her heart was in her gut as she remembered that one night so many years ago. Blood had been everywhere. His face had been splattered with it and his teeth were bared like a rabid animal. He'd turned to smile at her as he smashed the side of her only remaining friend's head with a chair leg, so that she knew without doubt it was all her fault.

The only reason he hadn't killed the young girl was because of Paula.

Paula had distracted him and convinced him he'd already dealt a fatal blow. Paula, who had steered him away, so Karma could kneel at her friend's side and apologise.

When Father had returned a few hours later he'd been pleased to see the dirt under Karma's fingernails, having decreed she should dig the grave for her only friend by hand. He stood by her side over what Karma knew was an empty grave and had placed a hand on her shoulder.

"You're a good girl, Karma. You're my good girl."

He'd whispered to her and although she knew the grave was empty, the tears of grief were real. Because she could never see her friend again, to do so would mean death for the one person she truly cared about.

With a shake of her head Karma was back in the present, back in the warm car with her useless lawyer. Father wasn't here anymore. He couldn't take Zoe's friendship away from her.

She wouldn't let him.

Chapter Thirty-Two: The Farm

Karma was ten years old now.

And finally, she was behaving as Father required.

It had taken the loss of a few young souls but finally she'd gotten the message.

Stay in line.

Love Father.

Or someone dies.

It was an extreme lesson, even he could see that, but it was an important one. He hadn't wanted those young boys to die, well not entirely, but he had to send a message to both Karma and his congregation.

He hadn't missed the signs that her insubordination was spreading like quiet wildfire. Smouldering at the edges he couldn't reach to stamp out.

He'd tried.

Lord knows he'd tried. But her rebellion had taken hold in some of the more feeble minds, especially in the older children.

She'd never spoken to the boys directly. He still had her watched every waking hour, and dealt with any emotional ties as needed with a simple reassignment to a new nursery for the guilty party. So, he knew the poison hadn't spread directly from the source. She wasn't intentionally turning hearts against him.

But the poison had spread nonetheless. And killing those boys had stopped it in its tracks. Which was the best outcome for his new world. Their deaths had been what the movement needed. And that's what he told himself as he sat back and watched Owen publicly slit their throats under his bidding.

He made sure Karma had a front row seat to their executions. Noting the way she held her head up high, no tears shed for the adoptive siblings she had lost.

He was proud of her at that moment.

So, so proud.

From that day on she came when she was asked.

She accepted his presence in her room.

She even managed to smile through her tears when he lay with her.

He was proud of his special girl.

And he grew to trust her.

Not knowing it would be his downfall.

Chapter Thirty-Three: Zoe

I'd been smuggled out the back door of our previous hotel and in through the staff entrance of a new one, advised by Harry to stay sequestered in my room.

Quite why I'm still listening to him I'm not sure. The man turned against Karma, worked alongside a bent cop to frame her and yet he's proved his loyalty to me since my podcast dropped.

He'd been the first phone call I received after uploading the episode, and after he thanked me for keeping his name from my lips, he offered to arrange alternative accommodations for me. He knew I'd be swamped by press and interested parties as soon as it made a splash in the public domain.

And he hadn't been wrong.

A receptionist had given out my room number for the right price and I'd answered the knock from a journalist before quickly slamming my door. It didn't deter them, though. In the end Harry had to come up and throw them out of the corridor, which is when I finally decided to accept his offer of alternative accommodations.

Now I'm sat here alone, in another non-descript

hotel room, wondering if I've messed everything up.

Inspector Sandways will sue me.

There's no doubt about that.

And I didn't even think about the ramifications further than that.

By pulling apart Karma's case, I've set in motion the destruction of several others. In fact, I'd wager that every case and arrest Sandways has been involved in will be double and triple checked over the next few weeks. True that I've given innocent parties hope that they'll be freed, but what if they tar all his cases with the same brush and some guilty people escape prison when they really shouldn't?

And then there's the matter of Sandway's associates. Should he have any. Who knows how many times his palms have been greased by people I'm better off not making enemies of. What if by exposing him as the fraud he is, I've exposed myself to a new audience that won't take kindly to my exposé?

What have I done?

What have I done?

Anxiety has its claws in me and every time I try to move from the bed, every time I try to complete one of the coping techniques I've learnt over the years, it digs itself in even further. There is no escaping this. There is no light at the end of the tunnel for me.

My distributors pulled the episode in a matter of hours after it was reported on each one. They don't want to risk Sandways coming after them for aiding and abetting in my campaign against him.

Not that it's a campaign. It was one podcast episode, and maybe one or two anonymous posts on forums regarding it. From there it swept through true crime fans, and pirate copies are still out there. Which I suppose in a way is a good thing - it means my moment of emotional stupidity can live on and keep the truth going.

I'm not an irrational person. I'm not a spontaneous person.

Every decision, every trip, and even outfit is well thought out in advance. Whenever I'm eating out, I look at the menu the week before and decide what I'm going to have for my meal, down to the sides. I don't make decisions lightly.

So that podcast, that moment of madness is completely out of character for me. And there's only one reason for that.

Karma.

I took an uncalculated risk because of her.

For her.

She needed someone in her corner, and I was ready to run up to bat for her. Because she's special. Because she makes me feel things. Because she's her.

When the news alert landed in my inbox that she'd been set free, I felt such a sense of relief that a smile spread across my face despite the stress levels in my blood. It was all worth it, all the potential danger and legal ramifications, if Karma was free. She's done so much for the world, for society, that putting myself on the line is the least I can do to repay her.

Just as I'm wondering whether I'll get to see her again, there's a knock at my door. Thinking the journalists have found me again, I throw it open with a thunderous look, only to find Karma standing in the corridor, staring back at me.

"Hey," she says.

"Hey," I reply. Too shocked by her presence to string together something more meaningful.

"Can I come in?" she asks and regaining my composure I nod, making sure to check the corridor for stragglers as she enters my room.

The last thing I want is a photograph of her visiting

my room, the rumour mill would have a field day and that's exactly what she doesn't need right now. She's been the most spoken about person in the country the last few days, and I don't want to add to that.

"How are you?" I ask as she takes a seat on the edge of my bed. It should feel awkward having her make herself at home, instead, it feels natural and I'm happy to see that she feels so comfortable in my company.

"I've been better," she says with a slight chuckle. It was a stupid question to ask her, I should have asked her something else. Anything else.

She pats the space next to her on the bed and as though in a trance, I move towards her and sit down. Our shoulders are barely touching but it feels like the air in the space between our skin is vibrating. I want to reach out and touch her, to reassure myself that she's really here. But I don't. Because that would be crossing a line. And if I touch her at this moment, I don't think I'll ever be able to stop.

She's incredible, beautiful, and resilient.

She's everything I want and everything I want to be.

And she thinks of me as a friend. And I'm grateful for that I really am.

To reach out and touch her now would be crossing a line. The woman has lived through days of legal hell and to close the space between us would be taking advantage of her situation. And I don't want to do that. I won't do that.

So I sit and I keep my hands to myself. Keeping my eyes focused on my lap, waiting for her to unburden herself to me so I can make all the right noises and none of the wrong moves.

"What you did with the podcast, that was incredible." She reaches across the space between us and places a hand over mine. "I owe you so much".

I want to reassure her that she owes me nothing. That my podcast was nothing more than doing the right thing for the right reasons.

But that would be a lie.

Yes, I spoke out because what was happening to her was wrong.

But I also did it because of my feelings towards her.

Feelings that are separate from our professional relationship. Feelings that I need to keep to myself.

And yet there's the way she's holding her hand upon mine, stroking one of my fingers with her thumb. Squeezing it ever so slightly so I can feel the pressure of her touch upon my skin.

This isn't the first time she's touched my hand. The night of the Gala she held it as we raced for a taxi to escape the function. She barely let go of it in fact once we entered the bar.

Could Karma have feelings for me?

No.

Of course not.

She's just a charismatic person.

She doesn't know the effect she has on people.

There's no way this incredible woman is feeling the heat building between the two of us the way I am. People like her don't fall for people like me. It just doesn't happen.

And yet.

And yet.

"Are you going to go back to the Foundation?" I ask, breaking the moment between us. She's my client. I must remember that she's my client.

She moves her hand away from mine and lays it in her own lap. The message I hadn't wanted to send, but needed to, has been received. I watch as she bites her lip, considering my question, wondering what thoughts are racing through her mind.

"No. I don't think so. I'm tired of living for other people, always worrying about the impact my actions might have on the Foundation and its work. I want some time to focus on my own projects."

Her reply is so steady and measured, lacking emotion between her sentences. Because she's switched off, she's telling me a story and hoping I believe it. It's a coping mechanism used by sufferers of trauma across the world, if you shut down and present something palatable then you don't risk getting hurt. It's not quite a lie, but it isn't her whole truth.

Perhaps I should feel upset that she doesn't fully trust me yet. But I don't. Because I understand.

After what happened to me with my ex, I spent a long time building up walls and hiding behind them. Smiling when I didn't mean it. Telling half-truths to avoid connections. And what I survived is barely a tenth of what Karma has, so yes I understand why she's keeping part of herself from me.

I just need her to understand that she doesn't have to.

"You can tell me the truth you know, about anything. How you're feeling. What you want to do. I don't even have to talk back if you don't want to, I can just listen. I promise you that I'm here and I'm not going anywhere."

My words have had their intended effect, and she turns her body round so she's facing me. I draw in a breath and get ready to listen.

Chapter Thirty-Four: Target #32

Danielle was beyond excited.

She's been a bundle of nerves since the leaflet with the Medusa stamp had been shoved through her letterbox. Finally it was her time, finally the Network had taken notice of the independent work she'd been undertaking and were welcoming her into their ranks with open arms.

For two weeks now she'd been hunting every night, her body tingled with exhaustion but adrenaline kept her awake. Well that and the seven cans of energy drink she'd washed down her vodka with last night. It was all worth it now though. The constant worry about every knock on her door or ring of her phone.

She'd banked on her targets being too embarrassed to confide in anyone what had happened to them the night they met her. So far their silence had assured her of this but you never know when someone might say something they ought not to.

The men she'd punished had been run of the mill. She didn't have the resources the Network had so instead she'd had to make do with stalking nightclubs, trying to catch someone in a sleazy act or spiking a drink. Sadly, nothing that dramatic had ever happened whilst she'd been keeping watch, and once or twice she had to ask herself whether every man was truly a monster but she was certain they were.

And if you can't punish the ones directly committing crimes, you punish the ones you can to send a message. That was the first idea she was going to pitch to the Network, to convince them to cast their net a bit wider. Going after so-called innocent people to keep the general public on their toes. Was anyone truly innocent? Danielle didn't think so, and she was certain those at the head of the Network would agree with her.

As the wind picked up around her she thought back to a few of her conquests. Remembering the way the men had whimpered, despite the sedatives she'd plied them with, as she left them with a gift they wouldn't soon forget. Not that she'd ever admit it to anybody she was going to meet today, but she'd enjoyed the sense of power she'd felt as she'd leaned over their naked bodies. The righteousness it brought with it.

It had thrilled her in a way nothing else had before, and she couldn't wait to continue her work alongside the Network.

A car slowed down beside her and the door was pushed open by somebody she couldn't see. All the drama and the mystery only increased Danielle's heart rate. They were showing her, with their treatment, how special she already was to them. How many other recruits had a private car pick them up? Not many, she'd wager. It made the half hour wait in the smelly alleyway worthwhile.

Her excitement was only tampered by the woman waiting for her in the car.

Bland didn't even begin to describe her. Danielle had expected the woman who picked her up to be glamourous, fierce and a force to be reckoned with. She expected to be knocked over by the woman's charisma and prowess. Instead she found herself sitting next to nothing more than a mouse.

Her dark black hair was parted perfectly in the middle, like the kind of girl Danielle would have picked on at school. There were little silver snake earrings hanging from her lobes, the only part of her outfit that was any nod to the work she was transporting Danielle to. She was wearing an old Hoodie for Christ's sake. The only saving grace about her appearance was her beauty.

Even Danielle couldn't deny that.

She had naturally high and an annoyingly perfect cupid's bow at the top of her plump lips. Her complexion was clean and her deep almond skin tone meant it was impossible to place an age on her.

By contrast Danielle, whilst dressed up to the nines in black pleather trousers and a halter neck top (what she believed to be the perfect outfit for a high class assassin), was painfully aware of every wrinkle and spot on her face. A life of hard parties and anger had robbed any youth that may have been lingering around her features.

She wasn't angry anymore though. She was happy. Elated. Dizzy with excitement - all the cliches a child might have on their way to Disneyland. Because now she would matter. Now her work was being recognised.

The woman sitting next to her didn't even glance in Danielle's direction, and there was something in the air between them. Jealousy. That's what it was. This woman was nothing more than an errand grunt and Danielle was a rising star.

Without a word, the woman passed a blindfold across the space between them.

"Are you serious?"

"Just until we're at head office."

The woman's voice wasn't what she'd been expecting. It was rough around the edges, clipped as though words were painful to her. Beauty doesn't equal intelligence.

"Fine," Danielle answered abruptly, the sooner she arrived at her destination then the sooner she could pitch her idea and take her place at the helm of the Network. After her work with those men she'd picked up, how could she be expected to take a lower rank than that?

Her only regret was that she hadn't targeted more. There were only so many nights she could drag an unconscious body around. And it took a lot of energy to then make them pay for the crimes of their fellow men. But it had been worth it. That's what she had told herself with each thrust, it was all worth it.

With her vision now gone Danielle finally felt the slither of vulnerability snaking itself into her stomach. But she had done nothing wrong, she had nothing to fear from the Network. She was just picking up their mantle. Showing them how much their work meant to her. How she could help them.

Every bump in the road went through her and the journey felt like it took hours, but every time she ventured a question towards their estimated time of arrival she was met with silence. And despite the woman's small stature, Danielle was certain she shouldn't reach up to pull down her blindfold.

Eventually though she felt the engine slow. Finally they were here.

Finally she would get all she deserved.

Before she could remove her blindfold though she felt two sharp stabs in her neck and the world began to grow fuzzy.

"We brought you here to show you something, something important. Something I want you to remember for the rest of your life." It was the same voice as the one that had instructed her to put on the blindfold, only now the woman's tone was strong, crystal clear. She'd been underplaying her hand.

Danielle was afraid. This wasn't how it was supposed to go. This woman's jealousy of Danielle's good work had caused her to lash out. It was okay though, any minute now somebody would open the car door and discover what she'd done.

Just as she'd hoped she heard the car door open and a hand reached in and gently pulled her out onto her feet. She was safe now.

A set of hands reached up to where hers couldn't and undid the blindfold she'd hastily knotted around herself at the start of her journey. Her limbs felt so heavy now, but it was okay. Soon, they'd give her some kind of vaccine to counteract the effects of whatever she had been dosed with.

Her eyes took a moment to adjust to the light around her. It was bright and artificial. The car had driven her directly into a warehouse.

All around her were the faces of Medusa.

Every person standing before her was wearing a mask and a crown of snakes.

Was Danielle hallucinating?

She must be. Because this wasn't the greeting somebody like her should be receiving.

They should be stepping forward to greet her, not standing silently judging her.

"Danielle, just what do you think you've been doing?" The woman from the car was standing directly behind her but Danielle could barely move her head to face her. She could tell there were people standing either side of her, holding her up. She didn't have the capacity to take them in though, to see them for real. They were just figures helping her fight gravity.

"Righting wrong," she managed to choke out despite her fatigue. This was an initiation test, it had to be.

"No, Danielle. You've been sexually assaulting people. Good, honest people who have done no harm to anybody else. And you've been using our name to excuse your actions."

Danielle tried to shake her head, there had obviously been some confusion here - she hadn't assaulted anybody. Not really. She'd been doing the same thing as the Network, punishing sins.

"The only thing those men ever did wrong, was being born as men. That was enough to put them on your radar but it is not enough to put them on ours. We punish the guilty, Danielle. And we don't assault them, or dish out an eye for an eye punishment. We kill them. Do you have any idea how much research we undertake on each of our targets to make sure we aren't behaving like you? Do you?" The woman struck Danielle in the face, but she was too numb for it to sting. The hands that had been holding her up now let her fall and the ground greets her warmly.

"We stand for something. We work hard to make sure we stand for something. And then idiots like you come along who threaten to undo all of our good work. You have become the monster Danielle. You have become the guilty."

The woman kneels down in front of Danielle and lifts her head so their eyes can meet. And despite the haze around her eyelids Danielle wonders if the woman looks a little familiar. As though she's a face she's seen in a dream once.

"And we punish the guilty."

Danielle feels a sharp prick at the side of her neck again.

And then the world turned black.

Chapter Thirty-Five: Zoe

"Sandways was right," she says and I blink twice before processing her words. What was he right about? Why is she even bringing that man's name up?

"I don't understand," I reply, despite how stupid it makes me feel. Because I don't. I can't. She can't mean what I'm beginning to suspect she means.

"Sandways…was…right," she repeats, adding pauses between each of her words. Because she doesn't want to explain anything more explicitly than that. She doesn't want to own up to what she's done.

"Say it," I whisper, trying to hold the rage that's building inside of me because I could be mistaken. I could be reading something into her words that isn't there. Sandways may have said something to her whilst she was arrested that I'm not aware of. That has to be it.

It has to be.

Because if she's about to say what I'm terrified she's going to then all the time we've spent together has been a lie. All the moments we shared, moments where I thought she felt something towards me, have been a lie. If she gives me the truth I suspect she will, it means she's been manipulating me since we first met.

She stares at me, and the silence between us stretches for miles. There's a pleading look in her eyes, she's desperate for me to understand, to allow her to remain vague in her answers. Because if she's allowed to be vague then she can heal her guilty conscience, kidding herself that she's been honest with me, that I know the full picture - but I can't make it that easy for her.

I won't.

I'm too angry to give her another way to lie to me. I really liked her. Truly I did. I'd thought several times about what it might be like to hold her, to kiss her, to share part of my life with her. And to find out all of that was built on a basis of falsities is devastating.

I wouldn't go so far as to say I hate Karma Jones.

But I am certainly not fond of her at this moment.

All the moments I thought were organic between us were just a way to pull the wool over my eyes.

Because now she's hesitant to respond to me, I know what she has to confess. I know with all of my soul that she's about to break whatever was growing between us.

"Sandways was right. I am involved in the Network."

Despite knowing what words were coming, actually hearing them fall from her mouth, her beautiful mouth I'd stolen more than a handful of glances at over our short time together, turned my heart to stone.

Karma Jones was involved in the Network.

Inspector Sandways may have gone about in the wrong way, but he had been right in his suspicions of her.

And I helped set her free.

I stand and move away from her, not trusting myself.

    Conflicted by my emotions.

I respected the Network and the work they did.

I doubted the Network and the thoroughness of their research.

I cared for Karma, wanted to know every inch of her.

I doubted everything that had ever passed between us.

The Network only killed monsters.

The Network killed Mr. Williams and had yet to own up to their mistake.

Monsters deserved to suffer.

Their families were destroyed by their crimes and the spotlight the Network carelessly threw upon them.

"Since when?"

Perhaps she's only just joined, perhaps there is hope that she's been honest in our time together up to a point.

"Since always." She has enough sense to have not moved from her spot on my bed yet. A spot I thought she'd looked so natural in just five minutes ago.

The whole time I've known her she's been working with them. Working for them. Plotting murders without a care for those left behind.

Our first night together.

Oh my God our first night together we'd sat and discussed the Network in detail. Exchanged theories on who was behind it and what their endgame was.

She sat there and let me make a fool of myself. I thought I finally found someone who shared my interests in the darker side of humanity, when in reality she was the darkest side of humanity. She was a killer by association, and a liar.

"I know what you're thinking..." she began.

"Oh, I highly fucking doubt that," I reply turning my back on her. I can't stand to look at her right now. I've been such a fool. Blinded by admiration and lust.

The man in the bar. The man who I know without a doubt that she knew. She knew that night that he was going to be murdered and yet she'd still been able to dance with me, still been able to pull me close and make me believe she wanted to kiss me.

"You're thinking that everything between us has been a lie." She manages to verbalise my exact thought train but I'm not about to give her the satisfaction of being right.

"Between us? There's been nothing between us."

Part of me wants to turn around and watch as my words sting her. I want her to feel even a fraction of how betrayed I am at this moment. But I can't do that. Because if I turn and look at her, I don't know how I'll feel.

My anger might melt and I might comfort her. Or it will roar and I'll be tempted to strike her. Not that I would do so. I am not a violent person despite my simmering temper. There's only ever been one person in life that I've truly wanted to hurt, and even those violent thoughts have lessened with time.

"We both know that's not true."

The confidence she injects into her words, the way she purrs them across the room at me causes me to feel the strangest mix of repulsed and turned on. I'm turned on because she's verbalised and acknowledged that she's attracted to me. That all the accidental touches and lingering looks did mean something. I'm repulsed because she thinks she can talk me round. That somehow she can find the words to make me forgive her.

Would I have felt differently if she'd confided in me that first night we met?

If when I brought up the Network, she'd unburden herself of the guilt that work must bring her?

Probably.

I'd probably be even more fascinated by her than I was. It would have added to her mystique. And that was before the Network murdered my beloved teacher and never told us why.

"Why did Mr. Williams die?" I ask the one question that's burning through me. And if she gives me an honest answer, if she can tell me he deserved to die, that his wife deserved to become a widow hounded by online mobs, then maybe, just maybe I'll give her a chance to explain.

After all, what true crime fan wouldn't want to learn about the inner workings of the Network?

"Who?" she asks, and I know instantly that she won't give me the truth. She's still playing with me, even now with all the cards on the table she still thinks she has the upper hand.

"My teacher," I reply, playing along with her charade. Making out like I believe she can't remember.

"I can't tell you that," and finally these are the words that cause me to turn round and look at her. Because I can't believe she has the gall to keep yet another secret from me. That she thinks she has the right to withhold more information from me after all the lies she's spun.

"Karma."

I speak her name with the tone of a teacher trying to control a class. "You need to tell me the truth." I want her to know that this is it, this is the last moment she has if she hopes to build any bridges between us. That this is her last chance.

"It isn't my truth to share. You have to trust me, he was a monster."

"He was a good man! And the Network, people like you, can't bring themselves to apologise for making a mistake. If he was like the others, you would have published the dossier by now! But you haven't. Because you fucked up!"

My accusations, no, my confrontation of the truth has stunned her. Her mouth opens and closes wordlessly a couple of times as she tries to find the words to defend herself and her actions.

But she can't.

Because Mr. Williams didn't deserve to die.

And she can't admit that. Maybe it's because she's unable to admit that the Network are fallible. Or maybe she'll get in trouble if she voices a worry about them and the work their undertaking. Whatever the reason holding her back from admitting the truth to me is obviously worth losing any hope of reconciliation we might have.

"The Network doesn't make mistakes," she finally retorts.

"Yes, they do. They did."

"They don't make mistakes," she replies, more firmly now.

"They made a mistake."

"I don't make mistakes!" she shouts at me, finally standing from her spot on the bed, irritation emanating from every inch of her as though I've personally offended her.

Which, considering her words, I have.

The Network doesn't make mistakes.

She doesn't make mistakes.

Because she is the Network.

Chapter Thirty-Six: Zoe

"You can't be serious," I reply as she begins to pace the short distance between walls in my room. Clearly she hadn't meant to out herself as the criminal mastermind behind the Network, but I pushed her into doing so. Her pride wouldn't let her just sit there and listen to me telling her that she got something wrong. That she got Mr. Williams wrong.

"Please let me explain," she begins but I make a move towards the door to the hallway. I can't share oxygen with this woman anymore. If I felt betrayed when I thought she was a foot soldier for the Network, finding out she was at the helm made me feel ten times more foolish.

She'd orchestrated the death of so many people. Blown apart so many lives with her actions. Yes, it was true that 99.9% of them deserved the deaths they were dealt but Mr. Williams didn't. And those left behind with the fall out didn't.

If the Network, if Karma, truly wanted to help victims, then she'd have been able to recognise that the families left behind were victims as well. She'd have gone about things in a different way to save them from the pain of being associated with nonces and rapists. At the very least, a courtesy call could have been made to them before the dossiers were published so they knew what was coming and could get ahead of it.

But no.

In Karma's eyes, everyone was guilty by association.

Before I can turn the door handle, Karma's hand is once again upon mine. There's no tenderness in her touch now though, she's given up on the pretence clearly. Instead, her fingers dig into my palm as she squeezes my fingers together.

"I can't let you leave yet," she says and truth be told I know I'm outmatched. Sure I could probably deliver a swift elbow to her face and get out of the room but then what?

She has spiders in every cobweb across the country, I'll never be able to outrun her. And even if I make it to a police station, they'll laugh away my suspicions, given what Inspector Sandways did and my role in setting her free.

Would I confide in the police?

Would I turn her in?

I don't know.

As a law-abiding citizen I'd like to think that yes I would. I'd leave this room and instantly call the police to let them know what she's just confessed. I'd keep talking to them until they believed me, until they brought her back in for questioning. I'd stand in a courtroom, staring at her from a witness box, as I told the Jury of the conversation we've just had.

But I don't think I would.

I don't think I could.

After everything Karma has been through it's not surprising that she'd like to bring a little justice into the world. To punish those she deemed guilty for the sins of the adults who raised her.

And, despite considering myself an ethical person, up until recently, I had been one of the Network's biggest defenders. Correcting people when they referred to them as terrorists, because terrorists don't target sexual abusers. That's what vigilantes do. And I've always been a big fan of Batman.

If only they - she'd, been able to own up to their mistake when they killed Mr. Williams. If only she'd offered some kind of olive branch to the people left behind after the murder. If only she'd confided in me before I publicly defended her.

If only.

If only.

If only...

"Please, sit down and let me explain," without loosening her grip on my hand she leads me towards the bed. And we sat as we had moments ago. Only now it's not passion simmering between us. Now it's resentment and mistrust.

"You have every right to feel this way," she begins and my back stiffens at her patronising tone. Who is she to tell me how I feel and whether it's acceptable or not?

"I should have told you the truth sooner. But I couldn't. And it's not because I didn't trust you. You've never given me a reason to distrust you. But it's because I was afraid of this. Of this moment. Of the way you're looking at me now."

I wish she didn't speak so eloquently. I wish she hadn't found words that worked. Because my anger is starting to fade, and I really wish it wouldn't.

I want to stay mad at her, I need to.

It's a survival instinct to stay angry, because if I stay angry then she won't be able to talk me round. She won't be able to draw me in again.

"That's not an excuse," I say, desperately trying to keep the irritation in my tone. What is it about this woman that causes me to act against my better instincts? I never should have published that podcast defending her. Yes, Inspector Sandways had falsified the evidence used to arrest her, but he had been barking up the right tree. Before I met Karma, I never would have taken such a risk. I would have spent weeks making a pros and cons list, weighing up and imagining every possible outcome of speaking out so publicly against a member of the force, and ultimately deciding against it.

But when it came to Karma, all my logic flew out of the window. She turned me back into the emotionally spontaneous nineteen-year-old I'd once been. The young woman I'd been back before he had stripped me of all trust in the world. Before he'd took advantage of me, because I was confident enough in naming his actions that, even if I wasn't confident it was rape, I'd been a bubbly person. Somebody who would pull into the first bar or restaurant they came across, make friends with the patrons and try everything new. I was someone who laughed easily, who flirted innocently, and who had dreams of upping sticks and following my dreams.

After him, I became guarded. My shine rubbed off. I no longer spoke to strangers, made friendships with other people in the bathroom, lengthened my skirts, covered my cleavage, and chose an easy life rather than an exciting one. It was easier that way. Because if I did all of those things, then I could protect myself. The world, and the people in it, couldn't hurt me the way he had. Nobody could break your trust if you didn't give it to them in the first place.

But Karma instinctively called out to that long forgotten part of me in a way nobody else in my life ever had. Yes, I trusted Jake, but he was still kept at arm's length. I still remained wary to a point around him, because I'd been burnt by somebody I trusted before and I vowed that night never to make the same mistake again.

And yet here I was. Injured again by somebody I put my trust in.

At least she had only done it emotionally, I suppose.

"I have to go," I say as I move to stand, but her hand is still firmly planted over mine, keeping me rooted to the bed. I look down at it and then back up at her, let me go Karma. Please just let me go.

"I can't let you walk out of this room like this, we can't leave things like this. You haven't even given me the chance to explain," she protests, looking so deeply into my eyes that I know she can see my resolve melting. This woman is a vigilante. I need to untangle myself from her web before I sink any deeper.

"You don't deserve the chance to explain!" I shout. I hadn't meant to raise my voice, I really hadn't, but she was pushing my buttons with her lies and her pleas. She had deceived me, which was worse than lying to me, she'd pretended she was just like me, just an interested bystander in the Network. Christ, she'd even asked me how I'd present a show on them and their workings. I'd essentially pitched her my idea for the true crime tale of her own true crimes.

She'd made a fool of me.

And I was no good at being embarrassed. It made me angry.

Was I more angry at being made to feel like a fool, or by the deception of her lies? Or her lie by omission.

I don't know. All I know is that I'm hurt and I don't want to stop being angry at her. Not yet.

"Please come with me, once you see the work we're doing you'll understand," Karma asks.

The audacity of this woman. To believe that she can not only talk me into forgiving her, to understand her actions, but to expect me to run away with her to God knows where and become a part of it alongside her. Does she really believe I feel such a connection with her that I'll simply throw my life away simply because she asked nicely?

Because she'd be right.

Or at least she would have been if she'd told me the truth before I put my professional reputation on the line. Because now when the truth about Karma and the Network come out, I'd look like I was complicit in her crimes. The truth about Inspector Sandways and his false evidence would be questioned, and the truly innocent parties he'd locked away would remain where they were. Any lawyer worth their salt would use her as an example. And every Jury would drink that up, and keep innocent people in prison where they don't belong.

Hell, after all this, I wouldn't be surprised if the ramifications for the Inspector were lessened to a slap on the wrist once his superiors learnt that he at least had pointed fingers at the correct suspect. They'll say that he did the wrong thing but for the right reasons. He'll be looked up to by others as a maverick, willing to do whatever was needed to make sure the right person was behind bars.

And maybe the others he had imprisoned with false evidence were just as guilty as Karma was. But if they weren't, now they'd have even less chance of having their convictions overturned.

Just like with the work the Network undertook at her guidance, Karma wasn't thinking of the bigger picture when she undertook her actions, of the other people it would affect. She wasn't thinking about anyone other than herself and her goals. Which is why, despite the pull I have to say yes, I can't go with her.

"I can't do that." I choose the softer of the two words, I could have told her that I wouldn't do that.

That I won't do that. But I chose to be as kind as I can allow myself to be.

"But I have to leave, there's something important I've got to do."

"Which is?"

"I can't tell you."

I scoff, knowing before I asked that she wouldn't give me a response.

"If I go with you, will you tell me everything?" Maybe I can pretend to go with her and she'll give me the truth about Mr. Williams. Tell me his sins, why he had to die, and maybe I can understand. If I understand then it will all be easier.

"No."

She removes her hand from on top of mine now, but before I can stand she places both of her hands on my shoulders, her touch gentle as she lightly plays with the strap of my top. Under different circumstances I'd melt but right now her touch repulses me.

"Will you keep my secret?" she asks.

"Which one?" I retort and she has the decency to look guilty. Now she moves her hands up to my cheeks, holding my head in her hands and despite myself my eyes are drawn to her lips. If she kisses me, will I refuse her? It's what I've dreamt about since we first met but I never imagined it would be like this. That it would be during a moment like this.

I'm not sure if I'm imagining it, but I swear her face is drawing closer to mine. My synapses are firing on all cylinders as I try to work out how I'm going to react, and to how to logically react.

But it's too late for logic.

Because her lips are on mine.

And it's everything I thought it would be.

And everything I'd hoped it wasn't.

Chapter Thirty-Seven: Karma

Karma honestly hadn't meant to kiss Zoe.

It wasn't the sensible thing to do. It wasn't a safe decision to make.

In fact, the Network had advised her to report straight back to head office after her release. Alone.

They knew that Zoe was a weak link in the armour Karma had built since she left The Farm. That going back for the podcaster, as they called her, was a fool's errand.

And they had been right.

Even though she'd known all along how Zoe would react to her revelation, there had been a part of her that had hoped for different.

Hope.

Bloody hope.

She should have given up on hope long ago. She thought she had the night Father beat her companion to near-death. She'd sworn to the universe as she cradled the girl's bleeding head that she'd never hope for anything again, that she knew it was a pointless endeavour. And for the most part, she kept that promise.

Even on the night she escaped from The Farm she

didn't hope she'd find salvation. All she wanted was to walk away, she didn't care if it ended in her death, she just wanted to be free. So when she rang the first few doorbells and found no answer she wasn't disappointed. Because the universe never looked out for her, so she never asked it to.

She was surprised when Joanna answered her door. Even more so when the older woman had welcomed her into her home, offered her a drink and some biscuits and held her hand whilst they waited for the police to arrive. She'd never received kindness from any of the adults in her life, so it was a foreign concept to her. But there had been something about Joanna that was worth trusting. She knew instinctively, in the same way she'd felt it when she first heard Zoe's voice on her application. There was a kindness living inside both of them and despite her better instincts hope had started to flutter in her heart again.

There had been times growing up that she'd allowed herself to hope that Joanna would gain custody of her.

But, it never happened.

She'd hoped her various foster parents would allow Joanna to stay in her life.

But, they didn't.

They all believed that keeping the woman who rescued her around would just remind her of what she'd escaped. That it would prevent her from creating healthy attachments to her new families. Which was ridiculous. Seeing Joanna didn't remind her of the hell she'd lived through on The Farm, her memory could do that well enough on its own. And the attachments to her new families never grew because none of the families felt comfortable engaging with Karma about all she'd survived. They overcompensated by trying to make her life as full of sunshine and rainbows as possible. No negativity was allowed.

That wasn't what Karma needed to heal, though. All it did was highlight to her all she had missed out on. How wrong her childhood had been up to the point she walked away. It never helped, it only hurt. And they could never understand that.

The final time Karma had hoped had been on her eighteenth birthday, when she independently boarded a train to Joanna's town in the hopes to see her friend again. But Joanna had died. And nobody had thought to tell Karma. The new owner of the house had briefly told her the news on the doorstep, not wanting to invite a stranger into their home, and that's when Karma finally and completely gave up on hoping for anything.

Until Zoe.

Zoe changed something about Karma with her light tone and her thorough research. Karma had listened to every episode of Zoe's podcast twice, until she knew every catchphrase, every inflection and had picked up on every Easter egg. She was Zoe's biggest fan, and she'd never told her that.

Instead, she'd told her the one thing that would mean the end of whatever was brewing between them.

She'd told her that she ran the Network.

She didn't blame Zoe for being angry. Karma had wanted to tell her the truth the first night they'd met. The confession had been on the tip of her tongue the second Zoe engaged her in conversation about the Network. But she'd bit down on it, putting her duty to the Network and those they served above her instinct to trust this stranger.

It had been a mistake.

One that Karma was paying for now as she tried to forget the hurt expression on Zoe's face.

So she kissed her to try and explain everything. Hoping that through her lips she could somehow express to Zoe all that she means to her, that somehow kissing her would help her understand why Karma had kept her secret. Why she still had to keep secrets.

And for the briefest moment after their lips touched Karma had hoped it would work.

Zoe had kissed her back, hesitantly at first and then with more passion. Karma had accepted her invitation and gently lay the other woman down on the bed, positioning herself so she was laying on top of her chest, their lips never parting. Her hand roamed around Zoe's body, starting at her calve and working its way up, and up, and up until -

Until Zoe asked her to stop.

And Karma did so instantly.

Because that's what you do.

Stop means stop. And no means no.

No matter what had preceded it.

"I can't go with you," Zoe had said as they parted and the words that Karma had hoped to avoid were spilt out into the world. Zoe may agree on the surface with the Networks undertakings, but she couldn't let go of her damn teacher. Who got everything he deserved. Probably less than he deserved. And Karma couldn't tell her any of that. Because it wasn't her story to tell.

She just hoped that Zoe would trust her.

Hope.

Hope had never worked out for Karma.

So she accepted Zoe's final answer and with one last look at her face, Karma stood from the bed and walked out of the room, ready for her true purpose.

Chapter Thirty-Eight: The Farm

Paula was beginning to become a thorn in Father's side.

Whilst it was true that she was one of the founding members, she wasn't one of the two true founders and yet she was acting as though her word should hold as much weight as Erin's once did. She acted as though she was Mother.

He wasn't sure whether it happened directly after his wife's death, for the week he'd confined himself to his room, or when his teachings grew darker as he worked through his grief - but it had happened. Somewhere over the years, Paula had embedded herself into the congregation, at a higher power than she deserved. He'd been so taken with nurturing Karma to be his protege that he'd missed the betrayal as it spread through his people, but he could see it now. He noticed the way eyes glanced at her for confirmation after he gave an order, in the little nods she gave followers as they took on their daily checks.

Paula was overstepping her mark in a way none of the others would dare.

Owen and Ian were happy with their lot in life. The purpose he had given them. Owen oversaw new recruitments and took care of their induction onto The

Farm. Ian oversaw the mating rituals, a task he had volunteered for when they'd first begun. And both men excelled at their work, found joy every day in the cog they kept well oiled. But Paula.

Paula wanted more. That much was clear to Father now.

And that made her a problem.

Unfortunately for him it wasn't a problem a knife could deal with. He was a smart enough man to know that the good favour she'd gained amongst his followers would soon turn against him if she wasn't dealt with correctly. So no, he couldn't just execute her and be done with it - as much as he wanted to.

She had to be micromanaged, he had to take his time with the process. Let public opinion fall away from her slowly but surely. Undermine her wherever possible, because she was nothing like Erin and he worried that one day the blasted woman might try to drive a wedge between him and Karma as a way to achieve power for herself. The last thing he needed was Paula trying to usurp him.

So Father did what he'd always done best. He talked to people. To the right people of course. The ones who would gossip.

He would tell them of his concern for Paula. Point out that she no longer partook in the mating rituals. She showed favouritism amongst the children. That she took more than her fair share of the crops, despite never stepping foot in the fields. And slowly but surely, he watched as her confidence melted and compliance returned to her brain.

That was the problem with all women who weren't Mother. They were weak. They relied on the opinion of others to build their strength. Erin had never been like that. She hadn't cared what others thought of her, only what Peter, Father, had thought of her. And that's why she had been the true Mother to the movement.

Karma would be the same.

The girl may only have been ten years old, but already he could sense steel in her soul. And that's what she would need to succeed in taking over The Farm. All she had to do was to bend to his whim and his alone, once he'd broken her enough for her to see that then she would be perfect.

Despite his lessons about the dangers of friendship, the child still stole away from time to time, and none of his spies had been able to identify where for him yet. Frustration was building in him day after day.

Anger at Paula's cockiness.

Anger at Karma's defiance.

But he'd dealt with the first issue and he would deal with this one soon enough. One day the child would make a mistake. One day her companion would be outed and then Father could take action.

Chapter Thirty-Nine: Target #38

Paula knew what was happening the moment the woman crossed the street towards her. She'd been painfully aware of the Network's approach for months now, feeling their eyes upon her at every waking moment. It had taken until the age of sixty-two for her to understand true terror, and that feeling had lived with her for so long now that it was almost a relief to know it would be over soon.

Since leaving The Farm, Paula had tried her best to atone for her sins, telling herself that she had been nothing more than a young girl led astray. And whilst that may have been true when she first started the cult alongside Father, by the end of it she was a woman in her mid-thirties who certainly knew better.

And yet she continued to stand aside and let members of The Farm abuse children and each other. If her slowing appetite for participation herself had been noticed by Trish or the other founding members, none of them had made mention of it, but she'd never spoken out. Never told any of them that what they were doing was wrong. Because it was easier to stay silent, safer, she told herself, but no matter how many charities she raised money for, or children she'd fostered since, she couldn't shake the guilt. Deep down she knows she was as much of a monster as any of them.

There had been a part of her, a part that had swollen since the first murder was announced, that thought she'd be spared. That the kindness she'd shown Karma in the last few years of their lives together would spare her from judgement. She'd hoped her life would be given to her because she'd helped give life to another. She'd been the one to prevent Father from dealing the fatal blow to Karma's friend. She'd been the one to lead him away and convince him that Karma should bury the injured child. And she'd been the one who'd nursed the young girl's wounds and kept her hidden from everybody else for the rest of her time on The Farm.

But no.

The Network didn't care about that one kindness.

It didn't care about the risks she'd taken to protect the child. Or the loyalty she had shown Karma whilst doing so. It only cared for the wrongs she'd dealt out, and they were countless.

She only hoped they'd grant her a swift end.

Which is why she made no move to run as the woman in the black sundress approached her. Their eyes locked onto each other from across the street, and each knew what the other was thinking. The woman was going to kill her. And Paula wasn't going to put up a fight.

Paula.

It was so strange to think of herself by that name now. She hadn't used that name for twenty-seven years, since the night she was put in charge of starting the fire at the barn. The memory of which still haunts her. Those children, despite what Father said, were innocent and they most certainly hadn't deserved to be burned alive. But it had been an order, and Paula always followed orders.

She'd spent nearly three decades since going by the name Leah, and had built herself up into a totally new person under that identity. Somebody who would never harm another, let alone a child. Try as she might, she couldn't shake the truth. Not only had she harmed children herself, but she had actively participated, no, encouraged others to do the same. Believing, at the time, it was all for the greater good of a new society. They had been abusers. They had been paedophiles. And no matter how she dressed it up, or tried to excuse it, her actions had been evil.

The woman in black was at her side now, and she braced herself, ready for death, squeezing her eyes together as though that might save her from the fiery pits that awaited her.

"Karma Jones requests an audience," the woman announced, and although she used the word request it was obvious it was a demand.

Paula's knees began to shake as adrenaline coursed through her body. She'd had suspicions all along that Karma had been involved in the network, how couldn't she be given all The Farm had put her through. She hadn't realised though that the girl, now woman, ranked highly enough to request an audience from somebody who was surely on the execution list.

Perhaps that one good deed, many years ago, was about to come to fruition. Perhaps Karma was prepared to plead Paula's case, to tell her of the young girl she saved, before the jury decided her fate.

Her former friends and colleagues had all deserved their fate, because they had never repented, but Paula had. She'd spent the years since repenting for the sins of her youth and now it would be worth it.

She'd kept track of Karma over the years, as she was sure most of the founding members had, and had been almost proud of the woman she'd grown into.

Hoping in a way that her kindness had helped shape that. With every photo she saw of Karma she saw more and more of her friend Erin reflected back at her. The apple hadn't fallen far from the tree, looks wise, and now Karma was older than her mother would ever be. It gave Paula a chance to mourn for her friend all over again.

If she'd been allowed at Erin's delivery, then she knows she could have saved her friend's life. Paula's success rate in deliveries was one of the highest on The Farm. But in order to abide by Father's rule that all children should be anonymised from their parents, she had to make herself scarce. Father knew Paula would not be able to keep such a huge secret from Erin. That one day, she would point at Karma and let Erin know that she was her kin.

Given how physically alike the child was to her mother gave the game away though. Father knew the instant he set eyes on her in the nursery. And thus Mother was reborn.

Thankfully other children weren't as recognisable. It saved them from being singled out by him. But Paula had her suspicions that he had sired more than one child, with the amount of orgies they all had, how could he not have?

But still, Karma was his special project.

And he made that poor child's life a nightmare.

Which is why Paula hadn't thought twice about stepping in to save the life of her friend.

Why it was so easy for Paula to stand next to an empty grave and celebrate alongside Father that finally, finally he had broken Karma's spirit and she would now be easy to mould into a new Mother for the clan.

She followed the woman now, without giving any kind of response, she would save her words for their reunion. That's when they would matter.

A car was waiting for them and she willingly allowed a blindfold to be tied around her head.

The journey was shorter than she'd expected, but perhaps her awareness of passing time was clouded by her lack of vision.

Before she could fully step out of the car, a voice startled her, a voice she'd been searching for over the last twenty-seven years. The voice of the child she saved and raised.

"Paula. How nice of you to join us."

Chapter Forty: Target #38

Without waiting for an invitation, Paula removed her blindfold.

Just as she'd expected, a woman in her late thirties stood before her.

Oh, how she'd aged.

Time had not been kind to the young girl she saved.

The scars Father's beating had rained down upon her were still present, but they had faded with the years. Paula only noticed them because she knew they were there. She remembered bathing and dressing each and every one.

"Jones," she said, stepping towards the woman, her arms outstretched ever so slightly. She'd grown to think of the child as her own daughter over their brief years together, hiding out from the rest of The Farm.

Jones regarded Paula's greeting before scoffing to herself.

"I'm not much of a hugger," she replied and Paula took the hint. Allowing her arms to drop emptily to the side. She spent the first eight years of life after The Farm looking for news of Jones, scanning every photograph of the survivors as they grew, but she never saw the familiar face looking back at her. Figuring the girl had chosen to live under the radar, she never breathed a word of her existence to anybody. Not even when Karma changed her name to incorporate that of her friend.

Karma Ann Jones.

Karma And Jones.

It was so on the nose if you knew the truth.

Paula had taken comfort in this, seen it as a sign that the two girls were still looking out for each other.

As sisters should.

Because that was the other secret Paula had kept from Father and the others.

The night Erin died, two new babies had been delivered to the nursery. Side by side, in the same basket. Covered in their mother's blood.

Jones had been lucky. She'd inherited more of Father's genes than Erin.

Unlike Karma, who was recognisable on sight.

There had been no way to prove it. The woman who'd performed Erin's delivery had brought the babies to the nursery and then walked to a nearby barn and hung herself. The shame of having failed Mother was too much for her to bear.

Paula had been the only one who knew.

Which is why she'd always encouraged the two girls to play together. Hoping they would figure it out on their own. Her plan had backfired though, the night Father tried to kill Jones to teach Karma a lesson. He had chosen her because she was someone Karma loved. And Father didn't want to share Karma's love with anyone else.

Thankfully, Paula had intervened at the exact right moment, and now her surrogate daughter was standing before her a fully grown woman. She was so relieved, tears began to spill from her eyes. Jones was okay, she had lived, Paula had made sure she'd gotten to live.

"Karma wants to speak with you."

Jones turned her back on Paula and began to walk away, leaving the older woman to try and match her pace.

"Jones, it's so good to see you. I looked for you. I swear I did." Paula's words come out in a jumble of emotion and yet there was one missing, the only word that would make any difference to the woman walking in front of her. But Paula couldn't apologise, because she'd saved Jones' life and that should make up for any wrongs between them.

No matter how much babble Paula threw her way, Jones did not reply. She barely acknowledged the woman's presence aside from a few quick glances. This wasn't a family reunion, no matter what the older woman wanted. Jones only had one family member, Karma, and Paula meant very little to her.

She was grateful for the woman's intervention the night Father tried to kill her.

Of course she was.

And she was grateful for the care she had been given and for the protection she'd been gifted during those final years on The Farm.

But none of that made the two of them family.

Paula, despite what she may think, was a monster. And Jones slayed monsters.

Finally, they arrived at a door and Jones stopped walking. She expected this meeting to feel easier than it had. She hadn't expected to feel any form of conflict towards what was about to happen. And yet she did.

Karma had warned her that she might. Some form of survivors' bond between her and the woman who stood next to her. And whilst Jones didn't think it was quite that strong, she could acknowledge that there were tiny sparks of guilt in her mind as to what was to happen to the woman who'd saved her.

They weren't family.

No.

They would never be family.

And Paula was a monster. One of the worst on their list.

But she saved Jones' life.

And that brought with it some level of gratefulness that Jones hadn't foreseen.

Still.

There was a job to do today. And logically she knew that she owed Paula nothing.

If Paula hadn't helped Father recruit for The Farm then Jones would never have needed saving. She'd never have been born. And that would have been bliss.

"You never told anyone about me?" Jones finally speaks to Paula, who by now has learnt to bite her tongue.

"Of course not."

"Why?" asked Jones, curiosity clouding her judgment. She should not be engaging the target in this manner. No good could come of it.

"Because I promised I would protect you." Paula smiled at the woman holding the door open for her, proud of the part she'd played in Jones' life, hoping that this exchange would thaw the ice between them.

A response couldn't be birthed onto Jones' lips, she was too conflicted by the reply. So sure that Paula had kept her mouth shut to protect herself, never for a moment believed that the woman had done it to protect Jones herself.

"Paula, please come in," a new voice floated through the open doorway towards the two of them. A voice that Paula knew nearly as well as her own - Karma was calling out to her. Now was the time she would be forgiven for the crimes in her early years, now the two women would plead her case to the Network and finally she could live without constantly looking over her shoulder.

With one final smile at Jones, she stepped over the threshold and walked into a large room that was empty other than a single chair at the very centre of it.

"Sit down." Karma's voice commanded as she stepped into Paula's line of vision. Her face was serious and although Paula tried to make eye contact it was as though Karma's mind was elsewhere. There was nothing left for the woman to do other than obey.

It took six steps for her to reach the chair, and with each one she felt the tug of her feet trying to pull her away from this situation. Some long-buried survival instinct screaming out at her to run. It was a foolish instinct though. It didn't understand that she was safe here. She was with family.

"Karma, how are you?" Paula asked as she sat down, hoping pleasantries would go down well with whatever audience was watching her. She was certain there would be a jury somewhere, taking notes, ready to listen to Karma plead to spare her. All she could do was present herself in the best light and hope that Karma and Jones' words would carry enough weight with their peers.

"What do you think is going on here, Paula?" Karma was finally present in the room, but Paula wished her attention were still elsewhere given the way it burnt now it was focused on her.

"I'm here to plead my case with the Network." She replied, being sure to flash her most sympathetic smile to each corner of the room.

She watched as Karma held back a laugh.

"Who exactly are you smiling at? It's just us here, Paula. Just the three of us. Judge, jury and executed." With her final word Karma pulled a syringe from behind her back, and all Paula's hope turned to ash.

"No, that's not possible. I'm here for you to speak for me. To tell the Network about what I did for you." Paula was angry and now she knew there was no audience she stood up. She was done being obedient. Today was not the day she died. This was a cruel prank, and she'd never cared for pranks.

"What you did for me?" Karma spits back and Paula fights back the urge to slap the smirk from her face. She'd always been a difficult child and age had not wiped that from her. Jones. Jones would be her saviour.

"What I did for Jones." Paula spun on her heel, turning all her attention to the child she'd saved. "I saved your life, I nursed you back to help, kept you hidden. I SAVED YOU!" Desperation was causing Paula to lose control of her emotions; she hadn't really meant to shout that last part of her plea but sometimes with children, the only way to get them to listen was to raise your voice. It had worked on Jones in the past, it would work today.

"Yes. You saved me. But if you had never started The Farm then I wouldn't have needed saving." Jones' voice was steady now, somehow seeing the rage in Paula had reminded her of all the negative times they shared. It was true, Paula had saved her and cared for her. But she also spent hours screaming at her, beating her, locking her in solitude when she couldn't cope with Jones' emerging personality. There were two sides to every person and both of Paula's were rotten.

"If it weren't for me, you would never have existed!" How did these girls not realise that they owed their lives to Paula? To the founders? They were nothing more than a random collection of cells brought together by the matchmaking on The Farm.

"That would have been preferable," Karma's response was drawn and with far more strength than

Paula had expected, she pushed the older woman back down into the chair.

"You owe me!" Paula cried out as the syringe drew closer to her neck. Karma's hand didn't shake, not even a fraction, as she pierced the skin and held her thumb on the plunger. Looking towards her sister for confirmation of her next actions.

Jones walked towards the quivering woman in the chair and regarded her.

"You're right. We do owe you. But there are forty eight other people who don't owe you shit." With the final reference to the siblings they escaped with, Karma pushed down on the plunger and Paula's fate was sealed.

The two of them stood side by side and watched with interest as the woman who had helped create the hell they grew up in convulsed and eventually choked on her own vomit. Neither of them felt the urge to aid her or comfort her in her dying moments. Instead, they focused on the memories of all the children she hurt, the fear their peers had felt at her hands. The universe wrapped them up in its warm embrace as Paula's spirit moved from this land to the next.

This was what justice felt like.

Their silence was interrupted by somebody running through the door.

"I'm sorry to interrupt, but we've had news." The voice called out to them from the darkness.

"What is it?" asked Karma, finally taking her eyes from Paula's corpse.

"Zoe Lewis has been kidnapped."

The peace Karma had experienced with Paula's murder vanished in an instant. Her heart rate trembled as her pulse tried to keep up with her thoughts. She'd left Zoe safely in the hotel room. How could this have happened?

This wasn't the plan.

And now Zoe was in danger.
And Karma had a sinking feeling that she knew who was behind it.

Chapter Forty-One: The Farm

Karma's mistake made itself known quietly. As is often the way.

One night, as they lay together, Father noticed a red thread tied around her ankle. When his hand lazily made its way down her leg, she moved away from him. He made no comment, acted like his movement had been nothing more than the heat of the moment. And yet he'd known what her flinch had meant. The anklet was special. It tied her to someone who mattered.

After his business with Karma had been conducted, he made his way to the school hut. The place where the rest of the children slept. It was easy to slip into their bed chamber without disturbing them; they'd all been given their nightly dose of sedatives and as such slept like the dead. Father felt no guilt about drugging the younger members of the congregation into submission; they were too young to see the bigger picture of their lives on The Farm, and God would want him to lend this nightly helping hand to keep them on the righteous path he'd set out for them.

The alternative was that they rebelled. That they fled. That they told outsiders of the work he was conducting behind his fences. And that couldn't possibly be what God wanted for his chosen son.

So no. Guilt was not a feeling that whispered across Father's skin as he lifted each child's bed sheets and stole a glance at their ankles. It wasn't guilt that caused goose pimples to rise on his arms when he finally found what he had been seeking - a red piece of string tied delicately across an ankle bone.

It was rage.

It was jealousy.

It was annoyance.

Because how could his devoted followers, the ones he'd charged with keeping an eye on Karma and her associates, have missed this. This Earth shattering clue that at least a part of her heart belonged to someone else.

All the other children that had been sacrificed to try and teach her a lesson, to try and get her to see the light, had been a waste. They had not meant anything to her. They had just been random acts of kindness. This child, this child who lay slumbering before him was the true problem.

He watched as she smiled to herself in her dream, and he longed to reach out and steal the smile from her face, to squeeze the air from her lungs and to feel her heart beating in his hand.

But he held back.

Because killing her now, as she slept in her bed, wouldn't achieve anything.

True, her death would no doubt break Karma's heart, allowing him to fix it and rebuild it to his whim. But it would always be an imagined horror to Karma. She had to witness, first hand, the results of her betrayal for the lesson to truly sink in.

And it had to be worse than all the public executions he'd organised before. It had to be intimate, she had to realise how truly powerless she was to save the person she cared about. Only then would she see that the safest path in life was the one that led to Father's arms. Only then would she be his body and soul. Only then would she truly be ready to become Mother.

And so Father walked away from the young girl's bedside, cracking his knuckles as he did so. By this time tomorrow, he'd have dealt with the two problems that had been troubling him for months - he'd already put Paula's confidence back into the ground where she belonged and soon it would be Karma's turn to fall into line.

Chapter Forty-Two: Zoe

After Karma left, I sat for a while on the bed. Unmoving. Simply processing everything that had happened. All that I'd been told. And how I felt about it.

Had I made the right choice in turning Karma down?

Should I have gone with her?

There's no denying that I agree with most of the Network's undertakings. Sometimes, more often than not, a court of law doesn't achieve justice for victims. Guilty monsters were roaming the streets, and putting a little fear into them didn't do any harm. Perhaps it would make someone think twice before they raised a fist. Before they took something that wasn't theirs.

Monsters deserved to be slain. That's an undeniable fact that I stand by. There are certain crimes you never repent for, certain acts that should never be forgiven. And it might be extreme but sometimes I do believe that people should be able to kill their rapists.

But then there are situations like the one I lived through.

He took advantage of me being drunk, I believe that for definite.

I don't think he meant to rape me.

I don't think he knew that's how it felt.

So, given the chance, would I hand his name over to the Network and wait for his obituary to appear?

No.

I don't think I would.

What happened to me was bad, yes. Wrong, yes. But I've moved past wishing him pain, and I truly don't think I would want to kill him.

But victims of sexual assault should be given justice, in one form or another, if they wish it. And the Network was filling a void that, sadly, our criminal justice system was falling dramatically short on. So yes, I believe they had a purpose.

After all, if you're innocent, you have nothing to fear.

Unless you're Mr. Williams.

So far, he's still the only target of theirs that they haven't published a dossier on. He's still their only innocent victim. And, despite her bravado, Karma made a mistake when she ordered his death. I know she did. She knows she did. And I can't throw my life away for someone who can't admit to being wrong.

Still, when someone knocked on the door, there was a bubble of excitement in my stomach, a brief wish sent out to the universe that she'd come back to me. That she was going to give me the truth and that would give me a reason to go with her. Or maybe she'd stay. Maybe she'd turn her back on her side project and be happy living a normal life with me.

Imagine my disappointment when I opened the door, only to find a cloth quickly shoved over my face before the world went black.

I wake up in the dark, and it throws my internal

clock off balance until I recognise the sensation of a blindfold wrapped tightly across my face. My hands, on instinct, move up towards it but they're bound as well. Thankfully to my lap rather than behind my back but still, this small consideration doesn't make me feel more secure in my situation.

Has Karma done this? Would she do this to me?

Or maybe somebody in the Network has arranged for this, knowing that she was going to confess her crimes to me. It's not implausible to believe somebody she knows would act so violently to protect her from the fall-back. She inspires that kind of illogical passion in people, I should know. But Karma doesn't need to be saved from anything, I know that now and I should have known it the moment she was arrested.

Nobody saved her from The Farm. She saved herself. And she's been saving herself ever since via the creation of the Network and the security it offers her.

She doesn't need a hero or a white knight to come charging in to make everything right in her world. She is the one who is in complete control. I was behaving like everybody else, thinking she was a victim who needed my help when she was ten steps ahead, already securing her freedom in ways I couldn't fathom before I even hit record on my podcast.

Whoever has taken me hasn't taken into account Karma's reaction when she finds out what they've done. She'll be furious with them, I know she will. I haven't imagined a single moment that's passed between us, or the tension in every innocent touch. She likes me. She wouldn't have asked me to go with her if she didn't like me. If only things had been different.

If only.

If only.

If only.

The panic at my blindness recedes with each

second as I come to accept that sooner or later, Karma will undo all of this. She will demand that I am released and as the head of the Network, she will be obeyed. Everything is going to be okay once these wires are uncrossed.

I'm sure of it. I'm not delusional.

Am I?

As though sensing that I'm relaxing somewhat, the person sitting to my left grabs hold of my waist and squeezes it tightly. Trying to force the fear back into my blood, it's not going to happen though. They can play as many games as they like but ultimately, I won't come to any harm.

Karma won't let that happen.

She probably already knows I've been taken from the hotel room. Whoever's behind it hasn't hesitated to let her know the lengths they've gone to to protect her. In just a few moments, I'll hear her voice and maybe, just maybe, we can talk a little more before I return to my life.

I hadn't thought about the conversation we just had being the last one we'd ever have.

I only realised the weight of the moment as she walked out of the room. But I was too stubborn, too shocked, too hurt to call out to her and say anything that would carry the weight it needed to. To say goodbye to her properly.

She was never coming back. She was on the run now, her cause was more important to her than sticking around to be with me and despite my cloudy moral opinion on it, I had to respect her drive.

Perhaps I would explain that to her before we part ways again. Make sure she understands that despite not agreeing with all of her actions, I respect the good she is trying to put out into the world. The wrongs she is trying to right. Yes. That will be a better way for us to say goodbye.

Just as I'm fantasising about saying goodbye to her again, I notice a damp, warm feeling at the side of my stomach. I move my bound hands towards the sensation and can feel a thick liquid.

Whoever was sitting to the side of me hadn't been squeezing my waist, they'd punctured my skin.

I've gone into such a state of shock since waking up that I hadn't felt it.

My brain has shut off from my body, allowing me to tell myself stories and explanations full of hope and luck to keep me sane.

Karma wasn't coming.

This rogue member of the Network isn't intending on letting me leave this situation unscathed. Maybe not even alive. They have a plan for me and I don't know if I can get ahead of it.

Everything I've just convinced myself of, everything I've told myself was all a lie - I am in danger. I am in trouble. And I only have myself to rely on. I need to get hold of my emotions, I need to think clearly if I'm going to survive. I have to be smarter than they expect me to be. I have to hope they underestimate me.

This time, when the person sitting next to me in the vehicle runs a blade across my skin, I feel it in all its glory. Unable to hold back the shudder that tickles along my spine without the safety blanket of my fantasies to hide behind. No. I can't be afraid. If I'm afraid then I'm not thinking straight. And if I'm not thinking straight then I have no hope of survival.

Despite having my eyes blindfolded, I squeeze them tight, trying to summon up courage that's just out of reach. Like a child, if I can't see the monsters, then they can't find me. And I desperately don't want to see these monsters because every instinct I have is now screaming out at me to run, to get myself away from whoever has taken me, because they are the kind of monster you can't battle.

A low chuckle fills the air around me. A man's voice. It scratches across my skin, molesting every millimetre of it.

I don't know if it belongs to the person with the blade or not but it fills my brain, rubbing up against every neuron with its salty tone. Whoever this is, is enjoying my fear. Lapping it up like a true sadist.

I want to run; my feet push against the floor to do so, but it's a pointless endeavour as I'm quickly pushed back into my seat. There is no escape.

There is only me.

And that laugh that never seems to end.

Chapter Forty-Three: Zoe

They weren't exactly gentle when they moved me from the car. I can already feel bruises blooming on my skin where their hands touched me uninvited. And the whole time that laugh rattled around inside my skull.

"Hello Zoe," a voice said as the hood was removed from my face with a flourish.

His face was so close to mine that I could smell the coffee on his breath. Cappuccino with an egg sandwich for lunch and he chuckled as I attempted to jump backwards in the chair I was bound to.

The back of the chair cuts into my shoulder blades and I yelp out in pain. Which only increases the volume of the man's laughter.

Terror has a grip on my throat so hard I feel like I'm choking on my own tongue. Whoever this is, they intend to cause me harm. A lot of it. What the hell have I got myself tangled up in?

"Just in case you're wondering, yes this has everything to do with Ms. Jones."

Karma. This is all to do with Karma. Which means the man standing in front of me, who has no place in the Network, with salt and pepper soaked hair and eyes you could fall into, can only be one person.

Father.

"I know who you are," I manage to croak out. Hoping that my voice sounds defiant to his ears, rather than the pathetic squeak it sounds to mine.

"And who's that?"

He wants me to say his name. Or at least the name Karma knows him by.

"Father," I say, although every piece of me doesn't want to speak it. Because by speaking it, I've acknowledged his power over me. I've acknowledged his alias and all that it stands for.

"Bingo."

"Why am I here?" I might as well ask questions; the longer I keep him talking, the longer I live.

"Bait, my love. It's simple, really. Karma, Mother, cares about you. And by taking you, I've sent a clear message to her that it's time to step back in line."

"I won't bring her to you."

"You don't have a choice. None of us do. All of this is pre-planned, written in the stars. I didn't realise it at first, when she left. I thought it was a betrayal, but now I see it was part of her journey. The journey that ends with her by my side. She'll see how much easier life is back with me compared to life without me." Just as Karma had told me, this man loves the sound of his own voice. Hopefully, I can use to my advantage.

"Her life has been infinitely improved by not having you in it." My simple rebellion, the truth, earns me a strike across the face.

"You think you know her, but you don't. You don't know the first thing about her. Why she chose you to tell our story I'll never know. You are nothing, you have always been nothing, and by the time I am through with you then you will forever be nothing" He's drawing closer to my face now as he makes his threats, spit flies across my nose and I sneer in disgust.

"I'm the one she chose." I can't let him see me scared. Men like him draw power from fear, and he isn't having any more of mine. I'm going to die here, it's simple and it's true. And although I'm terrified of the how and the when, I can't stop fighting. Not now.

He thinks about hitting me again. I can read it on his face. Hate makes a person so transparent.

And yet he takes a step away from me, so I can finally breathe without drawing him down into my lungs.

"She only chose you to get to me. Why else would she speak so publicly about the life we shared, if she didn't want me to listen?"

This man is a complete and utter narcissistic psychopath. There is no other diagnosis. He truly believes, with his whole heart, that everything Karma has done since the day she fled The Farm has been to gain his attention. To reunite the two of them.

"If she wanted you to listen, why didn't she ever find you?"

"Because I didn't want to be found." His reply is simple and elegant, and I can see his personality shift before my eyes. Gone is the rage-filled maniac, and in his place is the soft-spoken man who drew so many followers onto The Farm. If you want people to listen, you should whisper. It does more than a shout. And this man is evidence of the power of that.

"She may be Mother reborn, but she is still years behind me in intellect. If I wanted her to find me, then she would have done so. It's as simple as that. But it wasn't time. She hadn't sent me the right message until she engaged with you. And until my friends were targeted by her little Network."

He knows about the Medusa Network and Karma's link to it. This man knows so many things that he should not. His webs clearly haven't lessened since he fled in fear from his own congregation and life's purpose.

"The Network has nothing to do with you," I speak with more confidence than I feel. For all I know, the Network's sole purpose is to hunt down Father. But it feels deeper than that, more important than that. He is just one man, and they are so many survivors rising up against those who escape justice. The story of the Network is not his story, and I won't let him take it to feed his ego.

"Oh Zoe, you could never be a part of the new world order. You can't see the bigger picture. It's all been about me. All of it. Don't feel too badly though, you weren't raised right, weren't raised like Karma. She's done all of this for me, for our future, and the future of society. She's a good girl, and good girls always come home."

He's posturing in front of me, expecting me to buy into his words as so many people still do. Because he must still have followers out there somewhere. He can't be operating alone. He can't have stayed hidden for so many years without the aid of others.

Father still has fans, clearly in very powerful places, and I hate him for it. I hate him for everything he did to Karma and all the other children. I hate his beliefs and his confidence and the way he's going to hurt me and kill me today. I hate him more than I ever thought possible, and although I am not a violent person right now I could hurt him if I had the chance.

"Good girls grow into strong women. And strong women don't take shit from men like you."

That comment earns me a swift kick to the stomach and I topple backwards onto the floor, the only reason my head doesn't hit the concrete behind me is I have the good sense to curl my neck towards my chest at the last moment.

I hear his laughter as he walks away and leaves me staring at the ceiling, and finally I let my tears fall.

Chapter Forty-Four: Karma

"This is a mistake, you know that, right?" Jones says to Karma as the two of them crouch down in a bush. They've tracked Zoe's location via her phone, thanks to a Network member on the force in the right department, and now they are staking out the building she's being held in.

Karma knows she is acting impulsively.

She knows that coming here is a mistake.

But she has to save Zoe. Because it's her fault she's at risk.

She never should have agreed to tell her story publicly. She shouldn't have gotten comfortable with the idea that Father was gone. That he'd died some unremarkable death somewhere. But it was hard not to think like that when decades had gone by without a single sighting of him.

Even her best intel gatherers had never been able to find evidence of him being alive.

So, over the last twelve months, she had grown confident that she was safe. She could tell her story without worrying about the ramifications.

She'd been wrong.

So wrong.

And she wasn't about to let Zoe pay for that mistake.

The idea that she might lay eyes on Father again terrified her more than she could ever verbalise. Jones at least had an idea of that feeling, but she hadn't been sexually abused by him every day for a decade. It was true that he did partake in the mating ceremonies as much as any other member of the congregation, had raped his fair share of children on The Farm, but it was always Karma he came home to.

Always Karma, he kept in his bed.

Jones checked that her handgun was loaded and passed Karma a knife. Her sister preferred a blade to a bullet, as she couldn't trust that her hands wouldn't shake if she lay eyes on her nightmare. The last thing she wanted to do was put anyone else at risk and a stray bullet would do that.

"Are you ready?" asked Jones, turning towards her sister, showing her sympathy. She understood a tiny fraction of what Father had forced Karma to live through. She had experienced the man's depravity and cruelty firsthand, and still bore the scars he had left behind.

"Yes," replied Karma, although her voice was lost to the wind. She didn't want to do this. Didn't want to risk confronting her demons, but she had no choice. Zoe needed her.

They crept towards the front door and found it unlocked and unguarded.

But that was a false sense of security.

In the first corridor ,they encountered two guards. Jones shot them both point blank through the skull before they could blink. She'd had more combat experience than her sister. Had spent her many years living underground hunting scum, practicing for the foundations of The Network. She'd taken more lives than she could count, and she didn't feel a fraction of guilt about any of them.

Whoever was guarding this place worked for Father. Which meant they supported him and his ideals. Which meant they were fair game.

Jones heard the woman's screams before Karma did. She didn't sound like she was being hurt, but she was certainly afraid. She must have heard the gunfire and yelled out in response.

They moved slowly and instinctively towards the sound, meeting no further guards along the way. Which was unusual and set an unusual feeling of distrust in her stomach.

This was a trap, Jones was sure of it.

As they stood in front of the door where the screams were emitting from, Karma braced herself. As soon as they opened it, Father would be there. He would be waiting for her. And she truly didn't know if she was strong enough to face him. But she had no choice.

Jones looked towards her, waiting for her sister to give the nod of approval before opening the door. She was prepared for Karma to freeze to the spot at the sight of Father, or even for her to flee, whatever her response was Jones would be there for her. She always had been and she always would be. It had been that way since they were born, since Paula told them they were sisters. She would always protect Karma.

The door opened with a creak and both women were surprised to find no monsters waiting for them behind it.

Just Zoe, bound to a chair on the floor, mouth open in a scream of terror.

"Zoe!" cried Karma as she ran towards the woman, slashing at her bonds with the knife.

Jones watched on, a new feeling creeping into her

stomach.

Jealousy.

Karma clearly cared about Zoe. Maybe even loved her. And Jones had never had to share her sister's heart before.

Chapter Forty-Five: Zoe

Karma leads me through a large door, her hand in the small of my back supporting me as we go.

I'm free.

I'm alive.

I'm safe.

Those are the three thoughts that run on repeat through my head, growing in volume with every inch of distance we put between us and Father.

The woman who helped rescue me is walking a pace behind us, and I get the feeling that she doesn't appreciate my presence very much. I get that feeling because she's repeatedly asked Karma to take me anywhere else but here. Because here, where we are, is somewhere very important.

It's the belly of the beast.

The Medusa Network's headquarters.

"Jones," Karma snaps, "this is the safest place for us all. Nobody knows it exists, and nobody else is here."

Jones.

Jones.

Karma Ann Jones.

Karma and Jones.

Oh my god. How didn't I piece it together? Back in

our first interview I'd asked her why she chose her full name and she replied it was to remind her she wasn't alone. I'd presumed, as I'm sure others had, that it was an homage to Joanna the woman who raised her. But we'd all been wrong.

Now I look at the woman escorting us properly, and I'm shocked at the resemblance that's there. Right underneath my nose.

She has the same lips as Karma, and although her skin is a lighter shade of brown, it's clear they share heritage. Karma just took after their mother more.

Jones is Karma's sister.

They walk me into a large office and Jones slumps down into a chair behind a computer screen. She makes no move towards the keyboard though, and instead turns to stare at me.

"So, you're Zoe huh?" she asks.

"Um, yes," I reply, not really sure what I can offer in the way of conversation to follow that.

"Thought you'd be taller," she shoots, before turning her attention back towards her sister.

The two of them are clearly in an unspoken disagreement, their body language although open is tense with unspoken words.

"We really should go somewhere else. Or at least call for backup."

"Why? We're perfectly fine here, only the Foundation knows about this building, on paper it doesn't exist." Karma replies.

"I'm just saying, we shouldn't stay long." Jones sighs and stands, stretching her back as she does so. "That was easier than I expected."

"Yes. It was." Karma's voice is unsure, although she's keeping her spine straight in a show of confidence. I, meanwhile, am standing exactly where I was placed when we walked into the room, the shock of what I've just survived sweeping over me.

"Is it over?" I manage to squeak out as my legs begin to shake, shock finally taking hold of me. Karma places a hand in the small of my back again and guides me to an empty chair.

"Jones, will you get Zoe something to drink, please?" she asks and Jones rolls her eyes but does as she's asked. Perhaps there is a heart underneath her bad attitude.

"I don't think your sister likes me very much," I say, and Karma looks taken back. As though I wouldn't notice their family resemblance and piece it together. "Karma Ann Jones, Karma and Jones, very clever."

She blushes slightly at my praise and busies herself moving some paperwork around on the desk next to us.

"Thank you for coming for me." All memories of the argument we had in the hotel room, the betrayal her truth had caused me, have faded. When you're kidnapped by a maniac intent on killing you, you don't tend to hold onto grudges as much.

"Of course. Did you...did you see him?"

I know who she's asking after. And I really want to tell her that no, it wasn't Father who kidnapped me. That he's long dead and he can't hurt her anymore. But I can't do that. I can't lie to her.

"Yes. I met Father."

She pales and her nose pinches at the bridge as she pulls in a deep breath, trying to stop the panic from engulfing her.

"So, he's here then. Okay."

I don't have the words to comfort her, and I don't want to tell her all that he said because that will only cause her more fear. Besides, we're safe now. She told Jones we were safe here. And so long as we don't leave, we'll stay that way.

There are bound to be some soldiers in the

Network that can track Father now he's made himself known, they'll be able to deal with him and finally Karma can be free of her nightmare. Jones is probably making calls already organising that.

"I need to tell you something," she begins and my mind races with possibilities. The last time she had to tell me something, she brought the world crashing down around my ears, I'm not sure I'm strong enough yet for her to do it again.

"Karma, can we not? I just need to not, right now." I plead, but she's already up on her feet, rummaging through a filing cabinet.

She brings a folder towards me, takes a deep breath, and puts it on the desk in front of me. She nods at it, desperate for me to open the mauve coloured cardboard and see her latest truth for myself.

I don't want to.

I really don't want to. I'm exhausted, mentally, physically, and emotionally.

And yet the journalistic side of my brain is screaming out at my fingers, telling them to clasp the thin material and reveal Karma's truth. Throwing a tantrum so heavy in my brain, I worry that it will cause a migraine if I don't obey.

So I do.

With trepidation, I peel back the cover and the first thing I see is a photograph of Mr. Williams. Kind, sweet, always supportive Mr. Williams. The teacher who encouraged me to make my mark on the world. Who didn't shy away from my blossoming interest in true crime and try to steer me towards something more palatable for a young girl. Who, up until he was murdered by the Network, listened to every episode of my podcast from its inception and offered me words of motivation each time.

On the photograph of Mr. Williams is a name

scribbled in Sharpie.

Ian.

But that wasn't his name.

His name was Graham Williams. He was a secondary school teacher in my home town who always saw the best in his students. His wife baked everyone birthday cookies so no child was left uncelebrated. He received a medal from the mayor for his acts of service in the community, for Christ's sake.

"Ian was one of the founding members of The Farm." Karma says, and once again her words tear my truths in two.

Chapter Forty-Six: Zoe

"It's not true," are the first words from my mouth. And I hate myself for them because I should at least let her explain why she thinks he's a monster before I disparage what she's got to say. Maybe then I can get her to see the error of the Network's ways and they can clear his name. His widow can go back to her life and everyone will be able to remember him as the man he was.

"Ian. Owen. Paula. Trish. I'll never forget their names. They were the inner circle that helped Father build and maintain The Farm. Owen oversaw recruitment. Paula was Father's right-hand woman. Trish dealt with punishments. And Ian ran the mating ceremonies."

Ian. Graham.

Mr. Williams.

Ran the mating ceremonies. The evening orgies where children were forced to partake in unspeakable acts. Picked like cattle from a line-up and taken away to be abused.

Mr. Williams oversaw that?

He couldn't have.

He's too kind to have done that.

She's made a mistake.

She must have.

"You'll find DNA evidence in that folder that matches him as the father of several of the survivors from The Farm. We have the same evidence on all of them. It's why it wasn't my story to tell. None of them ever hurt me, or raped me, Father wouldn't let them. But they hurt my siblings and it's not my place to publicly announce that."

"It can't be true," are the second words out of my mouth. Because I believe her, but I don't want to. What she's telling me doesn't align with my own experience of the man. It's jarring to imagine him doing those God-awful things, but the evidence is right here before me, he did do them. And by all that I've heard about The Farm he enjoyed doing them.

The man was a monster in sheep's clothing.

"I'm sorry, Zoe," she apologises for my emotions. And I'm struck by how selfish I'm being. She's apologising to me, when she's the one who lived through a hell created with the help of Mr. Williams. Ian.

"Karma," I take her hand, "you don't have to apologise to me. All you've done is tell the truth about him. You've done nothing wrong."

She smiles sadly, as though she only half believes what I'm saying. I wonder how she found the self-resolve to bite her tongue at the dinner we'd shared together, where I was talking about how sad I was about my teacher's death. She must have been desperate to open my eyes to the truth but allowed me to keep them shut out of loyalty to her family.

Jones chooses this moment to reappear, a cup of tea in one hand and a small plate of biscuits in the other. She takes in the scene of me and her sister and I notice a twinge of jealousy pull at her eyebrow. It flicks upwards just for a moment.

"Christ, you do look pale, here eat these," she says heading towards me, pausing in her steps only when she sees the open folder on the desk and Ian's face staring back at her.

"Karma, I thought we agreed?" she asks and the air becomes charged with irritation.

"Zoe knew him, Jones. Thought she knew him anyway. She had a right to know." Karma replies, taking the plate of biscuits from her sister and offering them to me.

The stillness in the room is destroyed as an alarm begins to sound. Jones looks over at Karma and the two of them freeze in panic.

"Someone's here," Karma says, looking at me as though I'll have the answers.

"They followed us! I TOLD YOU WE SHOULD HAVE KEPT DRIVING!" Jones is shouting at her sister, but as she does so she moves towards her and takes her hand. "We need to get down to the warehouse. The panic room is in there."

"We'll call for backup once we're in," Karma agrees and takes my hand with her free one. And then we run.

Our footsteps echo through empty corridors until we are in a large space, which must be the warehouse. There are unopened wooden crates lining the room in a methodical order. The venom. That must be the venom they use.

On the largest wall I can make out a giant list of names, but we're running too fast for me to read any of them properly. I do notice though that a great many have a line drawn through them. The targets. That's the list of the network's targets. I truly am in the viper's nest.

Just as we come into the centre of the room, I'm grabbed from behind and yanked away from Karma's gasp. She screams my name, but before I can match her tone, I'm hit three times in the stomach and all the oxygen in my body rushes out in one long swoop.

"Hello Karma," says a man's voice, and the world stops spinning,

Father is here.
Father has followed us.
We're all dead.

Chapter Forty-Seven: The Farm

He sent for Karma around 6 a.m., just as the sun had risen, knowing she hated mornings most of all. She never normally rose until nearly lunchtime, and even that was due to her being awoken. Father was certain that if she had the choice she would rarely leave his bed, and as much as he liked to tell himself it's because she cared about him, he knew it was more likely to be depressive episodes. Karma was prone to fits of melancholy just as her mother had been.

And what he once found endearing in Erin, he found irritating in her daughter. Karma was supposed to be better than the Mother who had come before her. She was supposed to be his successor, and she couldn't very well lead the congregation from bed. So every day like clockwork he demanded she be woken, bathed and delivered to his side with a smile upon her face. If he repeated the pattern often enough, it would become natural to her, second nature, and then he could begin teaching her all that he had to impart.

When she'd been a baby, he held her in his arms and had seen their whole future together. Except back then he imagined it to be a bump-free journey they'd take together hand-in-hand. He hadn't imagined she'd be so resistant to his teachings or indeed to him. In his dreams, she welcomed him into her arms and her mind, insisting passionately that he was the only person she needed in this life or the next. He never imagined that even a fraction of her heart would belong to another.

And yet it did.

As he waited for Karma to be delivered to his office, he regarded the young girl before him who lay bound on the floor. She stared up at him with a steely gaze. In another life he would have admired her resilience, her lack of fear, but in this life he hated it.

He wanted her to cower before him, to beg his forgiveness for trying to tempt Karma from him. To shake so hard with nerves that the ropes cut into her skin.

But she lay as still as a statue, simply staring at him.

Part of him wished he'd insisted on a blindfold for her, but he wanted Karma to be able to make eye contact with her one true friend as he issued this personal beating. He wanted her to see the love fade from her friend's eyes as the two of them learnt what the cost of their secret bond would be.

He wasn't going to kill the girl - as much as he wanted to last night whilst she slept.

The fact of the matter was that she was soon to turn eleven, which meant she would be of child bearing age, and he needed the congregation's numbers to continue to swell.

Unfortunately, most of the babies who had been born in recent years had been male, and as much as he needed soldiers behind him, he also needed nurturers. The ones who would bear the next generation of the congregation. So no, he couldn't kill her. But he could hurt her, and he was intending to do so. And once she was healed, he would be sure she was the main attraction of the mating ceremonies; the sooner she was pregnant then the sooner she had worth to him once again. The sooner he could view her as a commodity as opposed to a betrayal.

Karma barely flinched when she walked into the room and spotted her friend bound and gagged on the floor. There was a slight curl of her fingers into her palm that Father spotted and that was the final confirmation he needed that her heart had been ridden with disease. Sinful disease that prevented it from belonging solely to him.

Something about that movement broke him. Red mist descended across him, and for the first time in a long time, he struck Karma. An open-handed slap across the face that knocked her to the floor, so nothing major, but still it was a line he had never crossed with Erin. He never had to cross it with Erin. Dear, sweet, obedient Erin who had somehow managed to bring into the world a child the polar opposite of herself. Not for the first time Father wondered if God had let the wrong person die that night.

Rather than apologising for his temper though, Father turned his attention elsewhere. It would do him no good to take his anger out on Mother. She was an innocent victim in this. Corrupted by the demon on his floor.

He no longer saw the young girl as human. As a vessel for the expansion of his congregation. As something that needed to be preserved.

Instead, he saw a beast laying before him. An insect that needed to be ground out before it spread its poison around his people.

With this in mind, Father lifted the chair that lay at his desk from its home, surprised by his own strength as he did so, and he brought it crashing down upon the demon's back. He could hear a muffled scream from behind the gag as the satisfying snap of bones shot through his ears. This was good. This was what he needed to do. This is what God wanted him to do. God had sent him this girl, this monster, to provide him with an outlet for the frustration he felt towards Karma.

He shouldn't lash out at Karma. God had chosen her to replace Erin, to become Mother. So the girl on the floor was the conduit for his rage that Heaven had sent. And he was grateful.

In fact, he was so grateful, he shouted his thanks as he brought the chair down on the monster once again. It splintered as it crashed against her legs this time and he picked up one of the splintered pieces, holding it firmly in his hands he beat down against her flesh again and again until blood splattered all over his face.

It felt warm and right across his skin and so he continued until the screaming in the room faded around him. Until he had paused to catch his breath.

Father had lost control. And it had felt wonderful.

Chapter Forty-Eight: Karma

Karma has been thrown back into the past at the sound of his voice.

At the sound of Father.

Her legs feel hollow, and her arms feel heavy; every pint of her blood screams out at her to flee. To escape from the monster before he becomes reality. She takes in his aged face, despite the addition of facial hair he looks exactly as she remembers.

Crazed.

Dangerous.

Terrifying.

It's his eyes.

Those eyes that have haunted her every night for decades.

The eyes that used to gaze down on her as he held her down for their nightly ritual.

The eyes that had gleamed with blood lust as he tried to beat Jones to death in front of her.

The eyes that had sparkled with ego as his congregation listened to him speak with bated breath.

For so many years she'd wanted to reach into his skull and pluck those eyes from their stalks with her bare hands. She'd fantasised about holding them, squeezing them until they popped, the feeling of the liquid slipping through her fingers.

But now.

Now he was here in the flesh.

With his eyes.

Those fucking eyes.

And she couldn't move. She could barely breathe.

This wasn't how it was supposed to go. She practiced what she'd say to him over and over. How she'd verbalise all the pain he had caused her and others. How she hurt him with the truth of their relationship, that he was nothing more than a twisted predator and she hated every moment they'd shared together.

But the words would not come.

There were other people in the room, Jones and Zoe, but she wasn't aware of them and neither was he. They only had eyes for each other.

"My darling girl," he spoke with a softness she'd forgotten about. In all of the memories she'd clung to over the years he was angry. Always angry.

She'd forgotten the tenderness he also showed her.

The way he held her when she scraped her knee.

The kind words of encouragement he'd give as the two of them sat together night after night and he taught her to read.

The cake he snuck her after all the other children had been sent to bed without any supper for some minor infraction. He hadn't wanted her to starve, because she mattered to him.

She mattered to him.

All along he told her that she was special to him, that she was important to him.

And she'd forgotten all of that.

She'd forgotten the man behind the monster.

He was a man.

He was just a man.

Not a monster.

Not something to fear.

He was flesh and blood like her.

Flesh that had pushed itself where it was unwanted.

Flesh that had helped bring her into the world.

"Hello Father," she replies, finally having forced her voice from her chest.

Looking to her left, she finally notices the man standing behind Jones, with a knife to her throat. To her right, Zoe is cowering on the floor, having been struck in the stomach as Father made his entrance.

"Did you miss me?" he asks, no irony in his tone.

He didn't care to wait for her response, as he now turned his attention to Jones. Karma wanted to run into the space between the two of them, to help her sister now to make up for the past. And yet her legs wouldn't obey. Her survival instinct wouldn't allow her to move closer to Father. Because her entire mind knew that if she did, she wouldn't leave his side alive.

"And you! What a surprise to see you again, Jones. I could have sworn I killed you a while back." He waves his hand at the man holding the knife who retracts it slightly, whilst still holding a tight grip on Jones' arms.

"Should have done a better job, I guess," she taunts and Karma wants to call out to her. To tell her to behave. If she's a good girl and behaves, then Father will be happy, and if Father is happy then they are all safe.

He reaches out and clutches Jones by the chin, moving her head to the right and left as he surveys her.

"I barely left any scars," he says, admiring his past handiwork.

"Not that you can see," she replies.

Karma calls out to Father, aware that she needs to break his focus on her sister, and needs to bring his attention back to her. Despite how terrified it makes her feel.

She hates him.

She knows that she hates him.

And yet...

And yet he was Father. And she was raised to be Mother.

For eleven years she lived by his side. His company, her main source of companionship day in, day out.

She watches as he walks towards her, slowly, he's taking his time, enjoying the family reunion. She wants to run. She longs to run away and hide behind the sofa until this nightmare is over.

But she can't.

All she can do is stand still whilst the monster descends upon her.

She barely shudders as his hands place themselves on her cheeks and he leans forward and places a soft kiss on her forehead.

"Get away from her!" screams Jones as she struggles against her captors' hold.

"But she's what I came for." He rests his forehead against hers and looks into Karma's eyes. She returns his gaze, the vision growing hazy. This couldn't be happening. Not again.

"I know that the Network was just your way of getting my attention, pet, and I've listened. I've come back to life for you."

"Where have you been?" asks Karma, her hands moving up towards his face to echo his stance.

"I've always been there, darling. I never left you, not really. I forgive you for what you did. For leaving. You were so young, it was a stupid decision and I forgive you." He smiles as she thumbs his cheeks, wiping away the happy tears that were trickling down his face.

"Thank you, Father," Karma replies, her words soft

against the yells and expletives being flung towards them from Jones.

They'd always worried about how Karma would react to seeing him again in the flesh. Numerous conversations about Stockholm Syndrome and they had agreed that it should be Jones who dealt with him, because if Karma saw him again there was a risk she would revert to the young subservient girl she had been under his guidance. That he had broken her mind in places she couldn't ever have hoped to repair. That she would become Mother again.

And now he was here. Their moment of confrontation had been hijacked, and Jones wasn't in control. Father was. Just like old times.

"I forgive you for killing the others, truth be told. Your mother never truly liked any of them, so it makes sense that you wouldn't either." Now his lips were edging towards hers, the lover's reunion kiss he'd been waiting decades for.

Paula. Ian. Owen. Trish.

All of them had been targeted by the Network, and soon their crimes would be revealed to the nation.

Soon the irrefutable evidence that they partook in the rape of children would be revealed by the release of the DNA of their victims. DNA that would prove they brought children to life, the children who had escaped from the fire, the children who now grown would know that their nightmares were finally dead.

His lips on Karma's were tender and loving. Just as they always had been. His kiss spoke of promise, of forgiveness and of hope. Hope that his new world order could finally be complete, that he could finally ascend to his higher place once he had fulfilled his purpose on this planet.

His lips.

That shouldn't be on hers.

(a girl called) Karma

That should never have been on hers.

The two of them stared at each other, the moment, no care for the yelling or scre them.

"Fuck you," whispers Karma as her thumbs found his eye sockets and she pressed down.

Chapter Forty-Nine: The Farm

Father panted for oxygen as he finally let the splintered chair leg drop to the floor. By now it was more flesh than wood and he turned back towards the doorway to his office, ready to explain his actions to Karma. Knowing she would understand that she left him no choice.

Paula was standing by Karma's side, her hands firm on the young girl's shoulders. As though she had been holding her back, which couldn't be right as that would mean Karma didn't understand that Father had to kill the demon that had come between them. And that was impossible. He'd done this for her, for them, for the greater good - she had to see that.

Karma's eyes were red and dry, it was quite possible that she'd been crying as she witnessed the torture she'd put him through but for now she was stoic. Her lips, which were so much like her mother's, were down-turned in a frown, but she spoke no unkind words to him. He was grateful, as he didn't know how he'd cope in the face of her ingratitude right now.

Did she think he wanted to beat the demon to death?

No.

He came into this situation determined to let the other girl live, aware of her importance to his grander scheme.

But he had to end her life for Karma. So Karma would stay on the righteous path. On his path.

And if she hadn't been able to see that whilst he undertook his gruelling work then he may have lashed out at her again, and he truly didn't want to do that. So for the first time, in a long time, he was grateful for Paula's presence in his life. Despite the horrified look upon her face.

"Clean this up," he said and Paula stepped forward dutifully.

"Not you. Her."

Karma finally looked him directly in the eye and she nodded once. She would be obedient. She would do what needed to be done.

Paula insisted on helping, explaining that the child couldn't be trusted to make sure this death went unnoticed. And she was right. Paula did have more experience in cleaning up blood than Karma and so Father agreed. Pleased that the two women in his life who had been causing him so much grief were finally getting the message.

"Karma must dispose of her alone. You need to learn to bury your mistakes."

Once again, his protege nodded. A beautiful, singular acknowledgment that he was leading her down the right path.

Father couldn't be more pleased with how the morning had gone.

Chapter Fifty: Zoe

For as long as I live I don't think I'll forget the sound that Father's making right now. It's raw, and anguished and if you could bottle the sound of pain I think that would be it.

The agony from the jab to the stomach he gave me is finally fading, and I can breathe again. Which is a good thing, as I'm about to do something that's going to require my brain to think logically enough to do something stupid.

Jones is on the floor now, having been tossed aside by the man who was holding her captive.

The man who is now running towards Karma, rage contorting his features as he raises the knife in her direction.

I can't let him kill her.

I can't.

I glance at Jones, she's not moving, she can't help. No one else can help.

So I scream. I scream with the power of a hundred wronged women and charge at the man, who turns to look at me, stunned by the noise emanating from my lungs. I don't stop running, I don't even pause my pace as he turns his body towards me and growls.

A grown man shouldn't growl.

It's an utterly ridiculous noise. One that's clearly meant to frighten me into submission. Into stopping in my tracks and cowering before him.

I am so done being afraid of men like this.

The ones who think that because they are bigger, they are superior.

The ones who get a kick out of walking closely behind a woman walking home alone.

The ones who aggressively hit on bar staff because they know they won't face any ramifications.

Who laugh loudly and obnoxiously at the aging stand-up comedians routine about foreigners. Who think the world owes them something, that people, women, owe them something simply because they have a dangling appendage between their legs. Who proudly take to the streets and riot when the colour of a perpetrator's skin matches their agenda, but stays silent when it's one of 'their own.' Men like this have no place in a decent society, and I'm so done with making exceptions for them.

It's not all men.

But it is this one.

Which is why I find the bravery and strength to slam my body straight into his midsection. He folds a lot easier than I expected, crumpling to the ground below me, the threat to Karma neutralised.

Shit.

The knife.

I forgot about the knife.

It spins out of his hands as we hit the floor together, my chin bouncing into his, causing a ricochet of pain to vibrate down my neck.

"Fucking bitch," he screams at me as he pushes my chest away from his and punches me in the nose. Blood fills my throat at the impact but I can't let him get the knife.

It's all over if I let him get the knife.

I bring my knee up to his groin, up to that precious appendage that gives him the feeling of power and superiority and I bring it down between his legs as hard as I'm able. He screams in pain, far louder than I yelled when he hit me in the nose. I guess I've achieved what I wanted.

"How could you do this to me? Again? After everything I did for you." Father is speaking to Karma now, but I can't focus my vision enough to see them. The concussion from the blow to my face is setting in. She doesn't reply, doesn't hit back with a witty retort and my blood turns to ice. Instead I can hear the soft sounds of breath being choked out. He's strangling her. I can just about make out his frame leaning over hers.

How is he still standing? The woman took his God damn eyes and yet he's still standing.

Maybe he really is a higher being.

Maybe we've been doomed since the moment he walked through the door.

The man below me has regained his composure, I know this because he punches me in the face once again. This time hard enough to knock me off of him.

The ceiling above me is swimming, twirling in patterns I know are unnatural. I try to sit up but my arms have lost their strength.

I need to get to Karma.

I need to save her before Father chokes the life out of her.

The man is muttering to himself, calling me all sorts of words as he stumbles to a standing position. I listen, detached, as he feels around on the floor. The sound of the knife scraping against a hard surface as he finally grasps its hilt.

Soon, very soon, he will be upon me. He'll straddle

me and then stab the life from me. He'll want to watch the life leave my eyes, want to be bathed in my blood, he'll want to make this kill as personal as possible because I've shamed him. By attacking him, by stopping him, by fighting him, I have shamed him, and for that I will be murdered.

And Karma will die here. They will find our bodies in this makeshift headquarters, maybe soon, most likely not. And they will wonder what happened. What could possibly have happened that led to the murder of a podcaster and her client?

A small smile tugs at the irony of my future.

Where once I reported on cases of true crime, now others will report on mine. I will be the subject where once I had been the narrator.

Will they uncover the truth of what happened here? Will anyone be brought to justice?

Unlikely, given Father never answered for the crimes relating to The Farm. Karma will be killed by the man who brought her into the world, a man who knows how to disappear and stay hidden for decades. And the man who will shortly end my life is one of his foot soldiers, so he'll be just as protected.

We'll just be a statistic. Two more unsolved murders of women who should have known better.

I can feel the pressure of the man's body as he straddles me. He wants me to feel the full weight of him pressing down upon me, wants me to feel as helpless as possible. He wants nothing but fear to be running through my veins in my final moments.

But it isn't fear I feel. It's anger.

Anger at the unfairness of the world.

Anger that Father has been allowed to roam free for all these years, aided by God knows who.

Anger that my capture led to him finding Jones & Karma's hideout. That led to their downfall.

Anger that Karma is going to die today. A woman who survived so much horror that she deserved to live the best life possible. And that's going to be taken from her.

I'm so angry.

So fucking angry.

The man is pressing the knife to my throat now. I can feel its cool sharpness making friends with my skin. He's dragging this out for as long as possible. Wanting to punish me in this world as much as he can.

That will be his mistake.

I scream once again. Scream with all the rage left inside of me and bring my arms up to clasp his.

He isn't quick enough, didn't use enough pressure when he had the chance, when I wasn't fighting back and although I feel a slight cut as the knife penetrates my skin, I manage to push it away from my throat before he can make the fatal incision.

I am not going to die today.

I am not going to be a victim today.

I am going to fight with everything I have left.

And I am going to win.

There's another scream in the room now.

A female one.

Jones.

I feel the air move past me as she runs to Karma and Father.

I hear the sound of raised voices as she leaps onto his back, dragging him off her sister. Saving her life.

I hope she saved her life.

I hope with all that I have that she got there on time.

The commotion has distracted my attacker, drawn his attention from the battle with me and his grip on the knife loosens. He only has one hand on it now.

Without thinking through the consequences, I

lunge, pushing the blade away from me, his arm in my hand as I plunge it into his chest all the way to the hilt.

His eyes go wide and he pulls it out. A fatal mistake.

Blood gushes from the wound and I can hear the sound of air hissing as it escapes his lungs. He stumbles backwards, knife still in his hand, attention flicking between the blood-soaked blade and me.

I'm hot and damp, pints of blood already seeping through my clothes and settling on my skin. Blood that I'll never be clean from.

He collapses to the floor and I sit up.

I should help him.

I should apply pressure to the wound, call an ambulance, and administer some form of CPR maybe.

But I don't.

I sit and watch as blood ebbs and flows out of his body and he dies.

I killed a man.

I killed him.

Chapter Fifty-One: The Farm

On Karma's eleventh birthday, Father gave her a gift.

The ability to stay unchained and lucid on mating night.

The rest of the children were tied in the shed, as they always were. Ready to be picked and kept quiet with a small sedative. Forced to be compliant if they weren't naturally. Children were too young to see the bigger picture. It had always been that way at The Farm. It was one of the rules the founding members had drawn up.

Erin, Owen, Trish, Paula, and Peter had all been so young when everything started. All in their late teens or early twenties when they began their journey together. And so much has been achieved over the last twenty years. And despite the loss of Erin and Trish to childbirth, they had managed to grow the membership of The Farm to 800 members now. All of which hung on every word from Father's mouth.

And yet it wasn't enough for Father.

He didn't enjoy ruling over the congregation alone. He missed the other half to his soul.

Erin had been the only one whom Father had ever

truly listened to. The only one whose opinion on their new world truly mattered. Not that she'd ever had a differing opinion from his own in the time they spent together, but if she had then Father was sure he would have listened to her concerns and taken them on board. Because he had loved her. Truly and deeply he had loved her.

Which was perhaps why Karma had come to mean so much to him.

Why she deserved special treatment on this important birthday of hers. Soon her blood would come in and she would become the vessel he deserved.

With Mother back by his side then Father knew he would be unstoppable, and he knew that one day, very soon, the girl would be ready to happily accept her fate as his official companion.

Since that unfortunate incident that had resulted in the death of Karma's only true friend, she had become the perfect companion. Always attentive to his needs. Willing to do whatever it took to make him happy. The young girl was blossoming into the kind of partner Father required for his new world order to succeed. And he couldn't have been happier.

It's why what happened next wounded him so very deeply.

Chapter Fifty-Two: Zoe

I'm shaking.

I'm shaking so hard that I can't stand up. I want to collapse on the floor and pass out with shock but I can't.

Because it's not over yet. This nightmare isn't close to finishing, so despite the horror at my own actions seeping into my muscles, I stand.

I stand because Karma needs me to stand. Jones needs me to stand. Father is still alive, the threat against us is still real and I haven't come this far to give up on them now.

I hadn't meant to kill the man attacking me.
Had I?

No, I just wanted to save myself; that's why I pushed back so hard against him. That's why I didn't pause when I felt the resistance of muscle against the blade or when I felt the warm trickle of blood gushing over my hand.

I didn't stop because I was just trying to save myself.

I didn't mean to kill him.
Did I?

The shouts of rage between Jones and Father

prevent me from sinking any further into shock and I pull myself to my feet. The two of them are lashing out at each other, with the full force of their fury. Fists, feet, and words fly between them - accompanied by grunts when something lands.

I take a step towards them, ready to help Jones overpower the man behind this nightmare, when I catch sight of Karma. Lying on the floor. No sign of life emanating from her chest.

No.

No. It isn't possible.

The yell that stems from within my chest is the closest thing to a wail I've ever heard and although I want to run to her side, my feet are heavy and drag behind me, slowing me down, attempting to keep me from the inevitable heartache that her death will bring.

After everything that woman has survived, this can't be how her story ends. Dying at the hands of the man who caused all of her trauma. It can't end like this. The universe isn't that cruel. It can't be.

I fall to the floor and for a moment, just a tiny moment, I stare at her.

It's like she's Snow White, suspended in time, waiting for her Prince Charming to arrive. But he isn't coming. There is only me. I drag my eyes away from her resting face and before I wonder whether she's better off being left at peace, I place my hands on her chest and start compressions.

I feel the crack of her ribs and I know I'm applying the right amount of pressure. Somehow, despite the panic racing through me, I manage to count to thirty and then move towards her face. I pinch her nose shut and place my lips upon hers.

The last time this happened was in the hotel room. Just after she'd confessed to running the Network, after she'd unburdened herself of all of her truths. Now her lips are cold and clammy. Devoid of any life, let alone secrets.

I exert two deep breaths into her lungs before returning to compressions.

This has to work.

She has to live.

On the third round of compressions, finally her chest begins to move of their own accord.

She's alive.

She's alive.

She's alive.

She splutters, wretches and heaves - and it's the most glorious sounds I've ever heard.

I place a hand under her head to support her whilst her eyes regain focus. The deep red marks around her throat are angry and raw, he really did try to squeeze the life out of her. And he'd succeeded, at least temporarily.

"Jones," I cry out, wanting to let her know that her sister is alive. To share the good news that Karma is safe and still with us.

My biggest mistake.

Father takes advantage of his opponent's drop in concentration and with a grunt he lunges at Jones, knocking her off her feet and onto the floor. The thud as her head hits the concrete echoes in the room around us.

A sob catches in Karma's throat, a single word lodged behind sadness.

Jones.

Chapter Fifty-Three: The Farm

It didn't take long for news of Karma's disappearance to reach Father's ears, and when it did his heart shattered.

He'd truly believed the girl had grown to love him in the same way Mother had, so much so that initially he dispatched his Level Three and Four workers to scour the settlement and bring anyone who'd ever shown a passing interest in his special girl to him. Certain that jealousy had caused someone to kidnap her, to steal her from him.

She couldn't have left of her own free will.

She wouldn't.

When three hours of torture upon the relevant parties had passed, Father knew the truth.

She had escaped the Settlement. Disappeared into the night, and soon all that he'd spent twenty years building would come crashing down.

The outside world wasn't ready to accept his teachings yet, he knew that. He knew that those outside of his congregation would show disgust and horror at the things he and his followers had to do to bring about a better society. He could already hear the words they would throw his way.

Abuser.
Psychopath.
Paedophile.
Cult leader.

So many hateful little words that would tear apart the important work he'd dedicated his life to. And it wasn't time yet for his ascension; he could feel it in his bones. It wasn't time for him to usurp God and watch over the planet from afar. No. Father had to live. Peter had to live so he could keep his important work going. So he could show humanity that there was a better, fairer way to live.

Within five hours of Karma's escape, the Settlement was emptied of all adults. The children were too much of a burden to take with them, they would draw too much attention to whomever kept ownership of them, so they were left chained in the shed.

The idea to set fire to the shed had come from Owen and Ian. They pointed out that the children were the most damning physical evidence against them and Father had agreed. Their DNA could be used to make links to members of the congregation should any of them be stupid enough to get caught.

Paula had briefly argued against the three of them, claiming that the children would be easier to move than they assumed, but eventually she came round to the idea. In fact, she was the one who lit the flame right before the four of them left their settlement once and for all. Pausing on the outskirts to take in their failed new world.

Karma had ruined everything.

Karma would bring the police. Would bring scrutiny. Would bring hatred towards them and all of their loyal followers. All they could do was disappear into the night, with a vow to each other that although they would never be physically reunited, they would all remain spiritually connected in their fight for a better world.

Karma would be the downfall of a good and honest man.

And Father would kill her for it.

Chapter Fifty-Four: Karma

Karma is desperate to cry out to her sister, to let her know that she's still here and that she's coming to help. But the words are stuck behind a lump in her throat, a sign from the universe that her energy would be wasted.

Zoe is knelt by her side, her face a mix of relief and terror. Karma's chest hurts, a deep burning sensation that she knows has been caused by at least one broken rib.

It wasn't supposed to happen like this.

None of this was supposed to happen.

They'd spent decades planning Father's execution. Putting even more energy into it than they had the creation of the Network. Father may believe that the Network was all about him but he couldn't be further from the truth.

The Medusa Network had been born because of what they lived through at his hands, true. But it had not been created to bring about his downfall. That was a side mission for the sisters. The Network's purpose had always been about gaining justice for those society had failed. To extinguish the monsters that walk amongst us. It had never been about Father or The Farm. It had never been about Karma or Jones seeking revenge on those who had wronged them, it had been about seeking revenge for others who needed it. When those two missions crossed paths, yes, it was useful, but Medusa was about so much more than the two of them.

Medusa would live on without the two of them.

One of them.

Jones.

Karma knew that her twin had died. She'd known it the second she heard the thud of Jones' skull on the floor because she'd felt a piece of herself disappear into the ether. She was finally all alone in the world, and it felt terrible.

Zoe. There was still time to save Zoe. Sweet, empathetic Zoe. The woman whose voice she'd fallen in love with upon discovering her podcasts. Ending every difficult day with an episode, enjoying the sound of the lilt in her voice as she shared some of the worst stories imaginable. Zoe was a good person, and Karma couldn't let Father take her, too.

"Run," she rasped out to the woman who was still kneeling by her side, blissfully unaware of the beast that was regaining power just feet from them. They had to act now before he recovered from his fight with Jones. This was Karma's only chance to do the right thing.

It was now or never.

With this in mind, she found the strength to push herself up onto her elbows, ignoring Zoe's kind offer of assistance. She needed her to leave, and the only way she would do that is if Karma showed her the worst side of her.

"You've done enough." She made sure to lace her words with venom, wanting them to sting and poison the relationship between the two of them. "Go."

"I'm not leaving you," Zoe argued.

"None of this would have happened if he hadn't

followed you here. Jones would be alive if you'd never come here." It was all a lie; everything Karma was saying was a falsity. There wasn't a millimetre of her soul that blamed Zoe for what had befallen them all since they arrived back at head office. It had been Karma's choice to invite her into her life. Karma's choice to put her at risk. And Karma's choice to rescue her and bring her here.

Jones was dead because of Karma's impulsivity, and she wasn't about to let Zoe fall to the same fate.

Her words had their desired effect; she saw it in the way Zoe drew back into herself as though she'd been struck.

"That's not true," she protested, although there was no weight to her sentence. She didn't believe her own words. Guilt had already claimed her.

"Get out of here!" screamed Karma as she rose to her feet, one arm hugging her chest, easing the pressure on the bruised muscles within. With the other hand she pushed Zoe forcibly away from her, and her palm burned with shame as she drew it back into herself. There was a very real part of her that instantly wanted to apologise for the violent way in which she'd touched Zoe, but she couldn't allow her heart to rule her head.

Not this time.

She could hear Father chuckling between wheezes and she stole a glance towards him. He was pushing himself up from the ground, ready to fight again. There wasn't much time. Zoe needed to run and hide. If Karma wasn't successful, then she'd lose another part of herself. She'd be broken in a way she would never recover from.

"Just fuck off and leave me alone!" she said as she lunged towards Zoe again. But the podcaster was quicker than her and took a step backwards, avoiding Karma's outreached hands.

"Fuck you, Karma," she replied as she turned her back and walked away.

For every step she took away from Father, Karma managed to breathe a little easier. If Zoe had any sense, she would disappear and never look back. And if Karma had any sense, she'd kill Father, even if it meant ending her own life in the process.

Only one person was walking out of the warehouse alive today, and she just ensured that would be Zoe.

She didn't want to look at Jones, she didn't want to see her empty of the life that had sustained them both for so long.

Her sister had been the one who'd orchestrated their escape from The Farm. The one who had boosted her up and out of the window.

Paula had given Jones the chance to escape, leaving her front door unlocked when she went for a meeting with Father. It was Paula who had told Jones about the lapse in guards on the border, hoping the young girl would use the information to save her own life. But instead of rescuing herself, Jones had made her way to the barn, climbing through a window to save her sister Karma. Jones had no fear about the danger she was putting herself in by trying to find a better life for the two of them.

She'd been Karma's shadow as she walked alongside her, through the inky black night, to find salvation. And the two of them had exchanged cross words when Jones had insisted that Karma go alone to ring doorbells. Preferring to stay hidden in the shadows, excluded from a society that had turned its back on them for the duration of their childhood.

Growing up in her foster homes, Karma had always kept her eyes peeled for signs that her sister was still close by. Red ribbons tied to tree branches, fence posts, left on car windshields - all private notes from

Jones to Karma that she was still looking out for her. That she was always around.

No matter where they moved Karma in the country to, the ribbons followed.

The two of them were always together. Even when they were apart.

And it had been Jones who had been waiting by the side of Joanna's house when Karma found out her saviour, the only other person in the world to truly love her, had died. It had been Jones' arms she'd fallen apart in, arms that she'd missed for so many years.

But Karma had chosen a life in society. And Jones had not.

So once again, the two of them parted, but at least now they could speak openly to each other, or meet in a side street to avoid the growing publicity around Karma.

Where Karma had bounced from family to family, Jones had spent her time building up the kind of contacts most people avoid. Always working behind the scenes to make sure the plan they'd dreamt up on that long walk would come to fruition.

Even at eleven, the girls had known the adults who had abused them would get away with it. And they knew, instinctively, that there was evil outside of The Farm too. Because evil doesn't just exist in small pockets, it's everywhere people are, seeping its way through cracks and hurting those who were most vulnerable.

So they dreamt up the Medusa Network.

A way to punish the guilty. A form of therapy for survivors like them. Karma was in charge of building up her persona, making the nation fall in love with her and open their pockets. And Jones was in charge of finding those who could help, and those who needed help. By the time she comforted Karma on Joanna's doorstep ,she had already executed several targets and recruited troops to help with their work.

Nobody noticed the first victims. There was nothing to link them to each other. They were experiments as the venom was worked on and perfected.

Jones had always been there. And now the ribbon between them was severed.

And Karma didn't know how she was going to keep on living.

She knew she'd still search for red ribbons wherever she went if she made it out of this last interaction with Father, and she'd made sure it was the last interaction. She'd never quite believe Jones had died, there would always be a part of her that would hope it was a ruse. A mistake.

So no. She wouldn't look at the body.

She couldn't.

Because then she couldn't hold onto the hope that her sister was still out there.

That her sister was somewhere happy.

That her sister would come back to her one day.

Chapter Fifty-Five: Karma

Father's eyes were very badly damaged.

So much so that Karma was surprised he'd managed to put up as much fight as he had with Jones, then again, she knew better than to underestimate him. She just wished she'd been able to pop his damn eyeballs when she had the chance. It should have been muscle memory, given the number of times she fantasised about it as he lay on top of her in his bed. If her arms had been just a little longer, if she'd been a little stronger, she could have done it as a child and saved herself a lifetime of pain.,

Regrets.

That's what Karma felt at that moment.

Not rage. Yes, there was anger in her heart, but it was tinged with regrets for all she could have done, should have done in the past.

She should have escaped sooner.

She should have stepped in when Father was beating Jones, breaking free of Paula's grasp.

She should have killed him at every opportunity she had.

She should have hunted him down the moment she turned eighteen.

But she hadn't done any of those things.

Because those weren't the choices that had been available to her.

She'd just been a child when he'd been present in her life.

But she wasn't a child anymore. And she wasn't Mother anymore.

She was Medusa.

And Medusa always punishes the guilty.

Chapter Fifty-Six: Zoe

Words have never wounded me the way Karma's just did.

Jones was dead because of me. Because she and Karma had to come and rescue me from Father.

It was all my fault.

She'd put into words everything that had been running through my head since Father's arrival at HQ. It was all my fault.

She wasn't wrong. That's the truth of it. If I didn't agree with her then her words wouldn't have had the emotional impact they did. I may as well have killed Jones myself. I signed her death warrant.

Drowning in anger, I've already reached the main doors of the building, not realising how quick I'd been to walk away from her. To walk away from the danger she was still in.

She wanted me to leave.

She'd told me to leave.

She'd given me every reason to leave.

My feet stop before my brain has processed my thoughts.

She wanted me to leave.

She wanted me to leave.

She sent me away.

To save me.

Because she doesn't intend to walk out of this building alive. And she wanted to make sure I did.

How could I be so stupid? I'd reacted exactly as she'd needed me to. I'd left her. I turned away from her, exactly what I'd promised I would never do when we first sat down to record her podcast. She'd been so afraid to show me the truth of her life, of herself. Conditioned by a lifetime of people turning away from her truths, preferring to keep their mental health in check rather than accept her for who she was - trauma and all.

I won't do that to her.

I can't do that to her.

As much as part of me wants to keep walking out of the exit, to pretend none of this has ever happened, to return to my flat and my own safe, barely traumatised life, I can't. I can't leave her behind. She deserves better. She means too much to me to forget she ever happened.

I run back towards the warehouse, the sound of my thumping feet the only noise around, spurring me into moving as quickly as humanly possible.

As I skid back into the room I notice the glint of the knife in Father's hand behind his back as he looms towards Karma.

There's so much distance between us.

But I have to try.

I have to try and save her.

Chapter Fifty-Seven: Karma

She wasn't sure what had just happened, but she was covered in blood. Drenched in it. And surprisingly, it wasn't any of hers.

Father was knelt on the floor, arms desperately clinging to her legs as a knife lay protruding from his side. He looked up at her, through his hazy and bloodshot eyes and she heard the whisper of a beg on his lips.

"Forgive me, my child."

His voice was raspy and full of pain.

Good.

Standing behind him was Zoe. Sweet, beautiful, innocent Zoe, whose face was a mask of disgust.

She was staring down at Father, daggers in her eyes and her fists were by her side clenched. She stabbed him. She came back for Karma, despite what she said to her, and she stabbed the monster from Karma's childhood.

"You're going to prison for a long, long time," Zoe whispered at him as he murmured in agony, his eyes never leaving Karma's, never leaving Mother's.

"Help me, please," he begged between staggered breaths. Zoe scoffs in disgust but still begins looking around for something to stem the bleeding with. Because she's a good person.

Zoe is a good person.

And Karma is not.

With a flourish, she leans down, ignoring the way Father paws at her as she does so, and she places her hand around the knife. With one sharp tug, it's removed from his flesh and she hears his lungs sigh with release - now they are free to leak without any pesky blade in the way.

"What are you doing?" cries Zoe, though she knows.

Without giving a response, Karma kicks Father to the floor away from her, and then, without pause she's circling him, practically licking her lips. This is how it was always going to end, inevitably. No matter how well she and Jones had planned, no matter the revenge they'd dreamt up, this was how things between her and Father were going to end.

There would be no fanfare, no poetry in his end. No slow numbing of each of his extremities as they injected a lesser venom into each part. No recording of his last gurgled breath as he choked, that would be shared with any of his victims who wanted hard evidence he was finally dead.

No.

Fate didn't want that to be how Father's story ended.

That was more than he deserved.

If they'd killed him like that, he would be remembered. People would talk about his death, some may even feel sorry for the end he met. Because those people would never understand the pain he had inflicted on the children of The Farm - because they hadn't lived it.

Those liberal do-gooders would find some way to

paint his death as a tragedy. Whispering in pubs across the country amongst themselves that 'no one' deserved to go out the way they originally planned.

Their original plan had been cruel, and long, and drawn out over many days. They would take him to the point of death fifty times, one for each of the children who escaped The Farm. Pushing him and his body to the point of shutting down, before reviving him and doing it over and over again.

She and Jones had spent so many nights researching how much pressure a human body could take, sourcing adrenaline to restart his heart if needed and daydreaming about his screams.

But that wasn't what was going to happen.

That was too good for him.

If Karma enacted the plans by herself now, then he would know just how great an impact he'd made on her life. He would die knowing how much she'd been consumed by her hatred for him.

And she couldn't have that.

She wouldn't allow him that.

So she knelt down, silently ignoring all the ways he was trying to engage with her. His words melted into silence and she knocked his hand away every time he reached out for her.

The blade slid easily into his leg, she made sure to cut deeply enough to cause pain, but not so deep she would slice an artery. He was already bleeding out from the wound on his side and she didn't want to give him a quick escape from this world.

Over and over, she sliced at his flesh like a surgeon, until he was more cuts than man. Her hands were tacky with his blood, but her grip on the knife never wavered.

If Zoe had tried to speak to her during those minutes, Karma hadn't been aware. She was in a trance, her hands being guided by an outside force.

Love.

The love she had for Jones. For all of her siblings from The Farm.

She pictured each of their faces as she cut his flesh apart and listened to his cries. She remembered all the children who hadn't escaped, those he had sacrificed for whatever reason. The ones who weren't deemed worthy enough for reproduction. The ones who were worked to death. All under the guise of his better world.

He was going into shock now. She noticed the colour draining from his skin. It was surprising he was even still conscious, but he was a stubborn man like that. Probably still clinging to the hope that he could talk his way out of this situation. Fool.

Karma squatted down over his chest, not wanting to rest upon his body, not wanting to touch him with anything other than the blade.

She stares straight through him as she uses the knife to slice open the thin fabric that's protecting his chest from the world. By now he's lying in a puddle of his own blood from his wounds, he's nearly ready to move on. She just has one more thing to do.

The knife slides easily into his chest, lubricated by his own blood, and she peels back the layers of skin until she's staring at his chest muscles.

He's dead now.

She knows he is.

She felt him leave the room, felt the freeing calmness that came alongside it. Finally, she was free. Finally, she was safe.

But she had to be sure.

She hacks at his breastbone, flesh burying itself under her fingernails. Now she can touch him. Now he is nothing more than a body.

The ribs though are trickier than she'd expected. No matter how hard she pulls she can not get them apart. She can not get to his heart. She wants to hold it in her hand, to feel its stillness and know in all certainty that it's over.

"Karma," Zoe's voice cuts through the fugue that has descended around her and she turns towards it, suddenly painfully aware of the blood dripping from her face.

"Karma, he's gone, it's okay." The woman's voice is kind and understanding. Everything it shouldn't be at this moment.

She is covered in death. Blood and flesh seeping into her pores, changing the build of her soul and bones. She has become a monster and yet Zoe speaks to her with an understanding she can't possibly possess.

"Are you sure?" her voice sounds young, even to her ears. She is eleven years old again, looking for someone to give her the answers she needs. Looking for Jones to sweep in and rescue her.

But Jones wasn't coming.

She would never come to the rescue again.

Still now, Karma would not look at the body of her sister. Would not entertain the idea that her current status was permanent. Jones was just resting. Just taking a little breather from life. And if Karma didn't look at her then she didn't have to acknowledge anything different.

"Yes. I'm sure." Zoe's hand found Karma's. And despite the violence upon her palms, she took it. Gently threading her fingers through Karma's and pulling her to a stand. Leading her from Father's mutilated corpse.

"Okay," was all that Karma could say in response. Over and over, despite Zoe not speaking any further words.

Zoe stroked Karma's cheek gently with her free hand. Brushing away the drizzle of blood that lay upon it.

"I'm here, he's gone, everything is going to be okay now." Karma clings to these words. Engraving them onto her wretched heart, using them to paper over the cracks the loss of Jones has left behind. In this moment, she will allow Zoe to centre her, to aid her and protect her. But once this mess is gone, she knows she will flee. Because Zoe deserves better than Karma. She'd known that even before they'd met.

She'd fought her team, fought Harry, to make sure the contract for her life story tied her to Zoe. She'd been so intrigued by the woman that there was no one else she trusted. And although selfishly, she wanted to trap Zoe in the twisted web that was her life, to keep her by her side forever and always, she knew deep down that she wouldn't.

Because Zoe deserved nothing but the best.

And the best wasn't Karma.

Chapter Fifty-Eight: Zoe

I knew what she was going to say before she'd even started to string the words together in her mind. She was going to tell me to leave. Again.

And I would ignore her. Again.

Because despite how I felt about her lies, or my moral dilemma with the work she undertook via the Network - I cared about her. I really cared about her. And to be honest, when it all boils down to it I do believe that the guilty deserve to be punished.

I know that makes me a less empathetic person than I'd like to believe myself to be. Less of a liberal, less good. But there are some crimes in life you can never be rehabilitated from, some crimes that deserve the cost of your life. And if the Network were willing to do the grunt work, then who am I to judge the end result?

"We need to leave, Karma, before the police come."

"The police won't come, we're fine," she replies, squeezing my hand. Reminding herself that I'm here and I'm real. I notice the way she's keeping her eyes fixed on Father's body, as though she's waiting for him to breathe again and crawl across the floor to finish the job. I hope one day she understands that she's safe now.

Looking across the room, my eyes linger on Jones' body.

Jones.

The woman who had given her whole life in service of survivors. Who never existed as far as the world is concerned. She deserved so much more than the hand she was dealt, and she would be remembered by so few. It was a tragedy.

Karma hasn't once looked at her sister's body. Perhaps that's for the best. At least that way, she won't have to remember her like this, hair matted in a halo of blood and brains.

Slowly, I let go of Karma's hand, she makes no show of noticing, standing still as a statue, waiting for the monster from her nightmares to pounce.

I walk a few paces away from her, picking up a dust sheet that's laying in a heap across an abandoned table. There's a dull ache in my stomach as I move towards Jones and kneel down beside her. She looks so peaceful despite the trauma her body has endured. I hope she can be at peace now. Now that her sister is safe.

That's all that Jones ever wanted, I can tell that based on her actions the night they escaped The Farm. It would have been so easy for her to leave Karma behind, or to accompany her to ring on Joanna's doorbell. She could have allowed herself to be cared for and loved as she grew. But there was no guarantee that the State would have placed her and Karma in the same safe house, let alone the same foster family. Who wants to take on two traumatised children at the same time? Especially two who had been subjected to regular sexual abuse at the hands of multiple adults. It would have been too much responsibility, even for the most well-meaning of people.

By keeping herself off the radar, she allowed

herself to stay close to Karma at all times. Charged herself as her sister's keeper and lived each day looking out for her.

She's wearing a red ribbon upon her wrist, and the knot has come loose in the fight with Father. So I reach down and tie it for her, making sure to pull it tightly into a bow, so she can keep it with her forever.

"I've got her now," I whisper as I squeeze her hand. It's cold already, all life evaporated from her the moment she hit the floor. I hope wherever she is that she can hear me, that she knows her work here is done and she can be free.

I pull the dust sheet up and over her face, making sure to cover her entire body. I tuck it under the sides of her as though she's just fallen asleep.

"Thank you," I add as I finally stand, taking a moment to silently remember her even for the very brief time I'd known her. She rescued me from Father. She rescued Karma from Father. She's the closest thing to a superhero this world will ever know.

Returning to Karma's side, I take her hand again.

"Thank you," she whispers, finally turning her attention away from Father to look at me. She still won't look over at Jones, though I can tell a part of her desperately wants to. "I need to make some calls."

She doesn't let go of my hand. Instead, she leads me away from the room that's full of death and towards her office. And I'm grateful for this. I don't want to spend any more time in that room where I took a life than I have to.

I took a life.

Well, essentially, I suppose I took two.

I knew exactly where I was aiming when I stabbed Father. I was aiming for maximum damage. I wanted to strike a fatal blow.

I could have struck him somewhere else, anywhere

else, and it still would have saved Karma.

But I didn't.

I aimed to kill.

And that's okay.

Monsters deserve to be put down.

I sit next to Karma at her desk, our shoulders touching, as she makes a range of phone calls to members of The Network. They will take care of this mess. Our work here is done.

When the doorbell rings she takes my hand once again and together we let the clean up crew in. Both needing the physical presence of the other to keep going. We can process everything that's happened later. Together. For now we need to stay focused.

We stand opposite each other as we help carry the weight of Father's body and throw him down a disused well, hidden in the floors of the warehouse.

We grunt in unison as alongside reinforcements, we shovel cement mix into the hole above him, until he is buried in twenty foot of the stuff. Not that we expect sniffer dogs to come looking for him, the plus side to him hiding under the radar for so many years is that anyone who misses him will never come forward. How do you explain hiding such an evil force of nature for decades?

No. Nobody will miss Father. Nobody will file a missing person report. Nobody will even notice he has died.

He deserves nothing less.

Once the concrete is set Karma makes another call. To the Foundation to approve the purchase of the building. Construction of a new building under their banner will begin next week. Our secrets will be buried here forever, safe from prying eyes.

Finally, everyone but me and Karma, gently lift Jones from her resting place and remove her from the floor. Carrying her like precious cargo, they all walk with their heads bowed, tears silently streaming down faces. Karma pinches her eyes closed, refusing to open them until her sister has been removed.

She doesn't want to say goodbye. And I'm not going to force her.

Her hand is still in mine, sweaty now from all our exertion but I hold on tight. Threading my fingers through hers, palms imprinted on each other.

And we walk away from the building, ready to process all of our trauma in the company of each other. As we hit daylight, she turns to me and lets go of my hand as though it scalded her. Her face is cold, emotionless.

"You need to leave." Her words are clipped and she takes a step backwards away from me. She needs me to leave. Wants to save me once again from the mess that is her life.

"I told you I wouldn't turn away. I promised." I reply, filling the gap between us, putting my arms around her and pulling her into a tight embrace. I'll spend the rest of my life refusing to turn away if that's what it takes. But Karma is staying in my life - whether she thinks it's the right choice or not.

Epoilogue:

Two Years Later:

Two women are out walking a chocolate Labrador puppy. Their arms are interlinked and they smile at each other as they exchange a private conversation.

Their dog runs forward to greet a grey Staffie and they laugh before engaging the owner in conversation, the passing of a parcel between the three of them unnoticeable to the other dog walkers out on the beach.

As they wave goodbye to their temporary friends the taller of the women leans down to plant a kiss on her companions lips. For a moment they are locked in an embrace so sweet it laces the air with the scent of cherries around them. They are happy. They are safe.

Later that day, the two women wave goodbye to their dog as they head out towards the centre of town, having a light-hearted argument over who gets to drive before typing a postcode into their sat nav that they know off by heart. But today is different from that day two years ago, so much has changed in that time.

After leaving headquarters on the day they buried Father, Karma and Zoe have lived mostly away from the Network. It's self-sustaining now, Jones had made sure to build it that way, knowing that her sister wouldn't want to be tied to it forever. They still read every news article published about the targets, and make hefty donations where possible to survivors of the crimes.

Today they are on their way to the opening of a new head office for the newly named 'Jones' Survivors Foundation', the Karma Jones Foundation was dissolved shortly after Father's death. Karma wanted the good work it undertook to live on forever under sister's name and not hers. It was a way to honour all she had done for the Network, for Karma and for Zoe.

These days the Network has adjusted its calling cards. Thanks to Zoe.

A ring, made up of twisted snakes, with a note stating 'Innocent' is left with the usual calling card on targets. A way to remind the world that their families and loved ones were just as blind to their crimes as the rest of us. It's a small change but one that she hopes makes a difference.

Notecards with the phrase 'Do Better' are delivered directly to the doors of those who knew and turned a blind eye to the target's crimes. A way to make sure they knew that Medusa was watching them.

Zoe and Karma did complete and deliver their podcast. They began working on it a month after Father's death and didn't stop until it was finished just five days later. They lived in a shared hotel room for the duration, recording day and night whenever Karma felt up to it. The finished production still resides in the top ten podcasts on most streaming sites. Zoe kept her promise, and never once turned away, no matter how horrific some parts of the story were.

After completing the podcast, Zoe moved into Karma's flat. And at Christmas, they hung mismatched ornaments on the tree with smiles on their faces. Zoe has even added to the collection herself over the years.

And now it's time to open the new building. To provide a new sanctuary for those who need to escape from abuse, who need somewhere to heal, to process what they've survived.

Karma proudly pulls Zoe into her side as the press snaps the photographs at the opening ceremony.

Finally, she is at ease.

    Karma is justice.

    She does not reward or punish.

    She merely gives you what you've earned.

Acknowledgements

Where would an author be without the village that holds us up? Probably crying alone into a cup of coffee.

Where to begin? Well, with those who read the 'dump draft' of this book and helped encourage me to keep working on it - Viv, Charlotte, Terri, Liz & Ramona - thank you for being my most trusted pairs of eyes.

This time around I have a team of first readers that give me honest, much needed, feedback (good and bad) in no particular order thank you to: Hailey, Monica, Ashley, Faith, Robin, Deanna, Shari, Cheryl, Thesera & Shauntelle for all your support and encouragement.

And she'll kill me if I don't thank her, given how many voice notes and text messages she had to wade through. A massive thank you and shout out to my editor Allison - you're one of my biggest supporters and I'm so grateful the world joined our paths together.

Thank you to you, dear reader, for taking a chance on an indie author. You really do help dreams come true every time you do that.

Finally, and I promise I'm nearly done here - thank you to my family, my husband and my kids for once again letting me disappear into my own imagination with very little complaining. One day I'll live in the real world I promise.

SM Thomas

For updates and information on future releases please visit

www.smthomas.co.uk

And join the mailing list.

Or you can find me on Facebook (**smthomaswrites**), Instagram (**smthomas_author**) and occasionally TikTok (**sm_thomas0**).

(a girl called) Karma

Printed in Dunstable, United Kingdom